THE CASA BELLA QUARTET

THE CASA BELLA QUARTET

A novel by

Bernard Milofsky

BryanDorsey Books, Publisher
Denver

Copyright © 2017 by Carl Milofsky
ISBN-13: 978-1544237992

BryanDorsey Books Denver

To the memory of my son, Arthur Daniel.

* * *

  Until I think I can stand it no longer. But there comes a-day or a month or a year or some crumbled boulder of time, vast and gone, when the rehearsal ends......I walk to the door, leaving my instrument. We rehearse again tomorrow, the same place, the same music, the same cruel obstacles. I leave everything. Perhaps some kindred beasts will gnaw at night.

  ----From Andrea's Diary

* * *

BOOKS:

FURIANT

DELIRANDO

LE STREGHE

Esca was searching furiously. He was a thickset man with greying hair, and as he lunged about the room he sometimes stopped in bewilderment and scratched at his pale face. The long, parallel lines would appear, paler yet, reaching from eyebrow to chin. It was impossible. What had happened was impossible. If only he could find his old journal, to go over everything from the beginning, maybe something would occur to him and help him to understand. He gazed wearily at the disorderly room. It was a little volume, a little red —

Again he threw himself into the violent search. It wasn't lost, surely, it wasn't lost. Surely. It was only hidden in the bookcovered walls, or on the littered disk, chairs, floor. Somewhere. But where? Had it been "borrowed" after a wild interlude? Or stolen by one of the four? Their facile hands could do anything. He paused. What if it had been one of the — the five?

Even now he hated to think of the fifth and he became unreasoning in his urgency. He plunged at this torn leaflet, that ragged slip of paper, rushing back and forth fruitlessly and with and increasing sense of despair.

Suddenly he uttered a small cry of joy, and of concern. He had found it.

Now he hurried to his study and sat down at a large oblong table. His thick fingers fumbled hastily through the pages until he reached the beginning. For several moments he stared at it, breathing deeply. Then he began to read.

JOURNAL OF THE CASA

BELLA QUARTET, BY

WILLIAM ESCA

FURIANT

I should like first to tell of Otto. Marcus Aurelius Otto had barely reached his majority when his fortune was wiped out in the great depression. His father was dead and now his mother and two sisters expected him to provide for them. For he was head of the family.

But Otto had led a sheltered life and he was in no way prepared to meet this emergency. As he faced the angry, frightening climate of Austria in 1930 he felt bewildered and helpless.

Mama pointed out that Otto had been given an excellent classical education. Might not something be done with it? For he was a graduate of the University of Vienna, an authority on the Chaldean language, a mathematician, an extremely talented. painter (his portrait of Olga Hallant still hangs in the Stuttgart Museum of Art), and a member of the national chess team. And he even played the violin pretty well. Surely some one of these accomplishments could be turned, to account. Still he hesitated.

Now Otto was a small, ugly fellow whose red hair was shot through with a premature grey. Perhaps it was his ugliness which made him withdraw into the hermitage of his intellect. Or maybe it was only that he was afraid to venture into the great world. But in any case he seldom managed to get away from his studies, and on the rare occasions when he tried to find work he was never successful. For he was shy and awkward and his many academic achievements meant nothing in the harsh arenas of Vienna. As the weeks passed the situation of the Ottos became steadily worse and soon there came a time when they had nothing to eat. And Otto was plagued by anxious, tearful complaints. A fine man they had at the head of the house.

But now a curious thing happened to Otto, something which drove his mother wild with rage and despair. He fell desperately in love with three women.

Otto had been studying musical composition with Hugo Storch at the *Neue Academie der Tonkunst.* And he composed a sonata for string trio which was to be performed by three young ladies at the spring concert.

Otto had not met the young ladies (he had never met any young ladies) but soon he was asked to attend a rehearsal. The day came when he entered Storch's study and was introduced to Olga Hallant, Maya von Eber, and Andrea Dante. As he peered out through his shaggy, studious eyebrows he simply noted, dimly, that here were three rather plain young women.

It was when they began to play his composition that he was aroused and made fearful. They played like women possessed. It was not enough to play loud. Their instruments deafened him, the very walls trembled with resonance. And when the fiddles sank to a whisper his ears strained to hear the susurrus of tone and Otto began to know the dread of sound. He was afraid to breathe, awed by the experience, unwilling to disturb it with even the small, innocent noise of exhalation.

When the trio was finished Otto stammered, *"Meine – meine Damen, ich – ich habe Sie alle sehr lieb."*

For in his meeting with them a torrent had been released., and he did not know or care where it carried him. Never had anyone been so in love. And this love was to last for twenty years.

The Casa Bella String Quartet came into being at the end of the school year. I was not to meet them for some time. What I have written so far has been assembled from the scattered conversations of the decade which we spent together and, of course, from conjecture on my part.

They got along well from the start. This was unusual, for most string quartets do a great deal of fighting and bickering. But not the Casa Bellas. The girls were flattered by Otto's obvious devotion and gradually they came to love him too. And although there were honest differences of opinion from time to time, Otto was always able to settle these differences amicably.

They spent the summer in a frenzy of work and as a result their first concert in Berlin was an unusual success. They never returned to school, since their career was assured after this debut. I have the program here as I write. It was made up of two long works. Beethoven's Opus 130 and the Schönberg D minor quartet. I think this is probably one of the best programs which can be contrived out of the entire chamber music repertoire. In the beginning this single concert was all they could play and they repeated it everywhere.

And triumph accompanied them like a happy shadow. Every major composer in the world began to dedicate compositions to the Casa Bella Quartet. I owned a recording company at the time and even went to England to record them 1934, 1 believe.

When they came to America in 1939 they included Hartford in their itinerary and I met them again at the home of a friend, Minnie Watteau. My wife, Thede, was anxious to meet the quartet and so we went to see-whether they would remember me. They were surrounded by people and we had to wait for some time before I could, speak to Marcus Otto.

Finally my chance came. "Good evening, Mr. Otto. Do you remember me? My name is William Esca and I recorded the quartet in England a few years ago."

"Why, of course. How good to see you again. How very good."

"And this is Mrs. Esca."

Otto's bow to Thede was the beautiful polished, result of a thousand concerts, of command performances before the crowned heads of Europe, of playing for nobility and for famous states, men. It was quite a bow, and. I could see that Thede was ´flattered by the reverence of Otto's "*Enchanté, Madame*" as he kissed her hand. Amazing. Thede hardly ever feels flattered because, if I do say it myself, she is a beautiful woman who has been adored all her life. Adulation usually makes her Uncomfortable.

Now Otto called the others and they all remembered me. With some enthusiasm too. But I didn't feel complimented, for I have found that when concert artists are on tour it is the rule for them to be terribly happy to meet anyone at all with whom they have even a nodding acquaintance. Or perhaps it is only that they are so glad to escape Minnie Watteau. Minnie's receptions are uniformly dull.

Luckily I turned out to be the only person in Hartford whom the Casa Bellas knew. Minnie, as one of the local social climbers, had simply commanded their presence at her reception after the concert and there they were, stuck until I happened along and rescued them.

After a while we went to my place. Everyone relaxed and we had a riotous time. Otto fixed up a magician's turban and did some amazing card tricks. I still remember one in which the black queen turned red at the approach of the black king. Or was it the red king. Anyhow, it was a wonderful trick.

Olga Hallant did nothing but sit and eat cashew nuts. She is a huge woman and must have eaten a pound of nuts that night. She seemed to enjoy them so much that after a while I joined her. It ruined my diet, but— well, everyone was having such a good time, why shouldn't I?

Now Maia von Eber offered to entertain us. I tried to take the beautiful, ermine neckpiece which framed her little blond, head, but she refused to give it to me. Instead she went to her case, took out her fiddle and began to tune Strange. She even played the fiddle with the neckpiece. Now she began to imitate other fiddlers. For the most part the subtlety of her mimicry was beyond me and. I could only understand her takeoff on one or two of our most prominent violinists. But Otto and. Olga roared, and Andrea clapped her hands gleefully.

Andrea was the *piece de resistance* for me. She had the most extraordinary ability to imitate people's voices with her viola. I asked her what kind of instrument it was and she played something which sounded like Mardini. "No, no," Maia scolded. "Maggini." Andrea ignored her and began to converse with me. It was maddening and hilarious. I could say nothing to her which she did not twist and. pervert. "How do you do." "How do *I* do? How do *you* do." "I'm fine," "So *you* say." And so on. Her pitch perception was so acute that she was able to create the illusion of language by imitating the subtle inflections of a human voice. The tragedy of Andrea was that she was mute. She hadn't spoken a word since childhood.

But that night the five of us took notes as she, played, and almost unanimously we wrote dawn the following remarkable speech:

"Todaaay I saw the most beoootiful drrreeesssss. It was grrreeeenn and bullloooo." Minnie Watteau, of course.

Afterwards Otto had an idea. He said, "Let's play something for these nice people."

"Of course," Maia said eagerly. "An excellent suggestion." Olga grunted and Andrea smiled and. nodded.

Otto said, "What will it be? You can name anything in the standard repertoire."

"Anything? But you don't have the music."

"We play from memory."

I didn't believe it. Surely they couldn't know everything from memory. I was willing to wager that I could think of something that they couldn't possibly know. I have always loved music and have gotten pretty familiar with the chamber music literature by listening to it on records.

But better make sure I had heard right. I said, "Can I really choose anything at all?"

"Well, try us."

I didn't want to embarrass Otto, but for him to imply that they had memorized the entire repertoire seemed so outrageous that couldn't resist putting him to the test.

"How about the second. Smetana Quartet," I said. "Not the 'Aus meinem

Leben'. The other one. The one he wrote when he was losing his mind."

Otto hesitated. "It is such an obscure work," he said, and paused. I could see that the request had made him uncomfortable and I smiled to myself. Knew everything, hey? "And we can only play it about half way through." He cleared his throat. "Would you like to hear this part of it? Or some other complete work?"

I was amazed at his honesty. How easily he could have deceived me. I said, "I would very much like to hear what you remember of this quartet. It interests me because of Smetana's mental condition when he wrote it."

And so they got out their instruments, sat down and tuned. Then the strange sounds began. There have always been one or two authorities who believed that Smetana was sane when he wrote this quartet. And as the Casa Bellas played it, the music seemed crystal clear, with a lucidity which was characteristic of Smetana's strongest compositions.

As I looked at the fiddlers I was struck by the abrupt difference in their personalities. A moment since they had been full of fun, Maia shouting and laughing at Andrea's mimicry, Otto performing his card tricks and wearing a ludicrous turban, Olga crunching handfuls of cashew nuts, and, now—how intent they were.

My impression of them had changed since the concert. I remembered them as they had come onto the stage only a few hours ago, and I remembered how disparate, even grotesque they had seemed, what a contrast there had been between huge Olga and little Otto, tiny Maie. Now there was no contrast. There was only a flood of sound whose beauty obliterated the world and its tawdry dimensions.

I looked at Otto. His strong, lined face was earnest and concentrated. His eyes were shut, and he would lean now toward one, now toward another of the quartet as his melody merged with the melody of this or that player, so that it seemed that a single instrument played both voices. Olga's breathing was stertorous, her eyes almost closed, save that now and then she opened, them with a look of longing. She was an excellent player and the magnitude of her bass was a floor upon which the entire edifice of the quartet rested with an unshakeable solidity. Now came Otto with the solo part. And now Maia. And I wondered how it is decided who is to play first or second violin in a quartet, for certainly Maia was Otto's equal... And with an ermine neckpiece, too. Why did she persist in wearing it? She hadn't in the concert, of course.

But of them all I thought that I preferred Andrea. She was a brown-haired, ugly woman with a wart on her snub nose, and a little potbelly. She was the only one who played with opened eyes, and she looked constantly at the others, as if in doubt. But her tone was the most beautiful sound I had ever heard issue from a stringed instrument. And what variety! At one moment it was dark and somber, and the next shrill and piercing, and the next, guttural and harsh, and the next smooth and lyrical, and on and on endlessly. And In all the years that I heard Andrea Dante play I do not think that I ever heard her use the same tone quality twice. She was a wonder to me. I got so interested, in listening to her that I began to ignore the totality of the music, and today I can only remember the viola part of the Smetana Quartet. I couldn't think why she had not impressed me so during the concert.

They finished, finally, and Otto said, "Who is willing to take a chance on the rest of it?"

Andrea shook her head tiredly and began to put her instrument away, polishing it and cleaning the rosin dust from its flat belly.

"At least we played some of it," Otto said with a laugh. "Did you like it, Bill?"

"I thought it was beautiful."

"The evening is young yet," Otto cried. "Come on, Andrea. Let's play some more."

But she smiled and shook her head.

Thede blushed. She seemed to want to say something, but for a moment she hesitated. Then she said, timidly, "I'd be very happy to play a Mozart Trio with you, if you don't mind playing with an amateur."

Otto was immediately enthusiastic. "Wonderful idea," he cried. "Wonderful idea. What do you say, Olga. Mozart?"

Olga was silent for a moment. Then she growled, "Very well,"

Thede's bravery surprised me. In all her life she had played only a few small concerts. Still, what of it. Otto seemed to be having a good time, and Maia—I noticed that I was already thinking of them by their first names. We must have gone a long way in this short evening. Perhaps that was what Thede had felt too. Now she came in with some music.

"Well, Otto," I said, "I'm disappointed that you don't know the Mozart Trio from memory too."

"Oh, we do. But does Thede?"

She blushed again. I had never seen her blush so frequently. "Surely you are joking," she said. "The trio can't possibly be part of your repertoire."

Otto laughed. "You are right, of course, I was just teasing you."

"Why do you memorize everything anyway," I asked.

"What possible reason can you have for doing so much unnecessary work?"

"First I will tell you what is not the reason, Billy. We certainly do not do it to show off. No, we memorize because we like to have our attention free to concentrate on the music, and on each other. In any case, if you *don't* know a composition you shouldn't play it in public, should you? And if you *do* know it, really *know* it, well then, what on earth do you need music for? I tell you, I hate the idea of performing with my nose in the score. I like to close my eyes and, play and play—"

Olga snorted. "Well, play then," she commanded. "Don't talk so much."

"All right," Otto said dutifully. And he began to tune his violin again.

Andrea had not finished, putting her viola away and now she placed it under her chin and drew the bow. The few notes sounded surprisingly like, "Shall I turn?"

Thede laughed. "You are wonderful," she said to Andrea who smiled and sat down next to her. Then she riffled through the music to see if there were any difficult page turns.

Now they began the trio. As I listened to this unrehearsed performance I thought it was every bit as good as that of the Smetana, which they had rehearsed. Indeed the playing of Otto and Olga was so excellent that Thede seemed to catch fire from it, to be moved and thrilled by the experience. Her face was not expressive of it, but I had known her for a long time and could always tell when she was excited. It was her breathing, the flashing of her eye, the toss of her auburn hair. I was proud of her that evening. And. even Otto said, "Brava, Thede Brava. We must certainly play again together. Now Billy. It's your turn. Do you play something?"

"Well,—not anymore. I've always loved music, and when I was a student at college I even played the clarinet in a wood-wind ensemble. As a matter of fact, we had a small season of six concerts which I managed. But heavens, it's been almost thirty years since I've touched a clarinet, so I'd better beg off for tonight."

"We're ready and willing if you are."

For a moment I was tempted. Wasn't there a clarinet in the basement? But then I decided that it wouldn't be a good idea. Everyone was looking at me expectantly, and I seemed to detect a feeling of apprehension in Olga. "No, thanks," I said finally. "I'd love to, but I guess I'd need about a year to practice first."

The evening ended when Olga got up and said, "We must go. Our train leaves in a few hours." I looked at my watch. Unbelievably it was three-thirty in the morning.

We shook hands all around and parted with, I think, mutual regret. We even promised to write to each other. I had no idea how soon I was to hear from Otto.

The Casa Bellas after touring both North and South America, were getting ready to leave for France, where they had lived since the advent of Hitler, when France was invaded by Germany. Now their plans had to be reconsidered.

One day I received a wire from Rio de Janeiro which read, HAVE DECIDED INDEFINITE STAY WESTERN HEMISPHERE. ARE YOU INTERESTED MANAGEMENT QUARTET. REGARDS. MARCUS OTTO.

I was mildly amazed. Why should he have thought of me? I couldn't understand. it. But in any case I wasn't interested. I had worked enough in my lifetime and was just settling into a comfortable retirement.

But Thede was enthusiastically in favor of my accepting Otto's offer. She was much younger than I, young enough so that the telegram represented, a great opportunity to her. Immediately she had the headquarters of the quartet all picked out. She knew of a wonderful house which was for sale, with plenty of room for all of us and a special little auditorium for rehearsal. In short, it was an ideal place in which to work and live and she wanted me to purchase it right way. No, she didn't mind at all if I looked at it first.

She was like a child, But I wasn't going to throw a monkey Wrench into my whole way of life simply so that Thede could have her hand kissed and be told *"Enchanté, Madame"* every time she met Otto.

After much argument I was finally able to convince her that going into such a venture at my age would be a mistake. And. so I sent a telegram of polite refusal to Otto, mentioning my pleasure that he had thought of me for such a responsible and intimate position and thanking him sincerely.

That night I received an extraordinary telephone call from Otto. How he was able to persuade a retired record manufacturer who had never managed anything but a college ensemble to take charge of a major string quartet is a saga in itself. As I remember, our conversation lasted more than half an hour—I couldn't get Otto to hang up—and must have cost hundreds of dollars. Finally, and with decided misgiving, I agreed.

But when the quartet returned to the United States I was encouraged to find that Otto was an encyclopedia of information about the management of concert tours. (It was only later that I found out about Otto's photographic memory. During our initial session together I could only think it astonishing, conceited, and a little silly that such a fine artist should waste his time memorizing Canadian railway schedules.) I received a short, intensive education and three hours after we began I was pronounced a graduate of the Otto School of Concert Management.

I was able to squeeze one reluctant concession from him. Music has always been important to me and I wanted to be allowed to attend rehearsals. At first Otto would not even listen to me. The idea was impossible. But I was insistent. I promised that they would not even be aware of my presence, that they could rehearse in my home, that they would be served meals at their convenience. I even promised that they could come up to my Maine estate during the summer.

And Otto gave in at last. Of course I was asking a great deal, for no one had ever been granted the privilege of attending rehearsals before. It was understood that I was to be a chameleon during rehearsals, to blend perfectly with my surroundings and to be neither heard, nor seen. And I was to be absolutely discreet about any untoward happening.

"Rehearsals can be enjoyable," Otto told me. "But they can also be violent."

When I think about Otto I can scarcely believe that his youth was isolated and. friendless. He was an utterly charming man, and when he smiled, and he smiled frequently, you felt a private embrace, warm, secretive, intensely personal. One could only love and, trust him. When he performed, transparent and noble thoughts played across his features, and I never wearied of watching his beautiful ugly face. If it is true that all human beings are partly female and partly male, I suppose that in a way I loved Otto. Or maybe it is only that I am getting old, and have never had any children, and wanted him to be my son.

Anyway, at the first rehearsal which I attended I noticed that they did not play from memory, but from the music, which was arranged on music racks. Later I asked Otto the reason and he told me that it was because they were forced to stop playing from time to time in order to discuss a musical question. Then they needed the music so that they could agree on a place to start anew. It would have been pointless to memorize all the possible starting places.

But to return to the rehearsal. Soon I began to see the reason for Otto's metamorphosis. The ladies were strong-willed and Otto needed all of his charm and tact to guide the rehearsal smoothly. In ten years of managing that unruly trio he had per-force become a diplomat. But he was also able to be stern, and at times even harsh and sarcastic.

He spoke in English for my benefit. "Ladies, we have been for five minutes trying to make a crescendo. May I suggest that we inquire into the meaning of the word? After all, unless we can agree on a definition we can hardly achieve unity in performance. Come, come," he purred, "who will volunteer to explain the term?"

"Why Ottsy," Mala said, "it means to get louder, everybody knows that." She looked at him reproachfully. It was true. Even I knew it.

Otto roared, "It does not mean to get louder it does *not* mean to get louder! What a stupid oversimplification! Get louder than what? You begin to play like a brass band and you expect to get louder. My God: Get it through your heads, all of you. Crescendo means piano, and piano means soft, very soft." His voice was hushed. "When you can play soft, then you can begin to think about getting louder, *not* before. Crescendo is a concept. In the present instance it means that we are in the valley of the shadow, and we are terrified." His face was ghast. "We cannot be heard," he whispered, "we are afraid to move. Our sound is like the light, ever-present but unnoticed. Gradually," here he paused, *"very* gradually we grow bolder, now we can be plainly heard, and still we gain strength, we emerge into the sunlight," the crescendo of his excited voice continued, "we grow again until the climax, and then," he shouted, " we sound like six brass bands. That, my ladies, would be a crescendo—why. Maia, my dearest dear, you are crying—whatever for?"

"Because you hurt her feelings, you big oaf," Olga snarled. "You are more interested in impressing Esca with your so-called eloquence than in considering Maia."

Otto was appalled. "But she knows how much I love her," he protested. As I watched him put down his fiddle I noticed the hurried care which he could use even in such an emergency. Then he quickly almost ran to Maia and bent over her tear-stained face. "Come, my darling, I am so sorry, so very sorry." He kissed her eyes, and she looked at him adoringly. I thought I detected a trace of envy in Olga.

"No, Ottsy, don't be s-sorry," Maia said tearfully. "I really p-played too loud. I won't do it again, I p-promise." He gave her a handkerchief and she blew her nose.

Andrea held up a sheet upon which, in large letters, had been inscribed the word LUNCH.

Otto's technique varied, of course, in different situations. I remember one time he felt called upon to criticize the gigantic Olga, always a difficult task. For this he chose an intermission.

"Olga, my dear, I have been thinking of all the cellists I have ever know. I can think of no one who approaches you in excellence."

"Of course," Olga said complacently. Her feet, unladylike, were on a table, and she was smoking a small panatela cigar. She calmly blew a smoke ring.

"In every department of your playing you are the supreme cellist," Otto went on smoothly. "Except that I once knew a man in Basle—"

Olga's feet crashed to the floor. She stared at Otto through narrowed eyes. "Go on," she growled ominously.

"It is nothing, Olga, my dear," Otto said apologetically. "Can't I know a man in Basle? He was a terrible cellist. Awful. But he could do one thing. Pizzicato. It seems that when he was a small boy he found an old, cello, without a bow. And all he could do was to pluck the strings. That's why he was such a bad cellist, you see. During his formative years he hadn't known the use of a bow. But his pizzicato: When he plucked the string it sounded like a great bell. I'll never forget it. Like a great bell, really. It's an art all right. And his speed: Why, he could pluck the string as fast as most people can finger the string." Otto sighed. "But one can't expect such skill from even the best player." It was Otto's turn to select a cigar. Olga was looking frustrated. "You understand, of course," he continued imperturbably, "that I wouldn't dream of criticizing your own pizzicato."

They were rehearsing a piece by Alban Berg, its theme set forth with lonely notes plucked by the cellist. I had thought them lovely. But the next day Olga appeared with a bandage on her right index finger. Grimly she removed the bandage. Grimly she sat down with her blister.

Otto was concerned. "Why Olga, what on earth happened to your finger?"

"You know damned well, you villain," she muttered, beginning the Berg piece.

The change was unbelievable. The heavy note shot through the air with a resonance which set the other instruments humming with a sympathetic vibration.

Later I said to Otto, "If that's how pizzicato can sound, I'd like to hear the man from Basle."

"Basle?" Otto was surprised. "Oh yes, Basle." He smiled, his wonderful, secret smile.

Ten years have passed, ten years exactly since I became manager of Casa Bella. Long busy years they have been, for the quartet has played almost nine hundred concerts under my management.

And during this time the thought has occurred to me often that the art of music is strange in that it rejects musicians. It could not exist without them, yet what a trivial amount of literature they have inspired. One could find libraries full of information about the great composers. But the great musicians have been largely ignored.

It seems to me that these artists are important, and that many more biographies should be written about them so that the world can know of their thinking, and living and dying.

It has occurred to me that it might be a good idea to write about the Casa Bella Quartet. Of course I have gotten to know them very well. They are rare people, each in his way a unique contributor to the composite personality of the quartet.

Olga Hallant has become my dear friend during these ten years. She is a huge woman with very black, coarse hair which she has always permitted to grow long. I don't remember that she ever had it cut.

Among her eccentricities was never shaving her arms or legs, or plucking her eyebrows. "Takes your strength away," she would say, Samson like and solemn. I could never be sure there wasn't a twinkle in her eye.

But she is indeed powerful. She owns a truly wonderful cello made by Dominicus Montagnana of Venice and it sounds like an organ when she plays. Olga nurses it daily, like a mother, cleaning its strings, adjusting its bridge, shining its fat, red belly with an old flannel. She is the only musician I have ever known who is herself able to replace worn-out hair in her fiddlestick. I understand it's a tricky job, one for a professional fiddlemaker. And her strings. She has built a tiny factory for them on my estate in Maine. Every summer the intestines of a freshly killed sheep are stretched out on racks to dry. Then Olga trues her strings to the required thickness with *eyes* that are calipers and wraps them in silver wire. And we are forced to eat mutton for weeks. Until Otto complains bitterly, "Let her fool with her murdered sheep. It sublimates her hostility. But does that mean I have to *eat* the sheep? The *whole* sheep?"' Otto hates mutton. But he never complains to Olga, only to me. Sometimes I think that he not only loves Olga, but is somewhat afraid of her too.

Well. I once asked Olga how old she was when she began to study music. It is incredible, but she began to study the piano at the age of two and gave her first concert when she was barely four years old. She showed me the program—Bach, Beethoven, Schubert, Ravel and an original composition. She had not begun to read music and played the whole program from memory. Her father, a teacher of piano at the *École Normale* in Paris, would play through these compositions until Olga could repeat them from memory. "The music is inside," she would say, "otherwise let it remain on the paper."

Her recollection of the first years of her life was very clear. I can remember a trip I took when I was only twenty-three months old. I know I remember and that no one told me later because my father gave me some wine to drink. I blackmailed him all through my childhood. Poor man. My mother terrified. him. She was a colossal Russian Jewess and really behaved like the man in the family. She controlled my father completely. Too bad. He was always so curious about things and she would never let him experiment. His only firm stand was that I should study music, the earlier the better. I don't know to this day whether I should be grateful." She paused for a moment remembering. "My father. He was tall and handsome and had such beautiful, brown curly hair." She sighed "Ah, my father. Well, but you wanted to know about my childhood. I heard my first chamber music concert when I was six and immediately wanted to give up the piano in favor of the cello. I called it a moo-cow. My poor father fought furiously against the idea, but with my mother's help I won. Father was right, of course. The piano is the only instrument with, which a serious musician should choose to spend his life."

"Why do you think so, Olga?"

"Well, a pianist reading an orchestra score, for instance, can at the same time play the music of nearly all the important instruments. It. is as though he were at the top of a tall tower looking- down at various tiny incidents which are likely to be ignorant of each other. Let me put it to you better. The point is this, that the piano is almost the only instrument which gives you not only a melodic but also a harmonic concept of music. Where was I? Oh, — "

She paused. Her beautiful eyes were reflective. Her features were in themselves distinctive even without the rest of her body. She had a large nose, for instance, a Roman nose, and a slight moustache over thick, almost negroid lips. But her eyes remain with me. Perhaps it was because through her eyes one saw the soul of Olga Hallant, and that was memorable, like a bright light which even after it has faded away remains imprinted on the retina, hurting a little.

I asked her once how she happened to choose Vienna as a place to study. "Well, when father died...." She shook her head, as though to rid herself of the thought. "My mother wouldn't let me study In Paris. We compromised at last on Vienna. Not that I regret it. But ah, how I loved my father." Her eyes glistened with tears. It was the only time I had ever seen them in Olga is eyes.

I remember her playing for me. A lady wrestler playing the cello. She grunted when she played and on some of the quartet recordings you can even hear the faint bass grunting when the cello predominates. The recording engineers tried everything to get her to stop, persuasion, pleading, flattery. But Olga would say euphemistically, "I breathe loudly when I play music. It means something to me. Those who love music will listen to the playing, not the breathing."

"But Mademoiselle Hallant," an engineer would object, "surely such sounds are not in the music."

"They are indeed in the music," Olga would retort. "All kinds of noises are in the music, wailing, gnashing of teeth, tearing of hair, everything. Don't you know that music can even sound ugly because music is life, and life can be ugly?" Then she would leer. "I can even show you a quartet by Haydn which is supposed to sound like farting."

Olga always won such battles. The quartet recordings sold so well that she could afford to be temperamental. If standing up for what you believe in can be called temperamental. And so today you can go into a shop and buy a Casa Bella recording and still hear Olga grunting merrily away.

Grunting was not Olga's only mannerism. She also stuck out her tongue while playing. The photographer would try to get her to close her mouth, but Olga would say, "Then no action shot. No tongue, no playing. How in the world do you expect me to worry about my appearance when I play something? Ha!"

Only one ingenious photographer ever succeeded in getting a good shot of Olga in action. He stood on the piano and got her from above. It is pathetic and humorous. You can't see the tongue for the nose. But somehow you can see Olga. The photograph is on my desk today. And if I close my eyes I can see the indomitable tongue and. hear the heroic onomatopoeia. The language of

Hallant. Divine Olga, tragic Olga. She said once, "Ah, if I could only marry and have children. How glad. I would be to leave this crazy life. I am so tired of being a gypsy, of living in trains and in hotels. If I want to look up a reference on—Mehul, for instance. What shall I do? Call the porter?" Once in a great while she would make a humorous, sardonic remark like this, but mainly she was a somber, tragic person.

I kept after her to play for me and one day she said, "All right. Let's go to my place." I had bought a large house with an apartment for each member of the quartet and two small, connected suites for Thede and me. We called it "The House of Casa. Bella." Now we went to Olga's apartment.

She took out her cello and I said, "What are you going to play?"

"Bloch. I feel mournful today."

The music was modern and I didn't understand the strange disharmonies. I was somewhat at a loss when she finished and couldn't think what to say. But I needn't have worried because Olga had scarcely put down her cello when she began to lecture me. "Otto has no patience with this piece. Indeed he has little use for Bloch altogether. Says he is sentimental. By the way, you didn't notice it, did you? The quarter tone, I mean.'"

"No, I didn't."

"Bloch will be vindicated one day. You can forgive a great innovator a little sentimentality. This quarter tone which you didn't hear will fracture the piano into an instrument with twice as many keys. And that is only the beginning. The human ear can hear fifteen thousand tones from bass to treble." She looked at me triumphantly. She was in a state of high excitement. "The ultimate," she said in a ringing voice, "the ultimate piano will contain them all."

I remember having had lunch with Otto that day. The war news was of Africa. Otto talked about Rommel and the Africa Corps, military science and Clausewitz, and ended with a brilliant dissertation on, I think, ballistics. I'm afraid I didn't listen very carefully. My mind was still immersed in Olga Hallant.

* * *

And Mala Von Eber. She was born in Württemberg, the third of four children. One day she rushed excitedly into the house crying, "Mama, mama, Franzl is going to teach me the fiddle."

Mama frowned. Franzl was the son of the Jewish tailor. But their bill with him was unpaid, so mama said, "Very well. But he must come here if he wants to give you lessons."

And so Maia began to study the violin. Her father was against the idea. He didn't like Jews either. "But Herr Von Eber," said. Franzl, "she has absolute pitch!"

"Oh," said Maia's father. "Well, let's see." And he took up the violin and played a note. "And what note is that?" he said, glaring at Maia.

"I don't know, papa," she said fearfully.

Her father sneered and stalked haughtily from the room.

"But Maia," said Franzl, "you knew what note that was."

"Well," Mafia said apologetically, "actually I didn't, Franzl. It was too sharp for 'B' and too flat for 'C.'"

Mafia surpassed. Franzl in a matter of weeks and in the springtime she applied for and won a scholarship at the Württemberg Musik-Kollegium. Two years later she was graduated, and at her recital she played a Paganini Concerto. She was thirteen. The director of the Württemberg Philharmonic heard Maia play and was impressed by her tremendous virtuosity. He tried to arrange a concert career for her, but was unsuccessful. She was too old. The public could not even be persuaded to come to hear prodigies who were much younger. And, so, fortunately, her education continued. And, three years later Maia was to receive a scholarship to the *Neue Akademie der Tonkunst* in Vienna. It was there that she met Olga Hallant, who was to become a valued friend and mentor.

      Maia's upbringing had been stern, and she was glad at last to be free. And yet she was not free. It was as though the restraints of her parents had forced her into .*a* rigid mold from which she could not escape. She had none of the gaiety and ebullience of her fellow students who were able to have a jolly time at night and with the unreasonable energy of youth keep up a full schedule in the daytime. And Maia had neither the money nor the temperament for competing with the other girls. She shared a room with Olga and spent much of her time despairing of herself and of the future.

      Since she was able to surmount with ease the most difficult violinistic obstacles Maia. had a great deal of time left over for her other studies and did very well in them. She was a bright girl and soon mastered harmony, compositional technique, and other secondary subjects. She even did some conducting with a small experimental chamber music orchestra. But she spent most of her free time with Olga.

Her new attachment undoubtedly did her a great deal of good. One can absorb much through the antennae which spread out from the Subconscious, and who knows what four years of Olga's grunting pounded into the slowly evolving pattern of Maia's artistry. It seems strange that her development was slow, exploratory. She had a really superior intelligence. But except from the standpoint of pure technique she did not progress very rapidly at first.

Perhaps for her that was the truest way. She learned slowly but surely how to interpret the works of the masters. They were long dead, and since every instruction is not written in the music, the art of bringing to life the subtle nuances of the great composers takes many years to acquire. And each artist has his own individual reasoning about the matter. The battles raged in quartet rehearsals for years over tempo, dynamics, phrasing. Photostats were taken from original documents in the Berlin Staatsbibliothek, the British Museum, from holographs in private collections. And not infrequently four solitary, implacable, contradictory positions were assumed.

Then Maia would take up her fiddle. The disputed passage would ring forth true and clear. One could see Papa Haydn nodding his head in solemn agreement. And, peace would reign. Until the next time.

Main's upbringing had surrounded her with defenses which were difficult to penetrate and several years went by before I could feel she trusted me. But there came a time when she would visit with me and ask my advice, like a little girl. She was a charming person when you got to know her well. Her taste in clothes is excellent and I remember thinking when I met her for the first time that she was one of the most attractively dressed women I had ever known. She was tiny, pensive, and a famous couturier had recognized and emphasized her wistful charm.

But the poverty of Maia's childhood was something she never forgot. And with financial independence at last, she became actually destructive of money, as though she hated it. There was nothing, should the notion strike her that she wanted it, which she would not move heaven and, earth to own. She would spend fantastically absurd sums and go to an endless amount of trouble to get some ridiculous heirloom.

Her neurotic behavior would get her into trouble occasionally. Once she bought an old fire engine which she found in a small town through which the quartet passed while on tour. The police objected to her speeding down Broadway with the siren screaming and she came to me crying with frustration. She owned a small barn near Nyack which she used as a warehouse and, in which she stored all the things she had acquired impulsively and then tired of, and I persuaded her to leave the old machine in the barn. This she did reluctantly and from time to time when she went to deposit something in her little warehouse she would climb into the high seat of the old engine and play reminiscently with the siren.

One thing remained to annoy her. She could never get rid of the brand of the fiddler, the little red mark which comes from contact of the neck with the fiddle. It takes many years of hard work to acquire but when the mark finally appears it remains, a permanent disfigurement. Once Maia gave up playing for a whole summer, applied creams, lotions, massage. No use, the little red scar emerged undaunted. She swore that plastic surgery would be the next step, but Otto frightened her with imaginative and grisly tales of horrible mutilations which the knife could inflict. "It's the badge of every successful fiddler," he would say. "Wear it proudly. And so Maia reluctantly gave up the idea of an operation.

But she would still affect expensive fur neckpieces. Quite stunning and original they were too.

* * *

And about Andrea Dante. She had started early, as most fiddlers do, beginning the study of the viola at the age of seven. Her father was the viola player in the village quartet and. Andrea stubbornly refused to begin with the smaller violin and make a gradual transition to the bulky awkwardness of the viola. She wanted to play the big fiddle right away so that she could be like her father. But the smallest instrument they had been able to get was much too big for her and as a result she had been permanently injured. Anyone who has heard her play can imagine the terrible intensity which in her earliest years, and lacking professional teaching, drove the wooden giant into her tiny vocal chords, day after day, year after growing year. In five years she could hardly speak. She was always a silent child and the swarm of brothers absorbed her mother's attention so that Andrea's silence went unnoticed too long. And then it was too late. A congenital weakness had been aggravated and she would never speak again.

I could never get Andrea to write to me of her early life, and I have had to depend on old Pietro, her father, to tell me what I know of it. Andrea's muteness was discovered one evening when she was invited to play a Mozart Quintet. The members of old Pietro's string quartet had pooled their resources and bought a bound volume of all the quartets.

Andrea's effortless superiority to her father had startled his colleagues. Old Pietro recalled the incident clearly. "Anna was a good girl, Mister Esca. Yes, she play the Mozart Quintet when she is twelve years. Then we see something wrong. Everybody is happy, everybody so happy. She is so good. But she is quiet, Mister Esca. Not even to thank my friends! And we think-is she sick?

"We go to the doctor. He think she play the viola too much. He can do nothing. We make her to stop the viola. But she will not. The doctor tell us it will not hurt her to play. The hurt is done.

"And we let her play. But she is quiet. Always she is quiet. She whisper. I blame myself. The viola is a danger. But how can I know?" Old Pietro sighed heavily. "Now she write on little paper. But the voice, it is gone, Mister Esca. Gone."

The eloquence of Andrea, however, did not lie in her voice. Even though she never got much training she became one of the best and most articulate violists in the world. But she wasn't satisfied. And gradually she learned how to compose by studying the works of the great masters. By 1950 she had finished about forty compositions for every imaginable combination of instruments, and she had even completed an opera.

Andrea did not study for more than a few months with the fine professors of the Vienna Conservatory. As a matter of fact her attitude toward, most of her teachers in Vienna was somewhat contemptuous and she always insisted that she was largely self-taught. I consider it remarkable that she was able at the age of twenty-one to have acquired with almost no assistance the knowledge, the discipline, the artistry which enabled her to fit into the foremost string quartet of her day.

One of Andrea's most fervent admirers was Otto. He said once, "When she puts a finger down on the string you hear a word. When she plays a melody you hear a poem. She has the gift of speaking hands." As they all did, but somehow with Andrea you felt triumph in the playing which rescued her from eternal quiet.

She had one outrageous and stubborn fault, a fault which it is hard to tolerate in any fiddler. And it is a measure of her greatness that she was allowed to remain with the quartet. She would not use the mute, the little piece of aluminum which is sometimes made to fit onto the fiddle and which softens its tone to a hollow whisper.

"I will not mute my only voice," she wrote. Perhaps Andrea was right to object to the mute. My impression of the viola is that its timbre is deep and dark and easily drowned by the piercing soprano of the fiddles and the powerful bass of the cello. I think the mute might well make it difficult for the violist to be heard at all.

This reminds me of a rehearsal which I attended several years ago. I was following the music of a Brahms quartet by reading the score. (For I seldom go to a rehearsal without a musical score. It helps me to understand what is happening.) Now the scherzo of this quartet was muted and the Casa Bellas carefully attached the little metal prongs to their fiddles. Except Andrea of course.

And then I noticed what seemed to be a mistake in the score. Brahms had indicated no mute for the viola. But Otto said, "Well, Anny, today you are vindicated. No mute for you."

The quartet never sounded so well, the balance of the four voices was never so perfect. Of this music Brahms himself had said, "It is the most tender and impassioned writing I have ever done." Perhaps in his inspiration he had found the truest expression of the string quartet medium.

Andrea always seemed, to be a little removed, a little different, from the others in the quartet. For instance, Otto, Olga and Maia always wanted to leave as soon as a rehearsal ended. I suppose the enforced intimacy of the group was such a constant thing that they welcomed the chance of not seeing each other for a short time.

But long after the others had left, Andrea would remain in her chair, motionless, inanimate. With an utterly tragic look on her face she would just sit and stare into the distance, sometimes for hours. I always felt sorry for her and many times I would ask her to come with Thede and me to dinner. In the early days of my management she sometimes accepted but of later years almost never. I couldn't understand why she rejected us. It seemed to me that we got along famously. One thing that had particularly gratified me was the, friendship between Andrea and Thede. At least in the beginning. It was always difficult for Andrea to mix with people but Thede was a rather quiet, somewhat introverted person and it may have been their mutual silence which attracted them to each other.

I remember a time when Andrea did come along with us. We had a gay time that evening. First we went to one of the best restaurants in New York for dinner. Andrea looked at the menu with astonishment and began to write on the beautiful linen napkins. "At these prices why should I use my paper? Down with this place. Let it be destroyed."

I said to the waiter, "Two dozen napkins, please."

Then Andrea wrote another note. "Don't you think we should take some of these excellent napkins home with us?"

Thede read the note and smiled. "Of course," she said. "Let's see, what else can we take. I think we should rob them if they rob us, don't you?"

"By all means. What would you like to steal?"

"What can we get away with?"

"How about stealing some plates? "Silver? Maybe the tablecloth?"

"All right, but how can we get out without being seen?" Thede turned to me. "Will you help us, Billy?"

"Why, of course. But—excuse me a minute. I'll be right back."

I went to the headwaiter and explained the situation. I gave him a hundred dollars and my address in case we stole more than the money would cover.

Andrea was a master of casual surreptitiousness as she smuggled the silver into my pockets and the dishes into her bosom. We left the restaurant simply bulging. The door had barely closed behind us when a dish crashed to the pavement and Thede and Andrea broke into a wild run laughing like little children. I was glad to see them having such a good time.

We made for our car and piled all the stolen goods into the rear seat. Then we went to the Diamond Club. I said, "Now the prices here are even worse. But please—no more stealing. I don't want to end up in jail."

"Sissy," Thede said.

"Don't blame him," wrote Andrea. "He had an unhappy childhood," and winking at me she broke into silent laughter. She had a charming, mischievous wink.

Andrea seemed to be having a wonderful time. She didn't even look quite so ugly, her face took on some color and became animated. "Let's have some champagne," she wrote. I called the waiter.

I determined, to do this kind of thing more often with Andrea. Of all the quartet she seemed to me to be the unhappiest. It could come off my income tax as a deduction for entertainment.

The orchestra began to play. "Perhaps Andrea would like to dance?" Thede said.

Andrea blushed. "I am a terrible dancer," she wrote.

"You are looking at the granddaddy of all terrible dancers," I said. I offered, her my arm and led her onto the crowded floor.

"Do you like dance music?" I asked. She smiled and nodded, She was really an excellent dancer and even gave me the impression, very subtly, that she was leading instead of following.

But after what seemed like a very short time Andrea wanted to return to our table. She wrote on a napkin "This has all been wonderful, but I have an early rehearsal tomorrow. Could we leave soon?"

"Of course," Thede said. "Shall we go, Billy?"

We took Andrea to her home in Brooklyn. She smiled as her lips formed the words, "Good Night."

She seemed to have thoroughly enjoyed herself, but it was our last social evening. Although she sometimes came to our apartment she never went out with us again. With the passage of time, she seemed to be moving away from us altogether. Several times I noticed a faint smell of alcohol on her breath and I thought that she might have made some new friends. But I knew that she was not in the habit of drinking because her behavior was quite rational. Somehow she became less and less friendly to us, especially to Thede I could never understand, why. Unless it is that when an artist becomes great enough, he becomes also incomprehensible.

Esca nodded his head slowly, sadly. How little he had known then — and how much was to happen in the following years. It hardly seemed possible now that the people he had been reading about were those he had known recently. Could the really have stolen those plates and silverware? He nodded his head again.

But perhaps it was now time to write a real history of the Casa Bella. True, a great deal had happened, but it was time that the story be told. Now where the devil was the typewriter? Ah, he remembered. It was in the trunk of the car. He had succeeded in getting it back last week from

Phil Burton. You loaned something to that fellow and you were lucky if he ever returned it. Esca stood, yawned, stretched. Then he went out and got the typewriter.

When he returned, he placed the typewriter on the oblong table. Then he got a package of typing paper, inserted several sheets and began to type.

The quartet had been engaged to come out to the Jonathan Bezhvelbisec estate to play at the wedding of the old man's daughter Joanna. I am an old friend of Joanna's and she had sent me an invitation. And so Thede and I had come with the quartet. Before the wedding I wandered about the estate for a time. Bezhvelbisec was a rich old fool and it was costing him a pretty penny to engage the quartet to play for half an hour. Still, Joanna was an excellent musician and what better wedding present could he have given her?

I tried to estimate the size of the place as I walked. Roughly a thousand acres, I guessed. And there was a, small concert auditorium on the first floor of the big, three-story house, a gymnasium in the basement and a swimming pool on the front lawn. And grouse and pheasant in the forest which spread out over a good two-thirds of the property. Or so the old man said. He claimed to have imported the pheasant from Europe. But I hadn't seen any.

I had walked about two hundred yards into the woods when I decided to go back. What was the use? I was too worried to enjoy the beauties of nature. It was my eleventh season with the Casa Bellas and for the first time I had badly shirked my duties. That morning I had reluctantly approached my desk with the intention of completing the arrangements for the quartet's forthcoming tour of the United States. And I had a feeling of guilty joy when Thede came in to remind me that we must leave for the wedding before I had finished. Now I experienced the guilt once more, but there was no gladness mixed in.

I hated the messy details. They made me feel like a coal miner. But now it was really the last possible moment. I should have attended to everything in the spring, but—after all I had been traveling with the quartet and didn't have time. Or did I?

But why torment myself? I was sixty years old and entitled to relax a little now and then. Nevertheless, I decided that when we got home I would absolutely stay up until I was through with the stupid business, no matter if it took all night.

The decision made me feel a little better and I decided to go into the house and congratulate Joanna. And I wanted to know whether she was pleased with Otto's choice of the Schubert G major quartet for the concert. I knew that she was a fine pianist and that she had studied in Europe with the great Ergauer. And what an excellent debut at Town Hall. I had dragged Otto to the concert but somehow the little weasel escaped afterwards and managed to get out of saying what he thought of the girl. What a slithery rascal.

Now the chef came out of the house and struck a large gong. Time for lunch. As I rounded a leafy curve in the walk I saw Maia walking toward me.

"Hello, Billy dear. Have you seen Andrea?"

"No, Mala, I haven't."

"She should have come on the train with us yesterday. It was agreed. The wedding starts in a few hours and Otto is quite. worried." She frowned. "And so am I."

"As some of my Jewish friends say, 'I should have your worries and Rothschild's money.' Has she missed a concert in twenty years? No. Have you ever been late? Yes. So relax. Don't give it another thought. She'll be here all right."

Olga strode up. "Billy have you seen Andrea?'"

"For God's sake. Anybody with brains hates to come to these shindigs. If she isn't on the afternoon train there will be plenty of time to worry. I'll bet anything she'll have a swell excuse all figured out. Something about she had to go to the doctor because her backside was itching. Relax, will you?" And I went into the dining room.

I did not see Otto at lunch, and afterwards I began to stroll idly around the estate looking for him. For a long time I wandered fruitlessly and at last I decide& to look inside the house.

I found him in the gymnasium, simultaneously swinging a pair of dumbbells and reading from a book perched on a music rack. "Otto! At last. I've been looking for you the past hour. And what are you doing with the dumbbells?"

"Too much sitting and not enough exercise, Bally Make is wonderful, don't you think? Oh, you don't speak German." He began to recite the poetry and his voice shook bathos.

"Otto, take your damned clothes off. You'll get them all sweaty. Bezhvelbisec will lend you a gym suit."

"What for? Andrea will be here any minute and we'll have to start warming up." He put down the dumbbells, went to his big violin case and took out a small cake of rosin covered with green cloth. Then he unclasped the long velvet sheath which covered his bow and withdrew its shining length. Next came the careful tightening of the bag's screw and the elevation of the slack ribbon of horsehair to a smooth elongated bridge of white. He applied the rosin with a strong flowing movement and with short heavy strokes as he reached either end of the bow. He used great pressure. The delicate fiddlestick buckled until it seemed ready to snap in two, the pressure forcing the wood through the white hair until a small brown tongue pushed through the opening.

When he had a finished Otto beat the bow up and down several times to free the hairs of any large stray rosin particles. Then he stood peering dawn the length of the stick for all the world like a bullfighter about to perform his final thrust. Suddenly he said, "Did you know there's one school of thought which claims that Ludwig van Beethoven was a homosexual?" His left eye was shut tight now as he examined the white strands, his face screwed up so that a corner of his mouth opened into a moronic cavity. "These fellows in America just can't rehair a bow properly."

"I suppose that everyone is bisexual, more or less. But in my opinion all you can say about Beethoven is that since every man leans a little more or less in the direction of being feminine, he might have leaned a little more."

Otto whipped his bow up and down as though it were a sabre. "You know," he said reminiscently, "we used to fence with these things at school when I was a child. I remember breaking a good Lamy bow once.

"Children do silly things. Sometimes everyone does silly things."

"The people who talk about homosexuality in Beethoven have very little to go on." He was examining another bow now. He had four all told in his large oblong case, and two violins, the narrow part of one placed against the wide part of another. "Bisexual of course doesn't mean homosexual. Anyway he could have been asexual, like me." And. Otto rosined his remaining bows, and one after the other he lashed them viciously through the air which protested with sharp little noises.

Then he returned them to his case. It was an unusually large case. Underneath the violins there was a special drawer which was divided into sections. For overnight trips Otto could almost use it as a suitcase.

Maia came in. "Well, she still isn't here."

Otto flared up. He walked furiously over the gymnasium mats, kicking at them.

"Calm yourself, I said. "She's probably getting her teeth cleaned."

Otto ignored me. "Dammit," he said. "What the devil can we do? Can we play trios?"

"If we had some music and a viola we could, but we have neither." Maia was dejected, "To hell with the concert, Otto. I only hope nothing has happened to her."

"To hell with her," Otto answered angrily. "I only hope nothing happens to the concert. Now why didn't you bring your viola? Dammit, haven't we rehearsed, and rehearsed for just such an emergency?"

Maia was hurt. "Please don't be so nasty. You know we haven't taken these precautions for years. Why should we have today? Suddenly? For no reason?"

Otto subsided, grumbling.

Now the door flew violently open. It was Olga. "No sign of her yet."

"*Where the hell could, she be?*" Otto shouted.

"She'll probably be on the afternoon train," I said. "Or maybe she's sick," Maia ventured.

"She'd have to be mighty damned sick to miss a concert. Besides I saw her just yesterday morning and she seemed in good enough health to me." Otto felt his wrist. "*She's* killing me," he cried. "My pulse has gone from eighty to one hundred and thirty-eight."

I was puzzled. "How in the world, can you tell, Otto?"

"Oh, for God's sake," Otto glared at me. "Because in the beginning my pulse corresponded exactly to Beethoven's Opus 18, No, 6, which is played at a speed of eighty beats per minute. Then I went up to ninety-two beats per minute, Opus 95. Then one hundred beats, the third Schönberg Quartet, one hundred and twelve, Assezvif of the Debussy Quartet, one hundred and twenty, last movement of Opus 18, No. 1, and finally, one hundred and thirty-eight beats per minute, slow movement of the same composition. How can you have reached the age of sixty without knowing how to take your pulse?" he said disgustedly. Then he walked over to the window. "She is killing me," he said morosely.

"Don't be a fool, Otto. Your heart can go over two hundred beats a minute without damage. And anyway it's only temporary. As soon as she arrives you'll drop back to normal."

"If she ever does." Otto stared gloomily at the landscape. "I know all about how my heart can beat two hundred times a minute. But what if it goes up to two thousand times?"

"Now stop worrying. Look, I'll tell you what we can do. Let's go comfort Bezhvelbisec. If I know him he's getting ulcers. You don't want to ruin a profitable connection, do you?"

"No," Otto muttered. "All right, let's go."

We went upstairs, but the wedding was getting underway and it was impossible to speak with Bezhvelbisec. He only glared at us horribly. I was vastly amuse& and found it difficult to keep a straight face. But Otto was in despair.

We drove down to meet the four-thirty train, but Andrea was not on it. And now I began to worry, too. I telephoned my home in New Jersey. where Andrea usually spent her days. She, of course, never answered the telephone, and Mrs. Bundy, the housekeeper, was away visiting her sister. But Ebbie, the maid, should have been there.

Yet no one answered. What to do. I decided to telephone the Dantes and asked the long distance operator to connect me with their home in Brooklyn. But although I tried to reach them several times their line was always busy. I came out of the telephone booth at last angry and frustrated and when Otto said, "Well, Billy? What news?" I growled, "Come on. There's little time left. The only thing I can think of is that Thede will have to play a Mozart trio with you."

Disconsolately we all got into the car and. I drove back to the estate. The wedding was lust over and I waited impatiently to speak to Joanna who was surrounded with people. The minutes crawled by and I became increasingly nervous. At last there was a tiny chance and I broke in quickly. "Joanna—-Joanna, I must speak with you for a moment. Tell me, do you have any of the Mozart piano trios?"

"Why, yes, Billy. It seems to me that I have all of them. Do you need, them?"

"Well, I don't know how to tell you this, but—our violist has not yet arrived. It's disappointing for you, I know. But this has never happened before and. I'm terribly afraid that she might have had an accident." -

"Poor dear. Now don't you worry about me. We don't have to have any music at all if you think it might be too difficult."

"No, I'll find out about it. I think my wife can play a trio with Otto and Maia." And I went off to see what I could arrange.

"But Otto, what else is there to do?"

"Oh, all right, all right. But are you sure she has the trio?"

Just then Joanna came up with a volume of music. "I have them here. All the

Mozart's. But please don't feel that you have to perform if you don't want to, Mr. Otto."

I took the music. "We'll be ready in half an hour," I said. "I've heard them do this beautifully, Joanna, and I think you'll enjoy hearing them too."

She clapped her hands. "Oh, good. I must tell my father. He will be so pleased." And, she ran off happily.

Otto sighed. "Well, I guess we'd better play it through once." He went to find Olga, and I began to worry about the best way to break the news to Thede.

The Mozart was brilliant, but Otto smiled grimly at the throng clustering around Thede. She was beautiful and tonight she looked radiant. Sad that physical beauty always supersedes esthetic beauty. Not that she played badly. For an amateur.

And then there was coffee and a gooey monstrosity of a wedding cake. We sat and smoked and talked until late at night. Gradually the wedding guests departed until only the musicians and Thede and I were left. Abruptly Otto stood and said, "I guess she just isn't coming. "Let's go. I'm sorry, Joanna."

"It was exquisite, Mr. Otto. Nothing to be sorry about."

But old Bezhvelbisec was still disgruntled. "Catch me hiring your quartet again," he said. "Faugh."

We took the one o'clock train back to New York. I was very worried. I couldn't imagine what had made Andrea miss the concert that would also prevent her from seeing that we were notified. Unless it was something very serious. But why hadn't I been able to find anything out by telephone? Why wasn't Ebbie there? I would give her a good talking to.

"Maybe she mistook the directions," Maia ventured. "There are two Jonesvilles and she could have gone to the other one."

"No, no," Otto said wearily. "I told her about that. And I'm positive Bill bought the right tickets because I saw them. I also saw him give one to Andrea, and—"

"Stop talking about it," Olga interrupted. "We'll fine out soon enough, for god's sake. Andrea is coming to rehearsal at ten-thirty. Now I'm going to sleep a little so shut up."

'But Thede said, "I move we call her tonight when we arrive. Otherwise I'll worry."

Otto smiled. It isn't necessary. I've been thinking about it and I'm sure I know what happened to her. Now, listen.

Do you all remember, Olga, Maia ten, twelve years ago when Andrea was nearly an hour late and almost missed a concert? She had simply gone for a long walk and gotten completely absorbed in her own thoughts. The concert altogether slipped her mind. I'll bet it's something like that. I'll bet you anything she simply forgot about the wedding."

Maia shook her head. "No, Otto, no If it were only that. But most likely she is ill. Frightfully ill."

"Then why didn't she let us know," Olga said indignantly.

"Maybe she. couldn't," Mala answered sharply. "Maybe she was just too damned sick. One can actually be in a state of not realizing what is happening."

"That's true." For a moment Olga sat thinking. Then she said, "She might even have lost an arm, or something. You know, a horrible accident might have happened to her."

"Or Maybe," Thede said, "she just went off with a simply fascinating man. But no matter what, I still think we're entitled to telephone the Dantes tonight. After all she did miss a concert and it is perfectly reasonable for us to be anxious about her."

"All right," I said. "All right "All call them as soon as we arrive."

The rest of the trip to New York was made in a gloomy silence broken only by the sound of Olga's raucous snoring.

The train got in at half-past three and I went directly to a phone booth. Everyone followed me and stood Waiting impatiently while I dialed the number. "No, no, Billy. You've got a wrong number. Start over again."

"How do you. know," I said irritably.

"Because I hear the damned clicks. And I can count."

Now a sleepy southern voice drawled into my ear. "Booker T. O'Halloran's residence."

"I beg your pardon," I said and hung up angrily. The little son of a bitch was always right. It was tiresome. Why couldn't he be human like everyone else? Very carefully I dialed again. But still the infuriating busy signal. I called the operator and asked her to check the Dante phone. But there was no one on the line.

Otto was disappointed. He said, "Tomorrow. I guess we'll have to wait until tomorrow. Dammit."

"Well," Olga said, "we might as well go." Wearily she dragged her cello and suitcase into a waiting taxicab. The others followed slowly. There was little conversation on the way home. Everyone seemed to have run out of ideas about what could have happened to Andrea.

But when we got back to the house everyone burst out of the taxicab and raced for Andrea's apartment. We were shocked to find that it was completely empty, as though she had moved away. Her viola, which she always left on her desk, was gone, and her few books and magazines. There was even no music on the music rack. Although Andrea did much of her living with her family in Brooklyn, and kept few things in the apartment which I had given her, it was now so unusually bare that everyone was frightened. Something terrible must have happened to her, an illness so severe, perhaps, that she might have been taken to a hospital somewhere.

Disconsolately we went to bed. But no one slept well that night. Except for Thede, who slept like a log while I tossed and turned. She even snored a little. After a while I sat up in bed and regarded her enviously. The young are wonderful I thought.

The next morning Andrea failed to appear for rehearsal. Now everyone was seriously alarmed. After waiting a few minutes Otto, with a furious gesture, reached for the telephone.

The number rang for some time. Finally a voice came over the wire and Otto shouted, "What in the world has happened to Andrea?" There was an audible click as the connection was broken.

I took the phone. "They must have hung up." I said reprovingly. "You shouldn't shout at people." And. I dialed the number again while Otto crowded close to me.

After a very long time Mama Dante answered, and I said, "Hello, Mama. This is Billy." Her voice was like the grave. "Andrea is—dead," she whispered. And into the shocking, thunderous statement came the tiny sound of the receiver being replaced.

It was an unbelievable thing to hear. Otto turned white. "No, my God, no," he gasped, and collapsing into a chair he buried his head between his arms.

"For heaven's sake," Male. said. anxiously. "What has happened?"

Characteristically, I began to think how best to break the news. But Otto began to sob brokenly, "She's *dead*, they say my little Anny is *dead*, oh, God. help me, what shall I do, whatever shall I do now, what—"

"How frightful," Thede burst out. "When, Billy? How?"

"Mama didn't talk about it at all. I—I had no chance to ask her because she just hung up on me. I'll ring her again."

Everyone was thunderstruck by the news. Olga could scarcely speak. "What?" she croaked, "What happened.?" But everyone ignored her.

This time no one answered the telephone. While I waited. I wondered what could have happened to Andrea. Illness? Accident? Even suicide?

At last I replaced the receiver. As I looked around the room I thought that everyone seemed to be in a state of shock and wondered if I looked as numb as the others. I began to wonder about Mala, who was staring into nowhere with an almost psychotic intensity. The shock was so great that she could only gaze helplessly, with a kind of quiet hysteria, into the distance. I spoke to her but she didn't seem to hear me. She only sat, her mouth set in a strange little grin, her head moving in a tiny, gesture of disbelief, whispering, "No, no, no, no,—"

At last I told Olga,. "I think you should take Maia to her rooms and give her a sleeping pill. Thede, you go along."

"Sleeping pill," Olga said wearily. "I need one myself." For a long time she sat, chin in hand:, staring gloomily at the floor,

"What a ghastly piece of news," she murmured. "'Could they possibly be playing some kind of grisly joke?"

Maia was still shaking her head with the same negative weary denial. And I lost my patience. "Put her to bed," I said: sharply. "Put her to bed. You Olga and you Thede. And slowly, mechanically, like sleep walkers, they left the room.

Now I came to a decision. "Otto," I said, "I'm going to Brooklyn. We simply .must find out what has happened. Anyway, maybe I can do something for them."

"I'm going with you."

Better not. Mama Dante had hung up on Otto, no doubt because he had made her angry.

"Shouldn't you stay here, Otto, and look after the girls?"

"No, let Olga take care of Maia. If I stay here she'll have to look after me too. Anyway, I have to go." Otto's eyes were red from weeping and he went to wash his face as I phone for a taxi. Then we went outside to wait. It came in a few minutes and we began the long ride to Brooklyn.

As we climbed the stairs the door opened and Gino Dante beckoned us silently into the living room. The entire family was present, Mama and Papa Dante, the four sons and little Teresa.

No one greeted us and I felt a little embarrassed. But Otto said, "Was it a sudden illness? An accident? How did she die?"

Mama stared at him through narrowed, hating eyes. "Who knows?" she said darkly. "Maybe she has enemies."

"My poor Anna," Papa moaned. "To die when she was so happy, so glad to live."

Antonio, one of the brothers, said, "But Papa, you are wrong. She was almost never happy in her life. Even sometimes she used to drink, to drown her sorrow that she could not speak, and had not a man, and—"

"How do you say this thing," Mama interrupted furiously. "I will tell the sorrow. It was because the bad, bad quartet. She tell me everything. Who is like a mother? She do not talk, but she whisper. We have many nights, my ears near to her mouth." Mama spoke angrily, with great force, and as though we did not exist. "Twenty years she play with the—damned quartet. Is this a life? Concerts, hotels, trains? And always the hurry, the nervous, the exciting, the rehearsals. And more rehearsals. And the *still* more rehearsals. The better she know the music, the still more the—damn crazy rehearsals. And all the time she want to *speak*, to have her *part* in the music. She can never say something. She can never say *something*. The bad Otto never listen to her, and the manwoman Olga always shout, shout her away, even when she shake her head *yes*, or not. Sometimes she drink, maybe. Can you blame?" And Mama stalked angrily from the room. But once the door had closed behind her, a faint weeping, muffled and anguished, could be heard in the hallway beyond.

Old Pietro stammered, "Do—do not be hurt, my friends. Mama feels so bad., she is so unhappy, she—"

Otto had been shaken by Mama's terrible words, but he managed to say, "Don't worry, Pietro. It's all right." My mind wandered. One of the faces began to speak.

I shook myself into a recognition of the face. It was Gino, the brother who had let us into the house. "...took a drink sometimes," he was saying, "but only sometimes." He wiped his eyes with a bandanna handkerchief and blew *his* nose. "She never bought any liquor. Only the pure alcohol to clean the strings. We used to go to the doctor together. He wrote on the prescription, 'Use as directed.' Ha. A big joke, no? Use as directed." He wiped his eyes again.

"May I say something, please?" asked Teresa.

Old Pietro smiled at her forlornly. "What is it, Teresina *mia*?"

"Well, Anny wrote to me in such a sad way, and only a few days before she—she passed away. She wrote, 'I sometimes feel that I do not wish to live.'" Teresa's voice was hushed as she said, "Do you think that—"

"No, no, Teresa..." Old Pietro was horrified. "No! Andrea did not mean it so. I will not believe."

Everyone was silent for a time. Then Otto said timidly, "Would it be possible for us to see her? Please?"

Pietro sighed heavily. Then he rose painfully and stood for a moment, lost in thought. He led the way from the room and we followed him. With every step I felt an increasing dread and as Pietro led us through a door and into a small room I felt myself to be on the verge of panic.

"'I bought this coffin for myself," Pietro said gloomily.

"Who could know—" his voice trailed away. Then, faltering, he crept from the room.

It was very dark and I switched on the light. The coffin was open and as we approached it the sudden appearance of Andrea's face was shocking it had not been composed and the expression of her final moments stared at us horribly, remorselessly. The glazed eyes were frozen in a twisted grimace, the mouth fixed in a curious grin, a projecting arm rigid in an accusing gesture.

Suddenly I felt like screaming. I couldn't bear it, how utterly intolerable it was that she should be lying in the impossible coffin. No, no, I could not accept the unalterable fact of her death, — wait, now she would surely come to life and wink at me, and wink and wink as she had, done so often. God! I fancied that her eyelid had indeed moved, and I shivered and felt cold. As I stared at her intently, trying to surprise another wink, Otto's legs gave way slowly and he fell to his knees. For a time he knelt by the coffin, then he kissed Andrea's frigid hand. His eyes closed and he began to whisper to himself.

Otto looked lovingly at the dead face. He began to stroke it, but as he stroked the entire body moved, as though his touch offended it, and he lurched back suddenly. He stared suspiciously at the corpse. It stared back at him, its look of amusement seeming to mock him. The stray limb sticking out of the coffin was like a nightmare from Dada.

Now Otto broke into an anguished, heart-broken sobbing. And. I decided that I couldn't listen to him any more. It was too painful, too distressing. I went back into the living room, where the family was still sitting about silently, and said, "Is there anything, anything at all that I can do?"

Papa answered, "No, Mister Esca, nothing."

There must be something. I said, "You should really have called the police, you know, and a doctor to examine her. When did she die?"

"On Sunday. At your place, Mister Esca. The colored girl she call me on the telephone, and three of the boys, they go and get her."

Gino began to cry. "How terrible It is," he sobbed, "that she should die so soon, without knowing the joys of a husband and children."

Matteo tried to comfort him. "But she had her music, after all. Don't cry, Gino. Please don't cry." Matteo was the youngest brother a beautiful boy and a favorite of the family. He put his arm around Gino, who dried his eyes with a sleeve.

Otto came into the room. His face was tear stained but calm as he said, "Can we do anything for you, any of you?"

And once more old Pietro murmured, "Nothing, thank you."

"I should like to express an opinion," Teresa cried. "It is this. I think that there will never again be such a sister."

Alessandro, a dour pock-marked little man who had been silent until now, spoke at last. His voice was strong and harsh, like Saar Italian wine. "She is better off dead," he said bitterly. "What did life have to offer her? Only misery, loneliness, heartache."

I thought that we should leave. Certainly we were not doing anyone there any good. I held out my hand to old Pietro and said, "Well, I guess we'll go now." Pietro shook hands without energy. "Good-bye, Mister Esca," he muttered.

"Good-bye," Teresa said mournfully. The others were silent.

We left the family to its grieving and began slowly to walk down the street. In a tone of utter discouragement Otto said, "Well, that's the end of the quartet. We could never find anybody to take her place. Never." He shook his head and walked in silence for a time. Then he took my shoulders and I felt the burning of Otto's eyes as he cried despairingly, "Why did God let it happen? What did she *do* that deserved such terrible punishment? Can you think of a *reason* for it? Is it not *insane*?" He turned suddenly away. "You have to discount what Mama said," he muttered. Then he faced me again. "You have to discount it, don't you?" he asked, hopefully, pleadingly.

"Of course. Obviously she was almost out of her mind with grief. She didn't know what she was saying, just had to lash out at somebody. And I'll tell you what I think about Andrea. I think that frightful, unjust things happen all the time and that her death was merely one of these things. What the devil can you expect out of life."

Otto drew a long breath. "She probably drank too much. She even used to smell of liquor." We came to a playground and Otto paused for a moment and watched the children at play. "Yes," he mused, "no doubt she would have a real drinking bout now and then. Not very frequently. At least it wasn't often that she smelled of it." He laughed grimly. "Pure cleaning alcohol. You can imagine. That alone would be enough to remove her vocal chords."

I was not offended at Otto's humor at Andrea's expense. I knew Otto far too well to be angry with him. Poor little man. He was deeply and terribly hurt. Apart from the ruin of his career he felt guilt as well as the wound of Andrea's loss. How tragic it was to watch his transparent suffering features as he tried to deceive himself with light and silly talk.

We walked down a side street. Along its gutters there grew several scrawny trees, and a slight breath of air caused their branches to move gently. It seemed to me that they were waving good-bye. Good-bye, I thought helplessly, good-bye.

After a long time, it seemed hours, during which we talked of everything under the sun except Andrea, I said, "We might as well go and see how Maia and Olga are getting along."

"Yes," Otto answered. "But they are suffering too, I know. One can't escape it, no matter how one tries." He waved to a cruising taxi.

We climbed in and. Otto leaned back exhaustedly. "What an experience, Billy, what a fearful, shocking experience."

I was becoming a little weary. I had suffered too from a deep senses of shock end loss, but it did not make me feel better to grind the pain in by going on about it for so long. I said, "Otto, listen to me. It is too distressing to think about any more, really it is. Why don't you try to forget about it for at least a little while, and I'll try too."

I might have known better. Otto wanted to suffer. He said, "But you know, Billy, it is simply not true what Mama said. You remember? About not asking Andrea's opinion?" It seemed to be a fear he could not rid himself of, and during the coming months he was to ask the same question again and again and to anyone who might possibly be able to reassure him. I grew to recognize the look on Otto's face when he was about to ask the interminable question, and I became very tired of it. Once I almost thought Otto was going to ask Ebbie, the maid, for reassurance.

But now I said, "No, Otto, of course it's not true. You were very sympathetic and patient with Andrea's handicap and you considered her opinions as carefully as you did anyone's."

Otto breathed a sigh of relief. "I could not live with myself if I had contributed in any way to this horrible thing, if I had caused her to be so depressed that she committed—"

"She may have drunk something by accident. Or perhaps she had a heart attack. But surely she wouldn't have killed herself."

We were silent for a time, then Otto said, "Do you know, Bill, she was no doubt the greatest viola player in the world. By far. And one of the very greatest musicians."

"I know."

"My God, how I loved that woman." And he began to weep again. "Everybody knows how I loved her. And oh, how tortured her face was in death. Whatever she died from must have caused her such—such intolerable pain." He began to rock back and forth in the seat of the taxi, moaning in the most heart-broken way. Now it became difficult for me to bear. The tragedy, Otto's real suffering, overcame my impatience with him and I was almost at the point of tears myself.

"Otto," I begged, "try not to think of it any more. It's no good tormenting yourself. It won't bring her back."

"I know. Nothing will ever, ever bring her back." He uttered a long, shuddering sigh.

The taxi drove up to the door, I paid the driver and we went into the house. Olga looked up when we came in. She said, "Maia is still sleeping—"

But Maia called from the stairway, "No I'm not. I couldn't even fall asleep with Olga's pill. Tell me quickly what happened, in Brooklyn."

Otto clasped his forehead. "You have no idea how dreadful it was," he cried. "Her face had a look of such terrible pain. And then Mama Dante accused us of never asking her opinion about how to play the music. It isn't true, is it? Olga? Maia? Tell me it isn't true, please tell me it isn't true."

And he began to cry. Great racking sobs escaped him, and he wept bitterly and as though his heart would break. I was embarrassed. I thought that a man should not cry openly and before women and. I was a little ashamed of Otto.

Olga and Maia stood uncertainly for a moment, looking at each other. Then Olga said timidly, "Please don't take on so, Otto. Of course we—we did, ask her about some things. But after all she was mute. She couldn't have expected to enter into the heat of the battle to the same extent as the rest of us, could she?"

Otto tried to control himself. A long sigh escaped him and he shuddered briefly. "I suppose she couldn't," he muttered.

"But that is not the point," Maia said sorrowfully. "Many times we voted against her, the three of us. She was a marvelous musician and she could not have been wrong so often."

I said, "But Maia. I don't see how you can blame yourselves for that. Is it a question of being right or wrong? Or doesn't it rather have to do with how an individual feels about the music?"

Maia shook her head impatiently. "Usually it does, Billy. But now about Andrea. You see, it wouldn't have mattered so much except that there was this antagonism which she somehow aroused in us. Why? What was it that she did? Why did we find it necessary to be against her? I have thought about it and thought about it but I have never found the answer." She made a tiny, nervous, pleading movement with her hand. "But in our own defense I have to say that she was so—what is the word—so inarticulate. One seldom knew what she was thinking, how she felt. Could we know it was important to her? She didn't behave as though she cared."

And Olga grumbled, "I am convinced, I have always been convinced that she was completely indifferent to us. And this is the truth."

"I shall never feel secure again," Otto mourned. "How can I know that either of you might not die?" The tears were still streaming from his eyes. Although by this time his face had become relatively calm, the tiny rivers continued to flow down his cheeks. He looked absolutely wretched. Beneath his bloodshot eyes were great, white, puffy bags. He appeared to have aged ten years in a single day.

I decided to take matters in hand. "Olga," I said, "if you have any Dormital I think you had better give some to Otto."

"No, no. I can't accept the luxury of sleep. I must think."

"Nonsense. Olga, give him a sleeping pill even if you have to force it on him,"

"Here, Otto." And Olga made a ferocious face. "Go on and take it. Take two of them."

"All right." And surprisingly Otto took the capsules, meekly, as though he were a little boy. Then he staggered off to bed.

Thede stole silently, almost secretively into the room. She wandered about aimlessly for a time, then sat down. "It's a tragic thing that has happened." She spoke formally, as though she were obliged to tender a condolence. "I feel so—really sorry for all of you. Is there anything at all that I can do?"

"No, Thede, thank you," Mala said with a surprising harshness. "We'll just have to get over it the best we can. Olga, maybe two sleeping pills would have succeeded with me. Can I have another?"

"Of course. Maybe I'll take some too."

Suddenly I felt utterly weary, felt an overwhelming necessity to escape the whole ghastly business, to get away from it, far away from it. I said to Olga, "Might I have one or two of them, please? I guess I could use some sleep after what I've been through today."

And, except, Thede, each of us swallowed two of the capsules and went to bed.

But for a long time I couldn't sleep. I only felt groggy, and I wondered whether the others were lying awake too. After what had happened who could sleep, pills or no pills.

Now, in that state between semi-wakefulness and dreaming, I seemed to hear music, distant music. It sounded like a piano. If the music had been tragic, a funeral march or a dirge, I would have thought it part of a dream and that it was my subconscious mind which had manufactured a background for Andrea's death. But the music was quite happy and gay. From time to time I sat up in bed, and listened carefully. But when I did this the music would vanish and. I would think I had been dreaming after all. Then my thoughts would grow fuzzy and. I would hear music again.

At last I decided that sleep was impossible. I felt hungry and thought of getting something to eat. But now as I sat up in bed the music did not stop. Strange. Indeed it grew louder as I put on a robe and. started down the stairs. When I reached the main floor I was surprised to see Otto sitting at the piano. On either side of him were Olga and Maia, their faces heavy and languorous with the failure to sleep. Otto's eyes were closed as he played. The scene had the quality of a surrealist film, three drugged people, almost asleep, one of them seated at a piano and playing, of all things, a sprightly Mozart minuet. From Otto's lips came the sound of deep sonorous breathing.

The next morning the police came. Their presence was harrowing to everyone, but they found something that no one had noticed. In a corner of Andrea's apartment one of them picked up an empty brown bottle.

They were casually thorough. Frightened Ebbie was questioned. "No," she said in a trembling voice, "there wasn't any screaming or anything like that. But Miss Andrea couldn't talk or make any sound so I couldn't have heard her no matter what. I just went in to clean and make up the bed and there she was lying on the floor. I'm telling you Mr. Officer I was scared silly and after they came and got Miss Andrea I went *as* quick as I could to be with my ma."

Everyone else was questioned and then the police left. By three o'clock the newspaper reporters had come and gone, taking with them a photograph of Andrea, and the house of Casa Bella was left alone to grieve.

The day of the funeral I telephoned the Dantes. Gino answered the phone. Yes, the autopsy report was ready. In, brief, it said that Andrea had drunk a great deal of pure alcohol. But in her body had also been found a quantity of the poison of denatured alcohol.

The police were satisfied that she had died accidentally. I thanked Gino and went to report to the others.

Otto was horrified. "How do you think she could have come to drink the ghastly stuff?"

I shrugged. "She might have been in a drunken stupor and drunk it accidentally. *Or*," I said, "maybe she wanted to kill herself with it."

"Those seem to be the only possibilities," Maia said.

"I think so. Of course, Mama Dante made the gruesome remark that 'Maybe she had enemies,' but one can't take her seriously. She was terribly upset the day we were there."

Otto said, "What I can't stop thinking about is this. She *might* have killed herself. And if she did there is the terrible possibility that at the last moment, when she was suffering so horribly, she might suddenly have been afraid of death, have changed her mind, have wanted to live, have wanted to cry out for help. And she *couldn't*! I tell you I just can't stop thinking about it."

"How do we know she suffered pain," Olga objected. "It looks like she was far too drunk to be able to feel anything at all."

"What is the greater pain," Mala said sorrowfully, "is the loss of Andrea. *We* are the ones who are suffering now, not Anny."

Thede threw up her hands. "Why don't we try to forget her, for God's sake, and the sooner the better. We can't go on forever this way, I think everyone has suffered enough and I'm going downtown." She went to the telephone to call a taxi.

I was puzzled by Thede's behavior and a little ashamed. Since Andrea's death I had not been able to stop thinking about her, no matter which way my mind turned. Thede had became closely identified with everyone in the quartet and. I couldn't understand her sudden indifference.

But now I began to worry about Andrea again. Somehow I felt guilty about her, although I could think of nothing I had done or neglected to do. I remembered Thede asking her to dinner many times and her almost invariable excuses. We had really tried as best we could to get to know her, even bringing her little gifts from time to time. For even though her family loved her dearly she was somehow the isolated one of the quartet. Andrea had always seemed to me to be alone in some kind of personal desert, and my heart had gone out to her in her loneliness. I knew that I had thought a great deal about Andrea, about what I could do to help her.

Nevertheless the feeling of guilt grew stronger as the days passed. Among my friends there had been an occasional suicide, and such a death would always affect me far more deeply than the natural deaths of other friends. All manner of hindsight and cogitation and anxiety would trouble me as I wondered what I could have done to prevent it, wondered what great sorrow had clouded their minds.

And now I tried to understand the dead mind of Andrea, the mind which was so doubly closed to me. Maybe it wasn't suicide. For wouldn't she have realized her importance in providing for her family? She was a moral person and wouldn't have harmed anyone, especially those she loved. But then, who could know? Perhaps the desire for death had been overpowering. Still, hadn't the police thought it was an accident? But what did they really know?

Wearily I began to search in the record library for the recording with the unmuted viola, placed it on the turntable and started the phonograph. For a long time I listened, and played the record again and again. And in the music was a sadness to make one weep.

The dismal afternoon held the threat of rain. It had rained in the morning and the sky was overhung with dirty grey clouds. We arrived at the cemetery in a despondent mood. Olga, fat, gaunt and a little old, comforted Mala who was sobbing bitterly, her eyes wounds from which red tears flowed. I held Thede's hand. Otto stood looking far away, to Vienna perhaps, to the Böhmer Wald, to his youth. The living past spread its years before us and the future seemed dead. The black casket shimmered weakly, reflecting the light of a dispirited sun.

The murmuring, convivial swarm of Andrea's relatives was everywhere. I was glad that I knew a little Italian and as walked through the crowd with Thede I listened to the talk with interest. It was curious, but it seemed to me that the corollary of an Italian funeral, if this one was an example, was an air of festivity, a carnival. One could feel it among the people, something of a holiday atmosphere. Even at Andrea's funeral—and hadn't she brought almost everyone in her family to America? Yet there was little sorrow. Or at least there seemed to be very little. Instead, the aunts, uncles, cousins, second cousins and more distant relatives, seemed only to be enjoying an exchange of comfortably philosophical thoughts. There was much pleasurably doleful headshaking as they discussed Andrea's life, her lack of men, her secret drinking. One original soul even ventured the opinion that she wasn't mute at all, but simply didn't like to talk to people. I went with Thede to join the others.

The simple ceremony was over and now Otto and I went to speak with Mama and Papa Dante. They stood apart in a corner of the cemetery, Papa bowed with grief, Mama weeping, the brothers and sister silent. Softly, tentatively, Otto said, "I would like all of you who have loved her to come with me. We will break bread and drink wine and listen to her play again. And know that she will always be alive and can never die. And I shall give you records, so that the memory of her playing can be with you forever."

Mama Dante straightened to her full height of some five feet. "*No*," she announced tearfully. "I must go home with Teresa."

But Old Pietro hastened to say, "We will come with you, Mister Otto." He felt embarrassed by Mama's attitude and his manner as he came with us was apologetic. His sons followed obediently, but I felt that they did not come willingly.

There was little conversation. Thede made canapés and. Maia got a gallon of wine from the cellar. We sat for a long time drinking and nibbling and. listening to records of the quartet.

At last Gino said, "There is no good picture of Anny." And Otto remembered that Andrea had always been the despair of photographers. But he had some rather good snapshots of her. He would give one of them to Gino.

Antonio said, "She was writing a book about the quartet. She had just started it. Now—" He shrugged.

"I wish for Tommasso to be here," Papa said mournfully. "Now all my sons should be here."

I noticed that Thede was crying. I was startled and. a little ashamed. After all these years to have misjudged her and to have thought that she didn't care about Andrea. I had seldom seen her cry before and. I wondered whether she felt guilty too. How strange are the emotions of human beings. Thede did not cry at the death of her father.

"Anny wanted to write how four people can play the wonderful music," Antonio continued, "and, still to hate the others. And still to love the others, because to play the best possible love must be. Then the music is like a medicine and for a little while the spirit is well."

"Why do we go to Vienna," Alessandro grumbled. "For the scholarship we go away from home. I was happy in our home. Lucca was near. A plenty big town. Vienna. Ha!" He snorted. "Anny was very good. She played beautiful. She was good enough for the quartet, no? She could get a job in Italy. But we go to Vienna. Ha!" He glowered at Papa, looked evilly at Otto, then subsided, muttering.

Now Antonio became angry. "You are a big man," he said sarcastically. "But only after. You are what they call in America, 'Monday morning waterbrain.'"

Matteo yawned, and Papa Pietro broke in quickly, "my little one, you are sleepy. Let us go now." He stood and thanked Otto for his kindness. Then he thanked the rest of us. The brothers followed his example, some courteously, some with barely concealed hostility. Record albums were distributed and the Dantes thanked everyone again and said goodbye

I was very tired but I thought I should not leave Otto yet. Be had tried to be friendly but had been rejected. Now he was obviously upset.

Maia said, "Don't pay any attention to them, Otto. People who feel miserable tend to take it out on others." And Olga grunted, "A bunch of peasants."

But there seemed to be only one thought in Otto's mind. "it's not true," he muttered. "It's not true. Andrea frequently made suggestions and He began to pace the floor, grumbling to himself.

"Of course she made suggestions," Maia reassured him. "Stop worrying about it, Otto dear. Now listen. I think we ought to cancel all our concerts immediately. It's not fair to let them know at the last minute. Can you take care of it tomorrow, Billy?"

But Thede said, "If you could play the viola, Maia, the concerts might not have to be cancelled. Maybe a few of them would, but I'll bet that in the majority of cases you could play string trios for violin, viola and cello."

Otto sighed. "No, my dear," he said disconsolately.

"And why not?"

"Simply that you wouldn't have enough balanced programs. There just is not enough of such music."

"But isn't there already a professional string trio in existence? If they can do it, why couldn't you?"

"No. I don't know. I don't want to—wait." He paused. "But if we would play *piano* quartets—Thedie, my lovely one, I think you have hit upon the answer." He took out his notebook. "Olga. Maia, come let us think of some programs. Let's start off with the Mozarts. Suggest something, will you?"

They began to draw up a list of possible programs with everyone peering over Otto's shoulder. The list grew with amazing rapidity and soon it included the satisfying number of forty-four piano quartets.

I said, "Some of these ultra-modern compositions aren't going to be received so well, Otto. Even in New York"

"You let me worry about that, Billy. The main thing is to find a pianist at this late date."

Olga was unhappy. "I feel like a ghoul discussing these matters so soon after the funeral," she said sadly.

"Oh, my dear," Otto pleaded. "You must agree. Don't you see that we have a moral obligation to cancel all engagements very soon, unless—" He looked at her appealingly but her expression did not change. For some time he waited anxiously, but she would not answer him. At last he said, "And—and anyway, don't you think *Anny* would have wanted us to find a way out?"

Thede spoke up. "Of course Anny would have wanted us to find a way out."

Olga shot a look of the most intense anger at her and I immediately sensed the reason. Andrea's death was terribly near still, and Olga could not abide anyone putting words into the dead mouth. It was a desecration to her; she would always feel that Andrea belonged to the quartet and to the quartet alone. Otto said, "Thede, I'm sorry, but I must ask you to let us decide about this."

Olga sighed deeply. "All right," she said reluctantly. "But who's the pianist going to be?"

What a relief. Otto went over to Olga and kissed her cheek. She pushed him roughly away. "Never mind that. Who have you in mind?"

"Van Clausteyn. If we can get him."

I was anxious about Thede, for she was going to rehearse with the Casa Belles until the question of the pianist was settled. It was a difficult task she was attempting and. I hoped that she would be capable of doing it well. I remembered the time I had first heard her play—God, it was a dozen years ago. Minnie Watteau had telephoned me one day and asked me to come over. She promised that I would meet a brilliant young pianist. These Brilliant young pianists of hers seemed to be numberless, and. I hadn't heard a good one yet.

But Minnie was Minnie and I had become resigned to her demands. That day It looked like she was going to woo me with beauty, for Theodora Karman was 'a gorgeous child of eighteen. But she really played quite well, I thought, and I liked her playing enough to suggest a course of study with one of New York's better teachers. I thought it might even be possible for her to break into the concert world with five years of study or so and careful promotion.

But Minnie was impatient and, wanted me to make recordings of Theodora's playing immediately. For why should she waste the bloom of her youth and beauty? One concert in Carnegie Hall would suffice. Then she could concertize and study at the same time.

In five years she would have America at her feet, in ten years the world, And Minnie was willing to finance the whole affair.

But they needed my help. After the concert at Carnegie Hall we would use the critical notices in the papers to build up Theodora's reputation, together with wide publicity of her recordings. It couldn't fail. Minnie had it all figured out.

I tried to point out that the notices might be bad. Theodora might not play well, or the critics might not like her even if she were very good. They were often wrong.

But Minnie was obdurate. One could always find a hopeful word or sentence in any write-up, and this could be used for publicity. Anyway it was worth a try. The main thing was to go ahead with the making of records so that their release could be synchronized with Theodora's debut at Carnegie Hall. What say, Billy? What say?

I looked at the young girl. She was very demure and beautiful. Finally I said, "I think the best thing to do would be to have somebody reliable listen to her. I'll try to get Ehrlich. But you must agree to take his advice."

We left it on this note. Left it forever, because a month later Thede and I were married. And we were very happy, confounding the pessimists in general and Minnie Watteau in particular. Although I was forty-eight years old when I married Thede, the last twelve years hadn't contained a moment, not a single moment that wasn't filled with joy. I was both husband and father to Thede, and she was both wife and daughter to me. My only regret was that there hadn't been any children.

Ah, well. To the rehearsal.

As Otto tuned his fiddle he spoke to Thede. The man fascinated her. She was always making new and. startling discoveries about him. Never had she known a violinist who could play and at the same time waggle his chin in conversation and neither had I. Several times it seemed sure he would drop his Stradivarius and we would gasp and then be amused and reassured as he caught the violin with his chin.

"Do you know the Fauré Quartet, Thede?" he said as he played its first theme.

"Yes, I know it pretty well."

"It is very good of you to help us learn this new music. There remain only three weeks before the season begins and in this terribly short time we must prepare at least four programs. You see, in some large cities several concerts are scheduled, sometimes in different places. There are persons who come to all our concerts whenever we play many times in a single city and we must not force them to listen to the same program again and again."

They began to play and as they played. I worried. I thought that this time Otto had surely bitten off more than he could chew. No, they couldn't do it, I was almost certain they could never do it. Not in three weeks. Surely they would be forced to relax their rigorous standards, for there was simply not enough time to rehearse. My mind searched out every possible result of inadequate preparation. I worried about bad critical notices, about the effect on the re-engagement of the quartet, about—God, the Fauré was almost over and I hadn't even listened to Thede. Hell and damnation.

They played the last chord and Otto looked up and smiled. "Not bad at all, Thedie. Now we'd like to run through it once more, just to get our bearings. Then we can begin to take it apart for cleaning and oiling."

But they did not begin to play just yet. Instead they discussed the question of who would play the piano. Maia and. Olga suggested several names, but Otto would consider only Van Clausteyn of Holland, Hankins of England and Ergauer, the

Austrian pianist. For some time the discussion went on and at last Otto, with an impatient gesture, cut it short by picking up the telephone and calling Van Clausteyn long distance. But he was not at home. Amsterdam said he would call back and. Otto sat down. "Fauré," he said briefly.

I was delighted. For a comparative amateur Thede was playing beautifully and I was pleased and amused to see Otto looking at her now and again with puzzlement in his grey eyes. Suddenly he stopped playing and said, "Excellent, Thede. Really surprising much better than the first time."

"I was nervous at first, Marcus. Honey."

"Of course. Although you needn't have been. We won't eat you. Now, just for the fun of it what do you say to some Mozart?"

"I thought we were going to rehearse Fauré," Maia objected. "Why did you stop in the middle?"

"Oh, let's just have some fun. Anyway don't you think it might be a good idea to wait for Van Clausteyn to call? Maybe he doesn't like Fauré. Some people don't you know. Before I spend a lot of time practicing the wrong repertoire I want to have a better idea about what we're going to play." He smiled at Thede. "Do you know the Mozart Quartets, my sweet?"

She smiled faintly. "Yes, it happens that I do."

Thede happened to know two piano quartets that morning and four in the afternoon. They played all day, stopping only at mealtimes. At dinner Maia. said, "I have been worrying about Van Clausteyn. It is not probable that he could be here for another week. Do you think the remaining two weeks would be enough even for him? And what about his own concert career?"

"Latest information is that he decided to retire last year," Otto replied. "And, you needn't worry about whether he can get ready in time. He is one concert pianist who knows all the piano quartets, quintets, trios, everything. His knowledge is encyclopedic, and furthermore he is perhaps the best pianist in the world. If we could get him for a season or two we might be able to decide on a course of action. For who knows when we might run into a very promising young violist? It might happen next month, and then again it might take a year or more."

"I've already received letters from viola players all over the country," I said, "and Andrea has been dead only a few days. I will probably receive hundreds of letters more, but we will have to wait until the end of the season to find time for auditions.

"Well," Olga said, "there's nothing we can do but wait until Van Clausteyn calls back." She sat moodily,, picking her nose, a discontented expression on her face. At last she came to a decision and rising to her full height of five feet eleven and a half inches she thundered, "No! I am *against* this whole idea. If you want to do piano quartets let's take two or three months and do it right. I can't get ready in three weeks and neither can Maia." She sneered. "And neither can you, my boy."

"We will simply have to rehearse on the road, darling," he said gently. "It is impossible to take two or three months off in this business."

"Who's in business," Olga shouted. "I thought I was an artist."

Otto shook his head "Do you think I am not an artist?" he said, and his tone reproved her. "Take my word for it. It is absolutely necessary for the career of the quartet that we begin this tour on schedule. We can do it, I tell you. The concerts are seldom consecutive. You know this as well as I. do. Mostly we will be playing only two or three times a week. We can rehearse in between."

Olga glowered at him, but She subsided, grumbling.

"I don't like to waste time arguing," Maia said. "What do you want to do now? Shall we play some more?"

"By all means." Otto turned to Thede. "What else do you know my dear?"

"Schumann?"

"Fine."

I was amazed that Thede knew the piano quartet literature. I had seldom heard her practicing anything but Chopin, and yet learning all this repertoire must have taken a great deal of time. And why? Could she simply have thought that it might be useful some day. Perhaps. Or maybe she just liked piano quartets?

At last Otto stood up, stretched and yawned. He looked at his watch. "Well past midnight," he said. "Really unbelievable that you are such a fine player, Thede." He stifled another yawn. "I guess we ought to close up shop for the day," he said sleepily. "If we can keep up this pace tomorrow we'll have covered a good deal of the repertoire we'll need, at least in the beginning;"

"Let's have some more coffee," Maia said. "I'm usually afraid of coffee at night because it keeps me awake. But I don't think anything could keep me awake tonight, and I feel like relaxing a little."

"I'll get some for you." Thede said. She went into the kitchen and Maia stretched out on the divan.

As Otto began to put his instrument away he was startled by the shocking, brilliant sound of the telephone. He lifted the receiver and said, "Who is it?"

It was Van Clausteyn and everyone held his breath while Otto spoke Dutch for a hundred dollars or so before replacing the receiver. "Damn it," he said unhappily. "He can't make it. He has just been appointed conductor of the Rotterdam Philharmonic. The regular conductor has had a serious stroke. Old Hoogeveene I knew him well." He sighed. "Too bad. What time is it in England?"

Maia and. Olga spoke almost as one. "Call the long distance operator," they said.

It was almost six o'clock in England. "Well, shall we call Hankins?" Otto asked.

"You might wake him up," Olga said,

"*Can't* it wait until morning?" Thede begged. "I'm simply exhausted and I want terribly to go to sleep, but I'm dying to be here when you call him."

"I'm dying too," Maia said. "Call him first thing tomorrow."

"All right, all right," Otto grumbled. "But if he's left tonight on a trip to Siberia I shan't forgive either of you."

The next morning everyone was tired. But poor Otto seemed to be utterly exhausted. I had the impression that he was keeping himself awake through an effort of will. Slowly, painfully, he began to talk about Hankins. Inexplicably he had changed his mind about him.

"He would in any case be only a stopgap remedy," Otto said wearily. I thought it must be the strain. The last few days had been hell for the poor boy. Now a lassitude seemed to come over him and his speech was slow and halting.

"We have to find and train a really gifted young fiddler," he mumbled. "That's the only way out." He coughed, and a new expression came over his face, in it were mixed fatigue, and bitterness, and rebellion, and outrage. I was puzzled and a little alarmed. In ten years I had never seen Otto look like this. There must be something new that was wrong, something that I didn't know about.

Now Otto forced himself to go on. The simple act of talking seemed to be painful to him and the words came out in little gasps.

"And why—" he swallowed. "Why should we—should we drag old Hankins out—of retirement? It would—be too selfish." He took a grip on himself and said, "Thede's playing is entirely adequate, I'm sure. I think we should let her be our pianist. I—"

Olga was speechless. But Maia interrupted furiously. "Otto! Wait a moment! Don't you think you ought to discuss such an important matter as a change in the quartet with me and Olga? Don't you think so? Really?" She stamped her foot angrily.

"Of course, of course." He seemed embarrassed and upset, "It's only that I've been almost driven out of my mind by—by Andrea. You know how it is, you feel the same, you can understand." He drew a long shuddering breath, then, more calmly, he went on. "So I have made a fool of myself. It is not the first time. Well, but look. Just consider the whole thing carefully now. Suppose we find a marvelous violist whom we will need to place under contract immediately. Then what shall we do with Hankins?" He frowned and began to count his fingers. "Secondly, I have had an idea. Wouldn't it be a good thing if we could organize a new kind of chamber music society with woodwinds and brass? We might, you know, we just might run into some unusual wind players. It's *possible*, isn't it? Now if we have Thede we are *flexible,* but it will not be so easy to get rid of Hankins. And another thing. Don't forget that the situation is too new for us to have come to *any* decision *as* yet. If we have Thede we can take our time to consider every possibility. If we have Hankins, then we cannot. Furthermore, you must remember that he is seventy years old. What if he gets sick in the middle of the tour? What will we do then? And what if we find nobody for several years? To spend so much time with us would be a sacrifice we should not ask anyone to make. Anyone except Thede, that is."

He had finished counting and balling his hand into a fist he struck it against a table for emphasis. "If I may say so—" he coughed again, an exhausted little cough. "If I may say so, I think Thede would work out very well."

I was alarmed. I had never, not in ten years, seen Otto look like this. He looked as though he was about to collapse. How haggard he was, as though—

Then I caught myself. To the devil with Otto, they were considering taking Thede into the Casa Bella Quartet, for Gods sake. It was tremendous. Tremendous. I wanted to shout, to sing, to—

Maia was talking and I cursed myself for having missed even one of her precious words. "—we can try it out," she said hesitantly. "What do you say, Olga?" But Olga only grunted.

"Why don't we all take the day off," I said. "If you think that Thede can play with you this season I'm sure that calls for a little celebration. Besides we're all worn out. Tomorrow's rehearsal will be better if we relax for a day, don't you think?"

And immediately everyone began to recover. Except poor Otto.

The next day Otto was ill. He suffered from fever, chill and intense, racking nausea. Maia was terrified and insisted on calling the doctor at once. And Olga hovered about the sick man like a huge mother hen, clucking and brooding.

At last the doctor came shooed everyone out of the room. He remained with Otto for only a few minutes, but it seemed a long time to us.

"It must be *serious*," Maia cried. "It's taking him forever."

I was concerned because it was so unusual for Otto to suffer from anything worse than a cold. But I tried to reassure Maia and said, "It's only that he's a very fine doctor.

Such a man always takes plenty of time to make sure of his diagnosis. But you can depend on what he says."

And. Olga growled, "And what if he says that Otto is suffering from cancer? The incurable kind? The kind that is so well hidden that they can't get at it?"

But they had no time to talk further, for suddenly the door opened and the doctor appeared, grinning and wiping his forehead. "Well," he said, "you're obviously the type of people that think nothing of wasting a busy man's time. There's not a thing wrong with him that I can see. Some temporary indisposition or other. If he doesn't improve in a day or two we'll give him some tests. But right now it looks to me like he's been worried or upset about something. I remember him from a few years back when he had that tonsillectomy. He was a nervous, sensitive patient then and he hasn't changed. Don't worry about him. It's probably nothing."

We breathed a collective sigh of relief. Now the door opened again and Otto appeared. "Well," he said. grimly. "And what's the real diagnosis?"

"I told you," the doctor said impatiently. "It's nothing serious. several days of rest will find you fit as a fiddle."

"Not likely. Very few fiddles are fit, doctor. Most of them are fought."

Everyone laughed, but Otto was grave. "I am glad to give up the struggle for a few days," he said gloomily. "Andrea was not the only one who wanted to escape from life." And he walked slowly into the bedroom and closed the door.

But it was only that Otto liked to be dramatic. The doctor insisted again that in all probability there was nothing the matter that a few days of rest would not cure.

After my first feelings of happiness and triumph had subsided a little, I began to think. It was a wonderful thing that Thede was going to play with Casa Bella, but I had to consider what the effect on the public might be. Musical circles would undoubtedly be suspicious of an unknown pianist whose husband managed the quartet, and there would, be gossip and rumor and speculation. And if she played badly the whole of America would buzz and sneer.

And another thing worried me. There would have to photographs, and Thede was a beautiful woman, and — what then? Was there not a danger that we might be caught up in the "pretty girl" syndrome so prevalent in the United States? There were already enough people who came to the concerts only to be seen by friends. If others began to come merely to watch Thede would not the quality of our audiences deteriorate? There might even be wolf whistles and cat calls. Olga and Maia wouldn't like that at all.

But oh, how I hoped Thede's playing would be excellent. Only let her perform sufficiently well and all our problems would disappear. Perhaps it would be a good idea if we were to use her maiden name. She had of course appeared as Theodora Karman during her limited career as a concert pianist, and to use the name again might help a little to camouflage the fact that she was Mrs. Eska. And so I thought, and planned and worried.

Working in bed, in defiance of the doctor's orders, Otto composed programs for the forthcoming tour. As far as it was possible these programs were designed to minimize Thede's role, and the piano trios and quartets were mixed with a generous sprinkling of string trios. For the first weeks Otto was still more cautious. There was to be only one piano quartet in each concert, as well *as* a Mozart duet for violin and viola and the customary string trio. He even considered a little known piece for viola and cello by Beethoven, but it was one of the master's least important compositions and he decided against it.

By Saturday morning my worries about whether the new quartet would be accepted were over. I had received a telegram from nearly everyone who had engaged the Casa Bellas for the coming season. They were all sympathetic and they all agreed to the substitution of the new piano quartet.

Now Otto released a long statement to the press:

Our hearts are buried with the great violist who gave meaning to our life as an ensemble. None of us wants ever to play string quartets again. But it is also true that we have played the standard repertoire many times and have even recorded it. With string quartets there comes a time when the good repertoire to exhausted, when one feels the need to perform the string trios, the piano trios, the piano quartets.

We are very happy to have Miss Theodora Karman as our new colleague. Certainly she is one of the most promising young American pianists, and we are looking forward with Miss Karman to a happy exploration of the literature for piano and strings.

The piece aroused nationwide critical comment, most of it doubtful. Who was Theodora Karman? No one had ever heard of her. Otto ignored the whole business, or at least he seemed to. But I wondered. I knew that Otto had an uncanny instinct for the box office and it was strange that he should appear to be indifferent to what was going on.

But what was more important was that almost two of the fatal weeks had passed and rehearsals were not going well. Perhaps it was to some extent because of Thede's sudden notoriety. She was so busy being interviewed that she had little time to practice I had never seen her surrounded, by so many personable young men. They made me keenly conscious of my age. I tried to be rational about the interviews and I realized that a young woman as beautiful as Thede must inevitably be attractive to young men. All the same, it was difficult for me. Sometimes one of the smiling young men would call me "Pop," and this would offend me greatly, perhaps unreasonably.

But what made me most unhappy was a remark Maia made to me one night. "You know, Billy," she said severely, "you ought to try to straighten Thede out."

"What's wrong?"

"Trivia. That's all that she has on her mind. Little bits of trivia. Now she's all wrought up about our gowns. She calls them 'time-honored.' Olga and. I have never bothered our heads about the gowns. They have served us well for years. And," Maia, continued indignantly, "she insisted so much that we finally gave in so that the rehearsal could continue. It was a lucky thing we could at least persuade her to agree on something dark. But now Olga and I will have to waste a lot of time shopping and we *haven't* the time. We have four string trios to learn." And she flounced angrily out of the room.

I went to see Thede immediately. "What's this about the gowns," I said sternly.

She shrugged. "I work hard all day, every day," she said calmly. "it's good for my morale to buy new clothes. And it does not take any extra time. No one can work for three weeks without a moment of relaxation. Shopping is my way of relaxing. And you can't tell me that getting away from the great white master now and then wouldn't be good for Maia too."

I didn't like it. I wondered how Olga felt about the situation and decided to speak to her and find out. It was rather late, but I was sure she hadn't gone to bed. She had slept badly since Andrea's death.

As I approached her apartment I saw that it was ablaze with light. Good. She was awake. The door was ajar and I walked in and saw her huge figure through a translucent curtain. She was in her little workshop. Back and forth she moved, back and forth, restlessly, tirelessly. I waited a long time but she kept up the interminable pacing. Certainly she must have heard me close the door. At last I entered the tiny cubicle and sat down. But she continued to ignore me. Now I saw that she was fussing with her cello bow. I cleared my throat, but she pretended not to have heard me.

Finally I said, "Maia has complained to me about Thede. Do you know about it?"

"Maia speaks for me," Olga growled. "But you must understand her. In many ways she is only a child, and you must give her time to get used to the discipline of the group. It is one thing for you and Maia and Otto to tear yourselves apart through overwork. You are used to it. But it's quite another thing to be asked to join the quartet and suddenly to find a whole new set of conditions imposed upon one's way of living." I cleared my throat again. "Look, Olga. Thede is simply delighted that she can play with you. You know that. And she does try hard. And she does rehearse conscientiously.

But don't you admit that one cannot keep it up twenty-four hours a day? And if it raises her morale to buy a new outfit, how can you object?"

Olga faced me with a look of tired scorn. She returned the bow to the cello case, then continued to pace, back and forth, back and forth. At last she said, "First of all, I can only say that if our positions were reversed I should not in the least be delighted. I should be terrified." Now she stopped her pacing. "And in the second place, it is certainly possible to work twenty-four hours a day. She should not eat without a score in front of her, nor sleep without the mill of her brain grinding dreams of tone. As I do not sleep."

And Olga stomped over to her whetstone and began to sharpen an end-pin, the long, thin rod of steel which, when fastened to the bottom of the cello, helps the player to anchor the instrument to the floor so that it cannot slip. Of late Olga had become easily aroused. She would seize her cello and hurl it into the floor with terrific force. Sanding didn't help much.

"Why do you constantly hone your end-pin, Olga? Such frequent honing isn't really necessary is it?"

"You can never tell. I might want to kill somebody with it."

I could think of no answer to this retort and after a few minutes I said good-night. Walking down the hall I passed Maia's apartment. She was practicing. Didn't anyone ever sleep in this house? I hesitated a moment, then knocked softly on the door. But the playing only grew louder. At last the piece ended and I knocked again. Maia opened the door and I saw that she was holding a violin. She said, "Hello, Billy. Come on in. Shall I fix you a drink?"

"No, thanks. It seems that no one can sleep these days, so I thought I'd keep you company for a little,"

"Fine. You came just in time. I was getting sick of practicing that damned piece."

"What damned piece?"

"Oh, I was trying to play Paganini's '*Le Steghe*'"

"Don't think I know it. "*Le Streghe*? Doesn't that mean something like a witch?"

"Yes, The usual translation is 'The Witch's Dance.'"

"Sounds awfully difficult."

"Yes, it is."

"You know, Maia, I'm amazed at your versatility. After all these years of playing the violin, overnight you have become a viola player. I think it's remarkable. And then in the evening you go back to the violin and play a difficult piece like '*Le Streghe*'"

"You are a dear innocent. There is not a good violinist in the world who could not play the viola instantaneously. The instruments are almost identical. No problem."

Now she decided to try on her new fur neckpiece and took it from the closet. Along its perimeter ran a beautiful white stripe. The fur was unfamiliar to me but this was not unusual. She was always experimenting with the furs of strange animals.

She went to a mirror and draped the neckpiece about her shoulders. I said, "It's lovely, Maia, but I can't imagine what kind it is, unless — would it be zebra?"

"No, Bill. Skunk."

"H'mm. I guess I'll have that drink after all."

She went to the refrigerator and, got out a bottle. "Martini?"

"Fine." She poured the drink and I began to sip it. "Not much time, Maia."

"Not much time for what?" She dropped, an olive into the martini.

"Before the tour begins."

"Oh. No, there isn't."

"Do you think you'll be ready in time for the opening concert?"

"I don't think so."

Now she began to clean her violin. I could think of nothing else to say and in a little while I left. Should I talk to Otto next? No, it might be better to wait.

It seemed to me as though the tang of the wind biting and swirling against the autumn leaves had affronted them into a flush of anger, and that their crimsoned cheeks tossed proudly, furiously against the wounded sunset. A rare, premature frost had combined with a dry spell to begin the fall transformation somewhat earlier than usual and the trees were alive with dancing color.

I loved the fall weather, I loved the brisk pace at which it accompanied me as I walked. I was glad that my dinner engagement had been cancelled. I hurried across the. George Washington Bridge, for I was eager to get home. If I arrived soon enough perhaps I could dine with Thede.

But I didn't want to miss my daily exercise. Nothing contributes so much to one's health as a few miles in the open air every day. Only it would, do me no good if I worried, and all day I had been thinking anxiously of Otto and his illness. Enough of it. Still, he had recently suffered his second relapse. His *second* one! Well, the doctor had said it was nothing serious. All the tests were negative and Otto would be up and about in a day or two. Nonetheless I wanted to see him. One could never really trust a doctor, any doctor, and I wanted to reassure myself. A gust of wind blew my hat off and sent it speeding down the street. It was pleasant to watch the racing hat. Ordinarily I would have been annoyed, but trifles didn't bother me then. The day had been glorious and I was happy. Bareheaded I walked toward the setting sun.

At last the three story building in which we had lived for the last ten years came into sight. It was a beautiful old house and I felt a strong affection for it. I had bought it for the quartet and regarded it as one of the most fortunate investments I had ever made. There were six apartments, one for each. member of the 'quartet, one for Thede, one for myself, a living room, dining room, a huge kitchen, two rooms for the maids, and a small concert hall. The Home of Casa. Bella, A good name for it, I thought.

As I opened the door I heard Otto's voice floating down the stairs, and in a flash of orientation I realized that a remarkable demonstration of one of Otto's theories of acoustics was taking place. His sickroom was on the floor above, at the other end of the house, yet every syllable was audible. His speech was like his playing, whose softest murmur could be relied upon to travel to the topmost balconies of the world is largest auditoriums. Those who had to squeeze and perspire over their fiddles In order to be heard would only move Otto to shrug and quote the late, great Franz Kneisel: "As more you press, as less comes out."

I eavesdropped for a moment, marveling over the phenomenon. I was captivated by the beauty and expressiveness of Otto's voice, by the clarity of each word, the subtlety Of each nuance. Listen, listen —

"Thede, my darling of darlings, of the women I have loved, you are the last, and the first. As they awoke me; so do you awaken me from my awakening, which was a sleep. It is for you that I betray my friend and my father. And to be frank with you, my dearest, I must tell. you that I also betray my mistress, who is music. It is strange that my mind is so clear. I know exactly that you will play only quite well. For the rest of your life, no matter how heroic your efforts, you can never hope to play any better than quite well. Olga and Maia will feel an uncertain distress, but they won't know that it is because you are only pretty good. And now listen carefully to, me sweetheart. Gradually, very gradually, the wonderful, amputated spirit of Casa Bella will *die* forcing us to become part of the music business, forcing us to play only for the reason that our bodies may survive could not speak so honestly to you., my darling, except that I know you love me, as I love you.

Could, we not rescue our love another way? Could we not with stealth, deceit, lies —

I staggered into the street. I felt feverish, and the night air seemed cool. A native instinct warned me not to go out without a coat, but I ignored. it and stumbled blindly into the gathering darkness. Briefly, inanely, I thought that Thede rhymed with greed.

I wasn't able to sleep that night. All night I tossed and groaned and yawned. Then, shortly after dawn, I began the monotonous daily ritual of showering, shaving and dressing. I knew that Mrs. Bundy would not be awake. Well, I wasn't hungry anyway. Later on I'd get a bite somewhere.

I went out into the chill of the early morning. It was cold and. I decided it would warm me to get something to eat. Then I would go walking, perhaps in Central Park. I went into an all night restaurant and ordered coffee and doughnuts. I forced myself to eat both doughnuts and to drink the scalding coffee. Then I paid the bill and left.

For a time I walked in a stupor. But after a while I realized that Central Park was pretty far away and hailed a taxi. We seemed to arrive immediately. I paid the driver, got out of the cab and began to walk again.

I had thought of Central Park because it usually comforted me to walk among trees. But now as I looked at them I had the depressing thought that they were never so hopelessly without the promise of life as they were in winter. But it was only September. Well, it seemed like winter anyway. I looked at the trees skeptically. Curious. I had always found them to have a certain beauty of form, even at this time of year. But now I wondered what earthly use they were, after all, except as materials for tables and chairs. Funny. Now the leaves seemed to be black, as though they had been scorched in a fire, and the trees were actually ugly. They were stilts with drawers sticking out of their sides. They were hatracks. They were turnstiles.

And then it occurred to me that my perceptions must be completely awry. I could taste nothing for instance. I remembered the tasteless dinner I had eaten out last night, the doughnuts this morning. I couldn't rely on any of my senses. Near a great rock two young men had built a fire. As I passed them the smoke was wafted toward my nostrils. But it didn't smell like smoke. Instead it smelled like some strange, gaseous poison.

With a feeling of alarm I noticed various other crippled aspects of the park. The very air seemed to have a new density and I had to force my way through it.

I looked at the young men again. Their faces seemed distorted and grotesque like monsters appearing life-like out of a forgotten nightmare.

For I long time I continued to wander through the strange, frightening montage that the park had become. I trembled as I walked and Central Park became ever more terrifying.

At last I came to Fifty-ninth Street, and staggered into a subway train. It was almost half an hour before a horribly ugly gargoyle seated across from me miraculously transformed itself into a querulous old lady.

The rehearsals were not going well. After three long, torturous weeks it had become obvious that Thede would never really play well. Otto was miserable and Olga and Maia were furious. As time went by, I wondered, why one of them at least did, not simply stop playing and refuse to go on. And I began to doubt that I could continue with the impossible situation. Now, now at any moment, Olga would put down her cello and walk out in a huff. I felt it, I knew it. She seldom looked at the music any more, but stared intently at Thede. And what could this mean? And Maia, Maia shook her head constantly with a tiny, almost invisible movement. But I saw it, the imperceptible negation. I saw it and Otto did, too.

But perhaps it was even worse. Perhaps they were afraid, afraid of Otto's relationship with Thede. If they knew Perhaps it was simply a subconscious fear which they felt and couldn't quite rationalize.

But the more I watched them the surer I was that they knew, that they were disturbed, even alarmed. Even outraged. Oh, if only some kind of precarious balance could be maintained, if only their envy would prevent them from noticing her playing, if only her playing would prevent them from being too envious. Surprising that it had taken them almost three weeks to become suspicious.

Thede was having trouble. After almost two hours of struggling with the Archduke Trio it seemed even more difficult for her than it had when they started. This was a new experience for her. All right, so she was an amateur. But why was she worse the third week than the first?

I sat and gazed, blearily at Maia I tried not to look at Thede, but she was a magnet which I found impossible to resist. At last I succumbed and glared at her; She looked different somehow. What was the matter with her?

Ah, yes. She hadn't fixed her face today. She wore no lipstick, no nothing. She was trying to be ugly so that Olga and Maia would like her. What a laugh. She looked like a ruddy, energetic angel.

Otto was stern, even severe with her, but she was quite cheerful and good-humored. How stupid. Here was Otto, doing his best to make Olga and Maia happy by jumping on her. The least she could do if she wanted to maintain the farce was to seem to be a little unhappy.

Now Olga criticized her for the twentieth time. "Please do not bang so, Theodora. I have told you before that you must cultivate the art of forceful playing *without* percussion. Do *not* lift your arms above your head to get the maximum force. You look like a lovely witch."

It seemed to me that there was something different about Olga's appearance. What was it? I stared at her for several minutes before I realized, that she had bobbed her hair.

Now it was Maia's turn to attack Thede. "Don't you realize that the piano is specially favored," she said sharply. "It is an orchestra, for God's sake, and each key is a different instrument, ringing free. Every time I put a finger on a string I choke its vibration to a certain extent. But do *you* have to put fingers on strings to play different notes?" She sniffed. "Of course not. You simply press different keys. *Please* use your advantage gently. Especially in the bass you sound like the subway,"

Now Otto cleared his throat and said, "Neither of you has sensed the *psychological* implications of noisy piano playing. The bad pianist, you see, not knowing what to say with his instrument, thunders away as furiously as he can. What he is trying to do and this may be an unconscious and therefore quite innocent subterfuge, is to prevent the listener from noticing his amateurism by using the diversion of noise. And sometimes he meets with success, for many an audience upon hearing such a bad artist will fall into a state of somnolence. Then it will applaud wildly as a kind of apology for having fallen asleep. Do you want that kind of reward?" he said, sternly.

She smiled at him demurely. "No, Marcus, honey," she said sweetly, "I don't."

I looked at her hatefully. Curiously, I blamed her for what had happened, and not Otto. I could not have said why, but I was convinced that it must have been Thede who had seduced Otto. I decided to leave. The farce was getting too painful.

But as I was walking out Otto called to me. "Billy! I wanted to talk with you. Do you think you could come on tour with us? I know it will be dull for you but there are a thousand things you could do to simplify our lives. We need someone to see that the piano is in tune and that it is in its proper place on stage. We need a reliable person to sit in various parts of the different halls to check on the acoustics of the new arrangement. And so forth. Of course we could hire somebody, but who is available on such short notice that we can trust?'

"Why can't you attend to these things yourselves?" I said testily. It might have been Thede's fault, but that did not make me feel kindly toward Otto.

"Because we'll have only so much energy, Billy. It will be bad enough to have to use up some of it rehearsing. You know that the concerts will never be quite as good if we have to spend ourselves in rehearsal. If in addition to this we have to attend to other things..."

"All right, all right. Give me a minute to think about it." So they wanted me to conserve their energy. I wondered how Otto's love life would affect his energy. How painfully funny. Well, perhaps I should go along and see for myself. Trying to detect a difference in the quality of the concerts would develop my ear. Yes, this time the tour should be really amusing for a change.

And so, perhaps fascinated by the prospect of observing my own cuckoldry, I said, "Very well. I'll do it. When are we going to leave?"

"Whenever you say. You're the manager. You know the schedule."

"I'll figure out the best time and let you know."

"Good. How glad. I am that you will be with us. What a good thing."

But I felt the intricacy of the motives behind Otto's invitation. He was troubled by guilt, loyalty, Thede, Olga, Maia, piano tuning, God knew what else, Otto was a complicated man.

Now Otto had long ago suggested to me that I try to arrange the tours so that the quartet could motor to a large city and use it as a center of operations. He did not like the idea of playing concerts helter-skelter and without a planned sequence. His idea was that after one or more concerts in the mother city, so to speak, it would be well if they could play in several smaller nearby towns before moving on to another larger city. This would do away with the tiresome business of packing and unpacking every day, solve the laundry situation, make available a competent fiddle repairman (Otto was always worrying about his fiddle and, never let a week pass without having its mysterious inner workings checked and rechecked), and in general provide the facilities, privacy and comfort which were sometimes difficult to find in a smaller city. And where it was possible I had so arranged the present tour.

Boston was to be our first headquarters and the debut of the new quartet was to take place in Kedzie Auditorium on October 5th. I decided that it would be best to start two and a half days ahead of time, and precisely at nine o'clock in the morning of October 3rd I got behind the wheel of my station wagon. Olga sat with me in the front seat, the others in the rear.

The weather was fine and as we drove along the highway I began to feel just a little better. I had been sunk in gloom ever since making my fatal discovery. I looked at Thede in the rearview mirror and was surprised when she began to talk. She was not a loquacious person and I had seldom known her to begin a conversation before. I gazed longingly at her tracially lovely face. Damn her to hell.

"I want you all to know how exceedingly grateful I am for this opportunity," she said, gazing pensively at the countryside. I nearly collided with a truck and reluctantly left the mirror. "When I was very small," she continued, "I became interested in the piano. And I practiced a good deal as I grew older." Her voice trailed away and she was silent for several minutes. Then, "When I was in high school I used to practice for hours and hours every day. I remember getting a pack of cigarettes and a coke and, playing the damn piano all day." I winced. I don't like profanity in women. Now I 'heard. the scraping of a match and, "Thank you, Marcus honey. As I was saying—"

But some time elapsed and she said nothing. For years I had been irritated by these little hiatuses. They would persistently interrupt her conversation while she thought what she was saying. At last she came out with it. "Everyone considered me a kind of tomboy because I never went out with the fellows. Music was the only thing I cared about. But one day a boy showed me how to play Dixieland jazz. And I sort of gave up study again and even arranged some concerts for me. And that was a lucky thing because if it hadn't been for Mrs. Watteau I would—I—would never have met Billy." I snorted and turned on the ventilator. The atmosphere needed clearing what with cigarettes and one thing and another.

I had been driving now for several hours and the monotony of the road began to dull my senses. I fell into a daydream and recalled wistful memories of our wedding. It had taken place on the Watteau estate under the angry benevolence of Minnie. Ah, how furious she was at the news of the engagement. But she finally made the best of it. Yes, she finally made the best of it. "It has taken me all these years to discover a first class talent," she would squeal. "And then you kidnap her from me. Right from under my nose. Really, Bill, I'd think badly of you if it weren't that any man would fall for Theodora. Isn't she the loveliest thing?" And. Minnie would flutter and bother, and swoop and bleat, and weep and blow her nose.

And she was right. Thede had been the most glorious woman in the world. I could even say that today, even with my fury against her. But was that in itself a reason for marriage? Why had I done it? I remembered my confirmed bachelorhood and the many women who had entered my life, and left it, easily and without strain. I remembered the adept and stubborn defenses which my forty-eight years of loneliness had created.

But the sudden smite of Thede's beauty had been irresistible. Now the ancient attitude which always and irrefragably excluded the idea of marriage began to crumble, dissolve, melt into a powerful new emotion which I had never felt before. It had been impossible for me to restrain this overwhelming passion for the young girl. What a tragedy. And where was the other part of it? I looked again into the rearview mirror. Ah, yes. He was asleep. Had he no conscience?

Suddenly Otto awoke and sat upright. He was sweating and his eyes stood out from his white face. "I was having a nightmare," he said. "I dreamed that I was walking along a high, narrow fence which seemed to be made of sand. At any rate it crumbled constantly beneath my feet. I had a feeling of desperate urgency and though I was afraid of falling, I began to run. Rain and sleet beat dawn upon me and thousands of little birds were flying at my face and eyes. As I ran I grew smaller and smaller and now my legs covered less and less distance until it hardly seemed that I was moving at all. My legs began to feel like they were anchored in concrete but when I looked down it was only sand and in frustration I began to cry.

"But suddenly I saw a gigantic shape coming toward me. It was a huge goblin of some kind and its face was hideously deformed. It threw itself at me but it was impossible to fight because it had a sticky, amorphous body that resisted force. Then the goblin seized me and threw me violently off the fence.

"The rain and sleet had stopped but the wind was deafening. I tried to cover my ears but when I did the shrieking came inside my head and I quickly uncovered, my ears.

"Now I was small and light and. I drifted slowly through an atmosphere peopled with weird, ghostly beings who threatened me, snarling unfamiliar curses whose meaning I somehow knew. Then as I fell they began to throw pieces of broken, rotted flesh at my head and arms and chest until I was numb with shock and pain. I tried to increase my speed but I couldn't and the torture continued. The wind grew warm, then hot, then blazing, and the burning air was suffocating. As I thought I could stand it no longer an unbearably ugly, grating voice screamed, "Next, next, you are neeeext, you are—"

"Next station, Boston," Thede's cheery voice interrupted. "Next station, B000ston." Otto, stopped, talking and stared gloomily out of the window.

The station wagon slid smoothly into a yellow-lined parking place in front of the hotel. Everyone got out and stretched. Maia yawned delicately and Olga ferociously. A liveried attendant took my place behind the wheel. "All of our luggage is in the back," I told the attendant. "It is labeled. Please see that it is sent to our rooms."

By this time Otto had recovered. He said to Thede, "We must attend to the matter of the piano immediately. I'll meet you in the lobby in half an hour. Billy, I prefer the Meringer piano, as you know. Please telephone Klaugen, their Boston outlet, tell them that we'll be up in an hour, and ask them to be good enough to have half a dozen concert grands ready. I hope we have better luck here than we did in New York." He paused. "Would you like to come along, Bill? You might possibly be able to help us. Arranging for delivery or something."

"Billy dear," Thede said, "I've been thinking about it and it seems to me that We ought to have separate rooms. I'll be getting up at the crack of dawn every day to practice and I don't want to be constantly waking you."

Clever, wasn't she. The bitch. But what could I possibly do about it? I shrugged and did not answer.

We agreed to meet in half an hour and I went disconsolately to the telephone.

We had been trying pianos for almost an hour, but Otto was still dissatisfied. Thede became impatient. "Heavens to Betsy. I have never in my life met such a fussy person. Marcus, honey, you know I don't play well enough to make such a bother."

"Precisely the reason why we must be particular," he answered wearily. "My dear girl, if you have to struggle with the piano as well as with your nerves, well then—we are lost indeed. Come, come. Try this one. No harmony, now. Only melody."

She began to pick at the keys with an index finger. "More softly," he cried. "More softly. We must teach the world the dread of sound. Now make me stra-a-a-ain to hear you. Now in the upper registers. Higher. Higher. Still higher, dammit. All right. Good. Now the left hand. Lower. Lower still. Now the extreme bass. Softly—the mu-u-u-ted threat of fate. I don't want to hear the key strike at all. I want only to be suddenly aware of an imme-e-e-ensely distant thunder." And so it went, on and on, into the late afternoon. Thede was exhausted, and Otto was sweating and bedraggled. But I enjoyed the experience immensely.

Finally, Otto selected two pianos, one for the rehearsals and one for the concerts. "To hell with it," he said, "let's go. Billy, be sure and tell them to deliver the rehearsal piano to the grand ballroom at the hotel." He wiped his forehead. "God in heaven, am I worn out."

I telephoned for a cab, arranged for delivery of the two pianos, and in a few minutes we were on the way back to the hotel-. Otto said, "I suppose the only thing to do is to get Van Clausteyn to pick one out and have it shipped here. Sometimes I think that that I could more easily find a fine Stradivarius violin than a really perfect piano. Not that the ones we chose are at all bad, but—"

He sighed and I thought I saw the flicker of a new expression cross his face. He looked—trapped wasn't the word. Perhaps the, expression was rather the result of the instant stifling of a rage. Yes, that was it. The stifling of a helpless rage. Well, Otto, my boy, seduction has its penalties as well as its rewards.

The concert was sensational, to the audience (the quartet was recalled to the stage numerous times with applause that was lavish and even vocal), to the critics (one critic said, in part, "What I heard was a miraculously achieved blend between two types of instruments essentially different in construction and purpose. The quartet sounded like one unified, marvelous, complicated music-maker. And the evening had a heroine, too. Theodora Karman is a really brilliant and beautiful young pianist.") and, to Otto (who said, "1 must tell you, Billy, since you ask me that I didn't think it could possibly be that bad." But he was Careful to say it in an aside. Obviously it would be safer not to commit himself before Olga and Mala.)

Dinner was late and gloomy. I thought I had never heard such a fortissimo silence from Olga. Thede was apologetic. She said, "I'm afraid I played too loud after all. I was terribly nervous."

I didn't believe her. I was sure that she had only been trying to steal the show by drowning out the others. She needed to do it only once to gain an important status in the eyes of the critics and of the public. In a way, perhaps Otto had done me a favor. At last I could see my dear wife in her true colors.

What a histrionic monster I had, been married to for twelve years.

We finished eating in silence. But Otto did not forget the inevitable farewell. "See you tomorrow at ten. No, wait. Better make it nine, better make it nine."

Early the next morning the final arrangements for the tour were completed. Jim Krikelaire, arrived from New York with his son. They had brought a small van in which to transport the pianos. They would also attend to the moving of all the musical paraphernalia, the music stands, the adjustable piano stool, the music itself. Everything would be delivered directly to the various auditoriums.

And now Otto told me I must learn to tune the pianos. But I absolutely refused. "Let me be," I said grumpily. "I don't want to do it. I don't know how to do it and just leave me alone about it."

But Otto wouldn't give up so easily. "Billy," he said cajolingly. "Good old Billy. You know I would never ask you to do anything unreasonable. Why, it's simple! Look, now." And he took me to the grand ballroom and. showed me a small machine. "This intonation instrument can detect immensely small imperfections when you want to tune a piano. You see, if any note is in the least off key a red light will flash. Then you tighten or loosen the string. When the red light stops flashing the note is in tune. Nothing could be simpler. Why, you will be able to tune a piano in less than an hour. Here, let me show you." And he inserted a piece of green felt into the piano.

"What are you doing that for?"

"Well, many of the keys strike not one, but three strings. We have to tune them separately, so the felt is placed between two of the strings to stop them from sounding. Then the third string can be tuned, without auditory interference." He took a long metal bar out of a case and inserted it into the piano. Then he played a note and began to tug at the bar. The note wavered.

"It's too complicated."

"Of course it isn't, Billy. Complicated indeed! Why, nothing could be less complicated. Oh, yes. There is something else I must tell you." He began to look through his pockets.

He already assumes that he can persuade me, I thought. Well, not this time. I'm tired of being a piece of putty in his hands.

At last Otto found a piece of paper. "Here "he cried. "Here it is."

"Here what is?"

"A chordal list. You see, if you want to make absolutely certain that the piano is in tune, you can check it with this list. It tells the number of beats per second which you should be able to hear when certain chords are played. Of course you will have to listen closely. I'll show you how to do it, then—"

"To hell with It," I snarled. "To hell with it absolutely. I'm willing to tune the damned pianos, I guess. But if that whatchamaycallit machine isn't enough, the devil take it. You can tune them yourself."

Otto smiled slightly. It was easy enough, he knew, to persuade someone who was already divided in his own mind. One had only to increase the pressure a little. He pursed his lips. "We-e-ell," he said reluctantly, "all right. But remember: Every day you must tune the concert piano. Faithfully. Every day. And the rehearsal piano once a week. You'll find it a simple enough matter once you get used to it."

"You can absolutely rely on my faithfulness," I said angrily.

Now Thede strolled through the ballroom whistling, "I Got Rhythm." She waved to them. "Hello, Bill," she called... "Hello, Marcus." They waved back and she walked on, her jaunty footsteps marking time to the rhythm of her whistling.

Otto made a face. He looked at me and shook his head unhappily.

I was comforted by Otto's discomfort. Well, every great love has its drawbacks. The thought gave me bleak satisfaction.

But Otto only said, "George Gershwin once complained to me that practically no one plays 'I Got Rhythm' in rhythm. I must teach Thede how he wanted it. You know, I met George on our first American tour. Was it 1935? Anyway, I was charmed by his freshness and originality. It is a shame that he was lost to serious music because he could have made a real contribution." Now he looked at his watch. "You'll have to excuse me, Billy. We rehearse in ten minutes and I want to wash my hands." He left the room, whistling briskly.

But the melody of his whistling seemed somehow to contradict the rhythm of his footsteps. What was that strangely intricate pattern, I wondered. It wasn't—yes, it was. Yes, yes it was. The founder of the Casa Bella Quartet was whistling "I Got Rhythm" in the original version. From Beethoven to Gershwin. Glorious, oh, really glorious. Of such is love.

The second, concert took place in Lynn, a city a few miles to the north of Boston, in the evening of October 7th. The next morning Otto suggested to me that I come to a conference they were having at one o'clock. It seemed that Olga and Maia wanted to talk about Thede.

Now it's beginning, I thought. I said, "Very well I'll be there."

We met in Otto's room. For some time desultory remarks of no importance were exchanged. But at last Olga began to talk with characteristic energy. "I think we should expand our ensemble," she said briskly. "I know an excellent horn player who would be glad to join us. For a start we could play the Brahms trio for French horn, violin and. piano. And I'd like to program it very soon."

"You haven't done a. thing to get a viola player," Maia muttered.

"It is because I *can't* do anything," Otto said indignantly. "There have been hundreds of letters of inquiry, but when can we possibly hold, auditions? We'll simply have to wait until there is time. What alternative do we have?"

"By the way," I said. I looked at Olga. "What did you think of Thede's playing last night?" That should stop all this beating around the bush.

Olga hesitated. "I think she did comparatively well," she said cautiously. "But to tell you the truth, Billy, I'm still worried about her."

"This is a temporary arrangement anyway," Maia exploded. "We have to find a permanent solution. Olga's horn player might help us at least to begin to solve our problem. He fits in with Otto's idea about founding a new kind of chamber music society. And I think our name has enough prestige so that we can start to organize such a society. For why shouldn't people have a chance now and then to hear the—the Beethoven septet, for instance? Or the Schubert octet? Neither of these unusual works is played more than once in a blue moon. And there are many, many such examples, not so striking, perhaps, but certainly very beautiful. The Mozart clarinet quintet. Wonderful piece. The Brahms and Schönberg sextets. I know, Otto, that you want to do these things gradually. But I say that we can at least *begin* immediately. Of course there will be many complications. But if Olga knows a horn player of high quality, I say give him a chance."

"Maia," Otto said wearily, "you are simply repeating my original idea, as you yourself pointed out. But the situation is certainly not desperate enough to warrant changing the program for any concert this week, or even next. If it were, we should have to cancel it. Are either of you in favor of this? Because I am not willing to play the Brahms horn trio without having a chance to restudy the score. And it would take an absolute minimum of two rehearsals. Olga, even if your horn player were adequate to the task. Which I don't doubt that he is," he added hastily, seeing the look on Olga's face. "But I have never played the piece and you'll have to give me a little time to learn the violin part. Hadn't either of you thought of these things?" He paused for a moment. "Then I must say that your suggestions were made emotionally rather than logically. What advantage would we gain? We need a pianist for the horn trio anyway. If you think Thede plays badly, I assure you that she can play just as badly in the trio. Worse, because I don't think she knows it."

"That is not my point," Maia cried. "We all know that it is not Thede's playing which is primarily at fault, but the way she looks at things. It is psychological. What we are trying to say is that a little competition might change her whole attitude."

"Of course," Otto said quickly "Of course. On the other hand there might be another way out rather than punishing the audience with a bad performance of the horn trio. And, my God, the terrible task of getting it ready. We have enough to do to perfect the repertoire, we have already learned. Now I had an idea, so, I asked Billy to be here because I wanted to ask his advice about it. What do you think of this," he said, turning to me. "If news of our conference were to reach Thede's ears, if she were to hear about the horn player, don't you think the effect would, be the same?"

I was a little puzzled. The solution was plain, yet no one had suggested it. It must be that they didn't want to hurt me. That must be it. Of course they didn't know that I couldn't be hurt any more. But it might be a good idea to hurt Thede for a change. "Why not try to get Hankins here," I said casually. "There will be complaints, of course. The patriots will say that American talent is not being rewarded. But if you like we can dissemble a bit and say that we had originally wanted to play with Hankins, that there was some doubt about his being available, and that he was able, finally and unexpectedly, to make it. Then we can tell the newspapers how grateful we are to Thede for her sterling help. Hankins' enormous prestige will take care of the rest."

There was a dead silence. Maia spoke first. "No, Billy," she said. "We can't do it. We are in a situation which we can't get out of without ignoring human values. The sacrifice would be yours, and it's like you to offer to make it. But there would be repercussions. Thede would be very angry with you because she would, know that you could have interceded." She frowned, "Anyway, maybe it's not being fair to her. She did play pretty well last night. No, I think that for the present it will be enough for her to hear about our conversation. Life is not a simple matter and it cannot have simple solutions sometimes." She sighed. "I think we'll have to wait and see how she reacts."

"All right," Olga grumbled. "We'll see how things go along."

A flicker of relief crossed Otto's wooden features. "Agreed," he said with an outward calmness.

I decided to get it over with and went immediately to the mezzanine where Thede was practicing on the hotel piano. Why didn't she use their own piano? Curious I approached nearer and. stood watching her, but she was absorbed in her task and didn't see me. Now the soft scale descended slowly into the realm of vanishment. Her control was improving daily and I could not help but be pleased, and then angry with myself. She began to play, very softly, the first of the Bach two-part inventions. In this piece the left hand was supposed to imitate the right hand in an echoing pursuit, like "Three Blind. Mice." But Thede had reversed the technique so that the right hand imitated the left. I thought that the invention would be much harder to play in this upside-down way.

At last I could restrain my curiosity no longer and said, "I see you like somersaults."

She did not seem in the least startled, and did not even interrupt her playing as she said, "What happened at the meeting?"

"Well—" I was startled by her answer. "They—we talked, about getting a horn player to enlarge the programs, but then decided against it for the present."

"I think it would have been a good idea to get the horn player."

Well, I thought, it didn't seem as though Otto's idea was going to work.

Now she was having difficulty with the invention. Frowning, she said, "You should be able to use any hand at any time in any place. So it's good practice to mix things up a little." She missed several notes. "Damn it," she said disgustedly. "God damn it." My dislike for her returned full force. Now she slammed the lid of the piano down.

We were silent for a time. Then Thede arose, took my hand and led me to a divan. We sat down and she stretched out her legs luxuriously, "Oh-h-h," she sighed. "What a relief to stop playing the stupid piano. I don't mind the concerts, but the practicing! It goes on and on."

I had a done my duty. Why should. I stay? But I said, gruffly, "Do you like the tour?"

"Mmmm!"

"That is, do you like to play with the quartet?"

"Mmm-hmmm!" She stood and stretched, then took my hand and led me back to the piano. I leaned against it as she began the Bach invention once more. This time she did not reverse her hands. After about ten minutes she stopped playing and crossed her arms on top of the piano, leaning forward to rest her chin against a tiny, powerful wrist. She closed her enchanting eyes and a moment of innocent, childlike sleep relaxed her features. I watched her quiet, regular breathing and thought that there was something calming, almost hypnotic about it. Now she opened her eyes, raised her large, heavy eyelids, and I was fascinated by the creases which suddenly appeared above the thick, curling lashes. It seemed impossible for this woman to move without the subtle implication of sex. She regarded me steadily as a tiny tip of blood-red tongue emerged and slowly traversed the length of her lips, protruding slightly as it passed the center of her mouth. My throat was dry and it was difficult for me to swallow.

"Hon-ney," she breathed. An essence of nectar was distilled, a lingering, almost plaintive command. She sighed.

I answered numbly, like an old, scratchy record, like a halting, dutiful echo, "Hon-ney—"

She sighed again, and now, breathing deeply, passionately, she whispered, "Let's go to bed, honey."

And I had complied. As always I had complied. But that night I stared sleeplessly into the darkness, thinking of the terrible fiasco of the afternoon. Was I really old at last? Or had my failure been caused by a subconscious resentment of her? No, that was only the petty excuse of an old man.

I tossed and twisted and threw the covers back. Now my mind returned to the beautiful sight of her nude body, to the remarkable auburn curtain which reached, well down her thigh, to the sharply outthrust plateau from which emerged two lovely, inquiring breasts, like avid question marks. And now I saw the ugly picture of myself in the mirror, with my contrasting, ridiculous paunch, and remembered my vanishingly faint passion, only intellectually powerful. Ah, had I never been young? I couldn't remember.

But with such a frenzied desire *how* could I have failed so miserably? What must she think of me now? How pathetic it was for me to have wanted to show her that I was superior to Otto. And how *galling* it was for her to have tried to comfort me.

And so I tossed the night away. And as the dawn arrived I came to an irrevocable decision. Never to interfere, not ever, ever to interfere. Let them have each other, let them always have each other. For me, marriage was a thing of the past. It was through, Over, done with, finished.

After the concert in Hartford, where Thede had lived as a young girl, the quartet was invited to a banquet in her honor. As a result everyone got to bed very late. But not before Otto mercilessly announced that there would be a rehearsal the next morning at six o'clock. I reminded him of the long trip ahead of them, and of the concert they had to play the following evening, but he was immovable. Olga protested bitterly. "Dammit" she cried. "Otto, you know that I hate to fly. And it takes seven hours to get to Baltimore by train. We won't be able to get much done anyway, so what use is it? We'll only lose sleep that we need and it will do more harm than good. Dammit. Double dammit."

Otto was apologetic. "My dear," he said gently, "I don't like it any more than you do. But it is absolutely necessary that we rehearse. I'm sorry. With luck it won't take very long. And Olga subsided, muttering and grumbling.

Only I realized Otto's motive. Thede had, made a few slips in the concert and he never lost an opportunity to attack her. Olga and Maia always felt much better after these attacks.

The next morning four bleary-eyed

musicians entered the rehearsal room. Their nerves were frayed and they gazed at each other with dull animosity. a had made the effort to be there too because I suspected that there might be some interesting developments. At the banquet several speakers had praised Thede so inordinately that their praise became insulting to the rest of the quartet. Usually Olga and Maia ignored anyone who flattered Thede as being too ignorant to be worthy of notice, but last night the native son claque had gotten out of hand and the tail had magically begun to wag the dog.

Thede had tried to control the situation by a modest speech in which she gave all the credit for her success to her colleagues. But this did not prevent Olga's temper from rising as one hyperbolic speaker succeeded another, and it had taken the combined efforts of Otto, Maia and me to keep her from leaving.

Now Olga was in a vile mood. She sat down and jabbed her cello viciously into the floor. Simultaneously she began to attack Thede. "Well, Mrs. Genius, I suppose wrong notes don't matter in Hartford."

"I'm sorry, Olga."

"Such an inflation of the ego because one has become third rate instead of fifth rate is unreasonable, don't you think?"

"I'm really very sorry. I guess homecoming made me a little nervous."

"Nervous! Ha, that's good. You have the nervous system *as* well as the sensibilities of a mule." She paused. "Ha, ha! That's very good, a mule. In everything except appearance you do resemble a mule. Intelligence, talent, sensitivity. What else? Even fertility, I suppose. Oh, but I forgot. Not persever—"

Otto stood up angrily. "Olga!" he said sharply. "May I remind you that I conduct rehearsals? And that while I have always, for twenty years, been able to speak with sufficient harshness when necessary—I repeat, when necessary—I do not think you can accuse me of ever having been abusive. If you cannot restrain yourself from saying vulgar things, then let me attend to criticism. After all, I think I know what good piano playing is as well as you do."

I was surprised. Otto had never dared to criticize Olga so openly before. Again I thought, of such is love. Olga was silent, but only for a moment. Then she got heavily to her feet and said, irrevocably, "I'm through." And seizing her cello in one hand and its case in the other she marched slowly and majestically out of the room. Her departure was like the clanging of a fire alarm and everyone began immediately to come awake. "My God," Maia cried frantically. "What shall we do? We have a concert in Baltimore tonight and must absolutely leave in an hour if we are to get there in time."

The tour, like all such tours, was merciless. It had no tolerance for human crisis, no patience with weakness of any kind, no matter how understandable and natural. Under the asinine banner "THE SHOW MUST GO ON!" artists have performed in a state of illness so severe that soon afterward they died. For music is a peculiar army. The artist soldiers are few, and the generals of the public many and indifferent.

I considered the situation carefully. I thought that they were in a dangerous predicament, for even if the concert tonight were cancelled there was the next concert to worry about, and the one after that, and who could say how long their female Achilles would sulk in her tent. Perhaps I should have been delighted, at the prospect of the tour coming to an abrupt and violent end, but somehow I wasn't. For the more I thought about it the more obvious it seemed to me that sooner or later everyone would kiss and make up. And if this was going to happen anyway, then ought I not to try and help them?

I said, "Now listen to me, all of you. We've got to fix this up right away. I think that Maia should go with me to see her, followed, by you, Otto. You got us into this mess and you ought to try to help us get out of it. I admit that Olga behaved badly, but shouldn't *I* have been the one to reprimand her? Why didn't you let *me* attend to it? After all it is—it is *my* wife who was insulted." I waited for some time but Otto did not answer me. He seemed to be utterly dejected. Too bad.

At last I continued. "Now here is what I propose. Since Olga is not an ordinary woman—you may conduct rehearsals, Otto, but you cannot conduct Olga—I shall always be present at future rehearsals. And though I have never said anything before, I shall intervene if anything like this happens again. Do you agree?" But Otto was sunk in gloom and did not reply. "Well, do you *agree*, Otto?" He stared dully at me. "Yes, Billy," he muttered. "Anything you say. Anything at all."

Sounds of violent packing came from Olga's room. I wondered how best to proceed, then decided to wait for the noise to stop. A little quiet would make my knocking more dramatic. Soon there was a lull and. I beat loudly on the door with the flat of my hand.

"Who is it," Olga growled.

"You have insulted my wife, Olga, and. I demand that you open your door."

There was a momentary silence, then muttered curses in French. Then another moment of silence, and the door was flung open. There she stood, the embattled Amazon. "Billy, my dear," she began, feebly, ingratiatingly, "you know that—that during rehearsals anything goes, and—"

"Then why did you get' angry at Otto?" I said sharply. "I'll tell you, Olga. Anything goes, but under one condition. That afterwards everyone kisses and makes up and is good friends again. This you were not willing to do. You were offended. Then I consider that I have a similar right to be offended. What would ordinarily have been an innocuous remark now becomes an. insult. We will expect your apology this afternoon." I walked to the door.

"Wait," Olga cried. I paused and turned to look at her. She was biting her lips and wringing her hands. Upset, wasn't she? I knew that she was an honest person and that her honesty would force her to return and apologize. It would be bitterly galling to her, but the only way out was for her to change her mind about resigning, and this would cause her to lose face. Rut how else could the "Anything goes" rule apply? It was a real dilemma and she began to blush and stammer. "B-billy, I—" She threw out her hands helplessly. I felt sorry for her, but the only thing to do was to maintain the pressure.

Maia had followed me and now Maia felt that she could stand it no longer. "Oh, my love, do not leave me," she pleaded tearfully. "Please, please do not leave me. I know that Otto is so unhappy, so anxious. Oh, oh, do come and be with us again. Please!"

Olga stood uncertainly, first on one leg and then on the other. And I decided that now was the time. I picked up the phone and called Otto. "Come up right away," I said.

Olga walked, slowly, disconsolately, to the window. She sat down and kicked off her shoes, then stared moodily into the distance. "What's the use," she muttered. "The same thing will only happen again."

There was a knock on the door and Otto entered, breathing rapidly. "Let's—" he swallowed. "Let's not be angry," he said apologetically. "Let's just forget the whole silly business. Shall, shall we forget about it, Olga?"

"Yes," I answered. "We shall forget about it. Now we have very little time, so let's get ready to leave."

But Olga ignored me. A look of desperation came over her face and she lurched to her feet, seized Otto, kissed him shamelessly and burst into tears.

Now they all surrounded her I telling them vainly to get ready. At last I gave up and, sat dawn on a sofa. What a scene, with Maia crying, Olga sobbing, Otto trying awkwardly to embrace her. The little man looked ridiculous next to the giantess. "My darling," he cried, "what does anything matter so long as we are together." And he comforted her until they did miss the train and I had to charter a plane.

Thede said, "All *right*, Billy. I'll do it. I've told you, I'll do it."

"Let me tell you once more," I said earnestly. "I'm sorry, but it's important. Now listen. When Olga open's her door, simply put your arms around her affectionately and kiss her. That's all you have to do. And even if you don't like the idea, put something into it. She will feel badly enough anyway, and guilty. You must make her feel that you are her friend, and that you forgive her. Be sure to give her warmth a great deal of warmth."

"I'll do everything I can," Thede promised.

She went down the hall to the elevator and in a few minutes she would be knocking on Olga's door. If it was her intention to hurt Olga deeply, she, with the infinite subtlety of a woman, would be able to do it. Outwardly her embrace would be friendly and no doubt she would kiss Olga and say endearing words. But over her behavior would hang the almost tangible covering of a sardonic *noblesse oblige*, of a caustic forgiveness. After a few minutes she returned to my room.

As she entered the room I looked at her anxiously. Her expression was inscrutable and my heart sank. When she said, "It's all fixed. We're great friends again," I was further depressed by her tone of voice. Ah, I could tell. I could always tell.

"Let's go," I said glumly.

We met Olga in the elevator. Her face was white, her lips trembling. Now I knew beyond doubt what must have happened, and my heart was heavy within me. I loved Thede, but I had long since stopped liking her. Now I began to hate her a little.

In spite of everything the concert was reasonably successful. Olga had managed to restrain her anger so that as far as anyone knew she was no more than normally irritable. Accordingly Otto suspected nothing and was in fine spirits. When the post concert crowd had finally dispersed he suggested that we have a midnight snack. Olga growled, "I'm sleepy," but everyone else wanted to go with Otto, and Maia persuaded Olga until she agreed to come with us.

Otto knew Baltimore well and took us to an excellent seafood restaurant. He was in rare form that evening, witty and humorous, and we had a riotous time. It was very late when we got back to the hotel and Otto said, "The devil take it. Let's not have a rehearsal tomorrow morning. What do you say?"

For several minutes the air was filled with happy shouts and with my shushings. Then everyone went more or less happily to bed.

We reached Washington early the next afternoon. The capital had always been a glittering romance to me, and after registering at the hotel I thought I would do a little sightseeing. But first to unpack. I went with the bellboy to my room.

I emptied both suitcases. What was

that slip of paper stuck in the lining. I pulled out an old program of the quartet. Yes, there was the dear, ugly face of Andrea. The forgotten woman. How strange that I hadn't heard a word about Andrea since her death. It must be that even to talk about her was too painful to everyone. So we tried to forget her. But did we succeed? I had not been able to keep from thinking about her, and I could not imagine that I was different. The others must think about her too. But then why didn't they talk about her? The catharsis of speech ought certainly to be therapeutic. A burden was lighter when it was shared. I must speak to Otto about it, I decided.

Now for my sightseeing. I visited the Capitol, the Lincoln Memorial, the Washington Monument. While looking at the Treasury Building it occurred to me that since registering at the hotel I hadn't once thought of Thede. Well. I continued happily down Pennsylvania Avenue. My what pretty girls. As I strode past the White House I began to whistle cheerfully.

But now it was four o'clock and time to go to Columbia Auditorium. The concert had been sold out for weeks and there was no doubt that many of the box seats would be occupied by political figures from all over the world. It frightened me a little.

In front of the hotel I saw Otto. He was leaning on his fiddle case and looking glum. "I never did like this barn we have to play in tonight," he muttered. "You need a microphone to be heard. Ah, well." He looked at his watch. "Isn't it about time to leave?"

We got into a waiting taxi. I was still thinking about the audience. Ambassadors from twenty European countries were likely to be present, and many of them were persons of culture and taste. They might spread either a good or an unfavorable report. Not that it should matter to me anymore, but I had become so identified with the quartet that it was impossible for me not to suffer the routine anxieties, just as did the artists themselves.

Except Olga. When we entered the main artists' room she was asleep. Yes, she was always indifferent to the business of playing concerts, always able to sleep. But before we could retreat she stirred and opened one eye.

"I'm sorry we busted in like this," I said. "I hate to awaken anyone who has to play a concert."

"It's all right." She rubbed her eyes sleepily. "I don't give a damn about the stupid concert.

I was amused. "But how can you not give a damn about it? You constantly amaze me, Olga."

"Aaaah," she yawned. "Who cares. An empty hall would excite me more. Who cares about people. What use are people.'"

"Oh," Otto observed, and as always I was struck by the expressiveness which filled the single syllable. Now the little man regarded the giantess affectionately. "Olga, my dear," he objected good-naturedly. "Whether or not you realize it I think you must care. Otherwise how could you, or how could anyone, play the 'Death and the Maiden' quartet twenty times a year? The only thing that makes it possible is our receptive, enthusiastic listeners."

"Is that so," she snapped. Now she was fully awake. "And what about our not-so-receptive listeners? What you should realize, my boy, is that the majority of people don't understand and therefore don't care about the music no matter how fine it is. Most come to concerts to be seen, and most applaud because it's the thing to do, not because they have any real enthusiasm. So if you can't get along without a bunch of stupid hand-clappers, then you're in pretty bad shape." She glared at him. "I'm surprised that you give a damn about the audience anyway.

Now that all the pretty girls are not out front I should think your interest would be localized a bit."

There it was at last. She was still upset about Thede and furious With Otto for having defended her. This was how my dear wife had helped matters. With a pseudo-anger I said, "Olga! Don't be a fool! You know as well as I do that Otto's only real interest is in music and in the great artists who help him to create it."

"Hah! Don't you believe it, my friend. He is not so simple. Listen to me and I'll give you an example." She sat up, cleared her throat and took a deep breath. Then she said slowly, accusingly, "Marcus Aurelius Otto is the only man in the world who can play so that your heart would break and at the same time *count the audience*! So," she continued angrily, "among other things he loves money. He would prefer that you didn't think so, but doesn't that *prove* that he loves money? Hah? Doesn't that *prove* it?"

Otto's face had grown taut with rage. He took a furious step toward Olga and for a moment I was afraid that he might strike her. I stepped quickly between them and held up a hand. "Rest! Olga, go back to sleep if you can. Never argue on the day of a concert." I shoved. Otto away. "Go on! Off with you. Try to get some sleep!" Maia stuck her head in the door and I pushed her gently out of the room. "You too, darling," I said. Maybe I oughtn't to worry, but tonight is important. You might think you won't be nervous but you can never be sure. There are 'Do Not Disturb' signs in the artists' rooms. Hang them on your doorknobs and try to sleep. I will call you in plenty of time. We will have a happy dinner after the concert."

A happy dinner. How unlikely it was with the seething that Olga had revealed. The rotting away of the quartet had begun. Of them all the only stable one seemed to be Maia, and there was probably something neurotic about her too that, even yet, I didn't suspect.

It was nineteen minutes after eight and Thede had not yet arrived at the auditorium. The concert was scheduled to begin at eight-forty and I felt angry and helpless. Otto was increasingly anxious. She hasn't any *right* to do this," he cried. "Damn it, damn it."

Maia tried to comfort him. "Don't worry, Otto dear," she said nervously. "Just be patient for another minute or two. She will certainly be here."

"We can play string trios," Olga reminded him. "Maybe we'll have a good concert for a change."

At eight twenty-one Thede walked in nonchalantly. "Where have you been," I demanded furiously.

"I was at the hotel. Sleeping."

"Why didn't you have them call you, for God's sake? And it's a stupid place to sleep. There are radios and phone calls."

"I couldn't hear a sound. There was no noise at all."

"Don't sleep at a hotel again. Especially for an important concert. And from now on I want you to be at the hall by seven-thirty."

"All right." There was a piano in the room and she sat down and began to play meaningless, irrelevant chords. Subtle, wasn't she? I felt like hitting her. Irresponsible bitch. She had upset everyone, and somehow I felt damnably guilty about it.

It seemed to me that the Washington concert was not very good. At first I thought that it might be the fault of the acoustics, for Columbia Auditorium was simply not suitable for chamber music. In its vast, empty reaches the sound trickled away into nothingness, and the rich sonorities became bleached and pale.

Then I remembered the flare-up that afternoon between Otto and Olga and wondered whether it could have affected their playing. I asked Otto what he thought of the performance, but was answered only with a gloomy shrug.

It was from then on that the concerts began noticeably to deteriorate. Not without interruption, for sometimes the quartet played, better and sometimes worse. But the long, zig-zag journey to obscurity had begun. In Richmond and Philadelphia their playing was of an indifferent quality and they came into New York with Otto angry and frightened.

In his voice was a tremor as he spoke to Thede. "Now you mustn't be afraid of these New York music critics," he said nervously. "You mustn't be afraid of them. They are a race apart, completely unpredictable. Sometimes they will even violently contradict one another. It's not the slightest use worrying about them." He took her arm and led her to a couch. "Now just lie down and practice breathing as I have taught you. Remember, if you can relax everything will go well. Try to sleep. We'll call you in time for the concert."

But Otto seemed badly shaken himself. Three mediocre concerts in a row was a new experience for him and he bit his nails with anxiety.

Tonight they were to play the new string trio by Hugo Storch, the atonal composer, and two piano quartets by Mozart and. Schumann. A difficult program. Thede still played, with the music in front of her, as did the others. For them to have played from memory would have been a piece of public arrogance.

It irritated me to see Thede peering at the tiny notes. It reminded me of her amateurishness. It reminded me that she was little better than a prostitute and that she had sold herself to Otto for a privilege which she did not deserve. And I was further convinced that she didn't even need the music and that she only liked to irritate Olga, who hated to be tied down to the printed page. For had Thede not been accustomed to playing from memory during her own short concert career?

How sly and petty and cowardly then was this way of attacking Olga. The more I thought about it the more it infuriated me.

At last I determined to speak to her about it and went to look for her. Where was she, damn it. She was not in the artists' room relaxing as she should have been. She was not at the hotel, or at least her phone did not answer.

I finally found her on the stage, practicing. For a few minutes I watched silently, then I touched her on the shoulder. "Thede," I said, "Thede, stop playing a moment." She turned to face me. "There is something you can do for me, something important." I gazed at her. It seemed to me that a fleeting expression crossed her immobile features. Was it an expression of fear? I couldn't be sure, but it didn't matter. To hell with her. I said, "Now listen to me," and looked at her sternly. "Listen to me carefully. I want you to play entirely from memory tonight. I don't want you to use the music."

"But Billy," she cried. "I can't play without it. I simply can't. Don't you know how difficult it is to remember all the string parts? Why, it's almost impossible! And I've never done it before. And this is New York, our most important concert. I'll be terribly nervous anyway, and—"

"It doesn't matter," I said. "I don't care if you make a million mistakes. I don't care if you break down, or get lost, or even if you forget completely. I *don't* want you to use music tonight. I've never asked you to do anything for me before. And I'm not asking you now, I'm telling you. No music tonight. Agreed?"

"But Billy, I *can't*," she wailed.

"You must." And I walked off the stage and went to look for Olga. I found her in the dressing room. "My dear," I said, "I've good news for you. Thede has told me that she knows how you feel about playing from the score and that she will try to play from memory tonight."

Olga's face broke into a wide grin. "How very good of her," she cried. "How thoughtful, how considerate. Oh, I must go to thank her immediately. Where is she?"

I was astonished. What an extraordinary person Olga was. Because of a single friendly act she was instantly ready to forgive a person whom I knew she had hated bitterly. She didn't question Thede's motives, she didn't reserve judgment she simply forgave.

"Where is she, Billy," Olga repeated impatiently. "She's—she's on the stage practicing. But really, I wouldn't disturb her now."

"No, no. I must thank her." And she was off with seven league strides. I ran after her as quickly as I could but I was almost too late. As I came onto the stage I saw that Thede was about to speak to Olga who was beaming happily. I frowned and shook my head warningly.

Thede hesitated. Then she said, "Of course. I would have done it before, but I was so nervous. You know how it is."

"Of course, my dear. But now you will see how much better and freer you will feel."

"I hope so, Olga. We can only try it."

The concert was successful, the audience enthusiastic and Otto terribly pleased. Afterwards, when the usual crowd had dispersed, we went to a German restaurant. No sooner were we seated than Otto slapped me on the back, grinned cheerfully and said, "Well, Billy! It looks like we're back in stride, hey? And. Thedie is getting to be quite a girl, isn't she? Look at her blushing. But I must say she played very well. And she didn't miss a note, by God!" He smile and kissed her on the cheek.

"Well, if you're so happy about me why don't you give me a contract?"

"Of course. Get our lawyer to draw one up, will you Billy? And ask him to make it ironclad."

All right." But why should she want a contract? She must have something in mind. Still, if Otto wanted his neck in a noose why should I object?

"There's one thing I'm curious about," Otto continued.

"What made you play from memory, honey?"

"Oh, I knew Olga would like it if I did."

Olga chortled. "If you weren't sitting on the other side of the table I'd kiss you on the cheek too."

Only. Maia was sad. Elbow on the table, chin in hand, she seemed to be sunk in gloom. I saw that she was dejected and I was puzzled. "What in the world is the matter, Maia? Everyone is so happy about the concert, but you look as though you've lost your last friend?"

"I don't know, Billy. But something is wrong, terribly wrong."

"What could it possibly be," Otto laughed.

She looked at him coldly. "Perhaps you could tell us, Otto. What do you think it could be?"

Otto gave an agonizing exhibition of a

man wrestling with an insoluble problem. He pounded his forehead, panted with exertion, groaned with effort. At last he shouted, "I have it, I have it!" And he grinned from ear to ear. "Female troubles," he cried joyously.

Everyone was convulsed with laughter, but Maia said dourly, "Very funny. Very funny indeed."

The tour continued. As one concert succeeded another, a new dimension of music came slowly into being, subtle, profound, imaginative, yet filled with Gallic wit and cleverness. For the programs had begun increasingly to comprise the world of Debussy and Ravel and Fauré. It was a ductile world, easily molded into exciting and unfamiliar shapes by the recreative genius of Otto. Transcending his past he entered, the new universe a conqueror, triumphantly seizing and claiming as his own the music of France.

And one day I complained, "Dammit, I scarcely recognized the Ravel last night."

"Two reasons," Otto explained. "First of all, Billy, you have probably never before heard it played by someone whose first desire is to be faithful to the composer's intentions. And secondly, French music will always sound a little strange when played with a German accent."

"Hmph. About Thede. D'you think she'll make the grade?"

"Well—" Otto was silent for the briefest of moments. "Er—I don't see why not, Billy. Ever since she's started playing from memory there's been an improvement, you know."

"Hmph." Was he lying? Or would the life of the quartet be prolonged for a time? I decided to ask Olga.

Tonight's concert in Newark was to include piano quartets by Schumann and. Fauré, and the concerto for violin and viola by Mozart. This was one of the great compositions of Mozart's youth and Otto had engaged a small orchestra to play the accompaniment.

I went backstage during the Fauré to conduct Olga and Thede to the box which had been reserved for them. Their duties for the evening would soon be over and I knew that Olga wanted to hear the Mozart. Inevitably Thede would come too, and sit in the box so the public could admire her. Damn her soul.

As I waited, I heard the faint sounds of violins tuning and it occurred to me that I ought to greet the conductor of the orchestra. He was Otto's friend and—what was his name. Ah, yes. Holberg. Josef Holberg.

I went downstairs. The fiddles were louder now and I could hear a stray oboe and French horn in the pleasant pre-concert cacophony. In the artists' room I found. Holberg walking back and forth with a score in his hands. He was very nervous and although I tried to reassure him he became increasingly agitated.

He spoke with a heavy German accent "*Der verfluchte Kerl*. He gave us no rehearsal. Almost no rehearsal. But I *agree* with him that without months of practice it is better to have no practice. I *agree* with him that one gets a spontaneity, electric drive. I agree that no rehearsing is better than only a little rehearsing." He sighed heavily. "But the cost is high, high. I am upset and what is worse my musicians are upset. Only one rehearsal!" He groaned and sitting down he buried his head in his hands. "And. *what* a rehearsal!!! *Ach, Gott im Himmel*! To play through the concerto *only once*! And then he yawns like a dog and says, 'Good-bye!'" Here Holberg's voice became a flute-like treble as he got up and performed a grotesque little pirouette, hopping on one foot, kicking with the other and waving a hand in a sardonic farewell. "Good-bye. See you tomorrow night." He groaned. "*Ach! Alles ist beschissen von oben bis unter wie eine Hühnerleiter.* You don't speak German? No. So I speak English. Listen. I engage the *best*, the *finest* musicians in New York. Maybe in the world. I pay them extra from *my own pocket*—"

I began to tire of the sad story. Of course it was a scurvy trick of Otto to play through the concerto only once. But it would probably be an electrifying performance. Still if it were possible to acquire ulcers in a single evening then no doubt the orchestra would eat milk and crackers for a long time.

At the end of the Fauré Holberg was still gaining in volume and energy. But soon the quartet came into the dressing room and Holberg dwindled to an angry muttering.

"Holberg," Otto said cheerfully. "And how are you today, old fellow?" At Otto's nearness a momentary palsy overcame Holberg. But then it left him and he began to tremble uncontrollably. He looked aghast with apprehension and sweat and his teeth chattered audibly. But Otto, without seeming to notice, said, "And how is the best conductor in New York? You are, you know. Now let's see. What was I going to say. Oh, yes. I've been thinking, old friend, and there are several things I want changed." And he began a complicated last-minute dissertation to an increasingly terrified Holberg.

Olga touched my arm. "Let's get out of here," she whispered. "Otto will commit murder to get a good performance." She growled, "Come on," to Thede, then stalked grimly from the room.

A bell rang to signal the end of the intermission and as the audience started to trickle into the hall the handful of musicians-began to people the stage. Gradually the sounds of preluding and improvisation increased until the concertmaster appeared. Then the orchestra tuned and was silent.

Now Maia and Otto, followed by Holberg, walked slowly onto the stage, bowing and nodding to the applauding audience. Olga looked sympathetically at poor Holberg who was white as a sheet. He chafed with impatience at the interminable applause. At last he could endure it no longer and rapped his baton angrily for the orchestra's attention. Then he brought down his arm swiftly in the movement which began the concerto.

There were fifteen players but the simultaneity of the opening chord was like the crack of a cat o' nine tails. Quivering arrows of sound fell like a rain of gold through the introductory passages and as Otto lifted his violin and Maia her viola I felt a tremor of fear. I could not help but feel that while these finest of New York's thirty thousand, musicians might not reach Otto's standards they were still pretty damned good. Perhaps they were too good. Perhaps—

Suddenly sounds of silver interspersed themselves into the heavy gold. Otto and Maia with their own little introductory passage were beginning the new material of the concerto proper and the orchestra was relegated to the accompaniment. Holberg's face had returned to its heavy German red and he was conducting like a maniac, his baton everywhere, the musicians aroused to a high peak of excitement. This was a new level of experience for them and they played better than they knew how to play.

Now the orchestra was silent as a cadenza for the two solo instruments began. How they fought, one superseding the other in a dialogue of joyous anger, on and on, until the orchestra's huger sound swept them aside like a mighty broom to end the first movement. Olga's hand crept into mine and. I saw that her eyes were filled with tears. Beyond her I noticed Thede. She seemed to be lost in thought. What could she be thinking of at a time like this?

No matter. The second movement was beginning and I turned my attention to the extraordinary opening theme. But was it extraordinary, or was it only that I was deceived by the amazing quality of these violins? I had never heard such a sound. Momentarily I feared for Otto who, according to the score, was soon to duplicate their melody. How could he possibly play better? Or as well?

And Otto began the theme of the

Andante, and the music became tragedy, an unbearable, dark grieving, enhanced, by the deeper darkness of the viola. Until one wondered at the universal conception of Mozart as the composer of gaiety and lightness and joy. Now the solo instruments engaged in the dialogue of another cadenza and the night blackened and the sounds were despairing.

When the final presto burst forth with a bewildering gaiety, mice suddenly scurried and trilled among the strings and drunken elephants stomped back and forth across the stage with a skittering and impossible speed.

Until Otto and Maia began to alternate in playing the final arpeggios. Beginning in her lowest registers Mala struggled upward untiringly. Higher and higher she climbed on the awkward viola until I thought she sounded like a piccolo. And as she finished the harp-like melody Otto began to duplicate it. Higher he played, higher and still higher until he seemed to have reached the upper limit of human hearing. I was forced to cover my ears. I turned to look at Olga, but she didn't seem to be uncomfortable. For some time I looked at her, and wondered at her indifference. Did professional musicians develop callouses in their ears?

Now I heard a muted roaring and

looked round. Otto and Maia were smiling, nodding, bowing. The orchestra stood at Holberg's signal to acknowledge the plaudits of the audience. The concert was over at last and the theatre resounded with applause: "*Brava,*" a man shouted. "*Bravo*" screeched his wife.

The applause continued and became an ovation which lasted for an unbelievably long time. Three thousand people rose to their feet, some stood on chairs. Even Olga could not remember anything like it, and she looked first a little envious, and then ashamed of her envy.

I was worried about Maia. She seemed to be in the last stages of exhaustion, in contrast to Otto who was smiling, waving to his friends, apparently enjoying himself. But he would no doubt take care of her if they could ever get off the damned stage.

I looked at Thede. She was working the crossword puzzle of one of the daily newspapers.

We found our way backstage through the private entrance and discovered that others had preceded us. Ah, yes. Autograph hunters. Devotees of one of the most fervent avocations in the world, experts in patience, persistence and ingenuity. Not knowing that

Otto never gave autographs a small queue had formed in front of the artists' room. Now they stood ready and eager, some with small notebooks and one with a large loose leaf affair.

Olga said, "I am sorry but we do not autograph." They stared at her unbelieving. She took off her wrap. "We do not autograph," she repeated. Then she went into the room with Thede and closed the door.

I explained that Mr. Otto felt that his signature had no importance, no relation to the musical event, but the people still stood around uncertainly. I waited for a few minutes, and then left to join the others.

The cheering audience had begun to subside but was still applauding as I closed the door. Thede was talking earnestly to Olga. —recruit one or two people from that Wonderful orchestra," she was saying. "The first oboe, for instance?"

"I don't know," Olga said doubtfully.

"But why not?"

"Because the thing that comes first is the music and, there isn't much music for oboe."

"Couldn't we play the Mozart Oboe quartet?"

"I don't know. Let's talk about it with Otto and Maia."

"Or do you prefer the first horn?"

And now I knew what she had been thinking about during the concert. Men, men, men. What an imbecile I was not to have realized it before. What an idiot.

But then I saw that there wasn't a single damned thing I could do about it. If she was going to have a million lovers she was just going to and there was nothing for me to do but endure it. But how painful it was. Why in God's name hadn't I been able to foresee what was going to happen twelve years ago? I would have needed to do a little simple arithmetic. Still, damn it—

Otto and. Maia came in with Holberg, Otto clapping him enthusiastically on the back. The conductor looked faint, but Otto wouldn't let him alone.

"—a great man," he was saying enthusiastically, "and I predict great things for you."

Holberg collapsed on the couch. "Otto," he whispered, "the people, please don't let them in yet. I want to rest a few minutes."

Otto smiled. "It's all taken care of, Josef," he said reassuringly. "I have already told the guard that no one is to be admitted until further notice. But what I wanted to talk to you about is that I plan to get someone to underwrite the expenses so that you can come with us on tour."

"Otto," Holberg said weakly, "for you I would do anything. He was silent for a moment-. "But—I have other commitments." He closed his eyes and stretched out his limbs, groaning a little.

Thede said, "I think we should congratulate the orchestra, Mr. Holberg. Would you introduce them?"

She wasn't wasting any time, I thought cynically. Surely she had not been interested-in the performance. Surely not. Only in the men, the men, the men. And I was seized by a sudden jealousy, a jealousy so horrible, so cruel, that I thought I could not stand it, but must cry out, cry out now, before everyone. I bit my, lip instead and was faintly surprised to taste something salty and warm.

"He's really too tired to introduce them," Otto said. "Then I'll just go out and bring them in myself." I saw a vision of Thede, triumphant among a mob of newspaper reporters.

Otto frowned. Then he shrugged and began again to try to persuade Holberg. But the conductor was adamant. He had commitments in New York and could not change them.

Olga had been pacing back and forth

in a corner of the room. At last she said, "Otto, what do you think of adding one or two of Holmberg's group to our ensemble? The oboist, maybe. Thede suggests it."

Holberg was immediately enthusiastic. Despite his weariness he sat up and smiled. "They are the best of the best," he said proudly. "But they are really not my orchestra. You see, in New York all the finest work is by the extremely small group of men accomplished. The cream of the cream came tonight. Mainly they are the independent, they do the most ex-pensive recordings, concerts, radio broadcasts and so on. So much money they make. *Ach*! Listen. You will not believe it, but of the six violins used in the concert tonight, three were made by Stradivarius. Amazing, no? And listen to the most extraordinary. If you want any one of them I am sure they would go with you. Such fine, sincere musicians they are. They would be willing a fortune to give up: Remarkable, no?"

"The Mozart oboe quartet," Maia said reflectively. "Nothing could be easier for us. Of course it needs a virtuoso oboe player, but for the strings it is childishly simple. We would lose hardly any time rehears—"

"Lo Presti," Holberg broke in enthusiastically, "I think nobody plays like Lo

Presti. Not in the whole country. Oh, what an oboe player and what a nice boy too."

Otto was uneasy. "Well," he grumbled, "There isn't much music for oboe ensemble."'

"We wouldn't need much," Maia said "I think that if we had this Lo Presti to lighten our burden just a little we would rehearse piano quartets."

The door opened and Thede came in. "First let me introduce the strings," she said complacently. Six embarrassed violinists entered and she read their names from a slip of paper. Everyone congratulated them on their excellent performance. Next came the other strings, the violas, the celli and the contra-bass, and then the oboes and the horns. They were duly introduced and congratulated.

I regarded them all with suspicion, but particularly Lo Presti. He was an amazingly young Italian boy, thin almost to the point of emaciation. He had burning brawn eyes and his huge, wild shock of jet-black hair crowned a sensitive face. He was very shy and left as quickly as he could.

I felt a bitter pleasure when he saw that Otto was also distressed. His distress was especially gratifying because one had to look closely to see it. But there it was. No doubt about it. Good that he was unhappy, and to hell with him too. To hell with both of them.

Otto was torturing himself by watching Thede. She in turn was furtively appraising the orchestra. The contrabass player was a handsome young man named. Brown and I could sense her silent, hopeless review of the chamber music literature. Ignoramus. Not to know that Schubert's Trout Quintet was scored for contrabass. And. I was damned if I would tell her about it.

After the orchestra had left Olga said, "It might be a good idea. I'm in favor of this—Lo Presti, if that's his name. You know, the oboe player. I think he is excellent."

And Mala agreed. "Yes, Olga. What do you say, Otto?"

Otto grumbled and seemed almost on the point of refusing. But suddenly he changed his mind and I knew why. He would agree to play with this Lo Presti, then find him unsatisfactory. He knew that he could find a thousand things wrong with anyone's playing even his own. Just let him have the opportunity and he could *cripple* this boy. And he would have no compunction about doing it either. After all, there was no other way out. He couldn't have him around, could he? Well then, it was necessary. No use feeling bad about it.

In his most agreeable manner he said, "Of course. Get in touch with him, will you, Billy?"

"I'll attend to it tonight," I said. And then I went to get the station wagon.

The rehearsal was at ten o'clock but Lo Presti arrived at nine-thirty. He wanted to be sure to have plenty of time to warm up. I answered the door. "Well, hello. Delighted to see you, Frank. Come on in and sit down. I have been wanting to talk with you."

"Couldn't we talk later, Mr. Esca? I really ought to get warmed up."

"There's plenty of time for that, my boy. Now first, tell me a little about your family."

"Well, my mother and father are both dead. I have two brothers, both older than me, both musicians. I guess we took up music because my father was an oboe player." Lo Presti was silent for a time. I was favorably impressed by this young man. He seemed sincere, intelligent, modest And. as he went on to describe his background I began to like him very much. Yes, he had been born in this country, in Philadelphia, and had studied at the great conservatory there, graduating three years ago. Yes, it would be wonderful to travel with Casa Bella, but it might take him a couple of weeks to wind up his affairs, depending on how many engagements he could cancel. No, there would be no difficulty about the Mozart Quartet. It had, been in his repertoire for many years. He did not inquire about salary, which I liked.

Now Frank said, "It's almost ten o'clock. Wasn't that when we were supposed to meet for rehearsal?"

"Yes. Come with me." As we went upstairs I asked him about his personal life. No, he had no girlfriends, at least nobody he'd feel bad about leaving. His age? He was twenty-two years old. No, he had never been to college. Music had always been his chief interest and it had seemed best to get his advanced training at the conservatory.

As we entered the rehearsal room we were surprised to see Holberg. He had taken possession of a large overstuffed chair and was smoking a cigar. "Hallo, Frank," he said. Jovially. "I told them you would come."

Otto, Olga and Maia were tuning gently. Thede was seated cross-legged on a sofa reading a score. They all greeted Lo Presti. He smiled nervously and sat down at a vacant desk. Then he took out his oboe, assembled it, squeaked a few times and said, "I guess I'm ready. Do you want me to play an 'A'?"

"No thank you," Otto said coldly. "We use a tuning fork." He sounded the fork by rapping it on his knee, then touching it to the bridge of his violin. A clear, bell like tone issued from the point of contact.

Lo Presti played "A" on his oboe. It

seemed comparatively flat. "As soon as the instrument becomes warm," he said apologetically, "it will be in tune."

"Why does it have to become warm," Otto said disapprovingly. "If you're a good oboist you warm it up before-hand. Otherwise you waste our time." He stood and said, "We will change this rehearsal to tomorrow at ten o'clock. Good day."

"But Mr. Otto," Lo Presti pleaded. "It will be the same thing. I live out near Coney Island. I did warm up this morn-ing but it took so long for me to get here that the instrument got cold again. Why don't we just begin? It will only take me a few minutes to warm—"

"That's no excuse," Otto interrupted. "You should have gotten here early. As I said, good day."

I said, "The boy is too much of a gentleman to tell you the whole story. He did come well ahead of time and he did want to warm up, but I insisted, on an interview and took up a good deal of his time. The fault is mine. Now go ahead and rehearse. As he says, the oboe will be warm in a few minutes."

"No," Otto said stubbornly. "We'll wait. Go ahead and play for a while."

Lo Presti was somewhat taken aback.

Warming up might take him several minutes. For a moment he hesitated, embarrassed. Then, reluctantly, he began to play the Mozart quartet. His tone cracked repeatedly, and no matter how he tried he could not avoid the unpredictable cracking. After a while he stopped playing. "I guess I'm ready," he said miserably.

They assumed playing position and Lo Presti made a tiny movement with his oboe. But Otto lowered his violin. "I have given the starting signal here for twenty years," he said sternly. "If you don't mind, I shall continue."

Maia and Olga looked briefly at each other. What an earth could be the matter with Otto? Since it was an oboe quartet it was certainly the oboist's duty to begin the piece. And they began to see a side of Otto that they hadn't known through all the years.

But what shocked everyone that morning was Otto's Cruelty. For an unbearable hour he tormented the boy with a caustic irony which shattered his playing. Hardly a measure passed which did not cause Otto to stop the quartet and make a gently sarcastic comment. Finally Lo Presti's performance grew pitifully bad.

At last Holberg rose to go. He looked weary and discouraged. "Please excuse me now," he said sadly. "It is so very nice you invited me." Everyone urged him to stay, but he said, "No. I must go now." He turned to me. "To the musicians' union you must come, Mr. Esca it is a riot. Quite an experience. And the men, they must be paid."

I was embarrassed by Otto's treatment of Frank and I wanted to make it up to Holberg somehow. But I didn't quite know what to do. Perhaps I would think of something. I said, "Will you come to the musicians' union with me?"

"*Ja*, Of course."

"Then shall we meet at Lindy's? At one o'clock?"

"*Ja, ja*. Lindy's."
"And Otto, I want you to come along."
Otto smiled. "Certainly. From what everyone tells me about the musicians' union I wouldn't want to miss it."

Otto and I took Holberg downstairs and showed him out. When we returned to the rehearsal room Olga put down her cello and stood up. Tremendously tall and threatening and ominous she was as she growled at Otto, "Either you let him play as he wants to, or I'll—"

"You'll *what*, my dear?" They glared at each other.

"Cut it out, both of you," I said. "We will stop now for a little while. Thede, you take Frank into the next room. I want to talk to the others."

Suddenly I was struck by a suspicion that Thede might well take advantage of this opportunity. Why had I given it to her? I was an idiot. As they passed into the hall Lo Presti lowered his oboe and it grazed her thigh. The mighty symbol, and a presaging of things to come. It was difficult not to run after them and stop what seemed a certainty. For Frank's sake as well as mine. I cursed myself as they left the room.

But no sooner had the door clicked shut than Otto was confronted by a furious Maia. It was rare for her to become aroused but now she was really angry. She turned on him like a little tigress. "Coward!" she said vehemently. "Fool! You have always pretended to be a human being. Drop the pretense. I know you for what you are! A cad! A despicable scoundrel! You made that boy miserable. Why? You changed him, in only an hour, from a fine artist into a—a wreck. Why? Why? If you didn't want to play with him you had only to say so. Why did you persecute him? What was your God-damned filthy motive?" She spat on the floor. It was incredible. Maia, the perfect lady. That she should do such a thing.

Otto was frightened. "W-well, —he's

only a boy," he stammered. "He has a long way to go." And then he added nervously, "D-don't you think?"

"Liar," Maia screamed. "You criticized, him like a fool. A dirty, stupid *fool*!"

At first Otto pretended to be indifferent, but as the tirade continued he began gradually to change. His face became screwed up, as if he were in pain. He tried to interject a word of protest, to assert his old authority, but Maia was in too much of a rage and shouted him down as soon as he opened his mouth.

Otto was an unlucky man that morning. When Maia paused for breath Olga, who had been hovering like a heavy vulture, pounced on him and tore savagely at his feeble defenses until he was ripped to shreds. Slowly her fists clenched and unclenched themselves and with each of the powerful movements Otto winced. Her breathing was labored and her face flushed. And I could not help but feel that such a rage must have been caused not only by Otto's behavior that day but by some ancient, deadly grudge, buried well throughout the years, nurtured through recent weeks and now, finally, exhumed. Up and down, the floor she paced, and now and again she would stop, glare at unhappy Otto, and unleash another burst of invective.

Only I could know that jealousy was the motive behind Otto's behavior. Perhaps Otto himself did not know entirely. But understanding and forgiveness were not the same. There was no forgiveness in my heart. I watched with relish while Otto suffered and did not think of interfering. The beating continued.

For a long time Otto was silent. But finally he cried," What the hell do you want me to do? I can't help it if I think he's a lousy player. What do you want me to do? What do you want of me?

"We want you to restore his courage," Olga spat. "We want you to give the boy back to himself. If anyone can work a cure it is you, who have made him ill."

Otto answered, dispiritedly, "All right, all right, all right."

We went into the next room, and the next room still, but Thede and Frank were nowhere to be found. Discouraged, I said I would try to have Lo Presti at rehearsal the next day.

Now Maia began to feel sorry for Otto. How miserable he looked. Now she seemed to regret the violence of her attack on him. Poor Otto. He looked lost. And so now she tried, to make him feel better. "Otto," she said gently. "You promised to meet Holberg downtown."

"Hm-m-m." He was lost in gloomy thought.

"Holberg. You promised to meet him downtown."

"Holberg," he mumbled. "Oh. Yes." He blinked and looked up. "Oh. Thank you, Maia. Thank you so much for reminding me." She could see tears of gratitude in his eyes. "Oh, thank you."

"It's all right, Otto." She smiled. "Go now with Billy. Have a good time. I'm sure it will be interesting."

Olga seemed startled. Only a few minutes ago they had been wiping the floor with the little— She looked curiously at Maia, but received only a warning glance in return.

Otto took a deep breath. "Come, Billy," he said. "We're due downtown."

"Just a minute I'll be right with you." And. I went and knocked at Thede's door. Then I opened it. They weren't there. I quickly explored the house and even searched the basement. Perhaps they were at the bar. No, nowhere. At last I went upstairs to meet Otto, thinking my inevitable thoughts.

We enjoyed a delicious lunch at

Lindy's and. Otto seemed to be in good spirits again. I paid the bill and we left.

"Now about the union," Holberg said. "It is a sight you will never forget. A thousand musicians gone mad. Let us go." He took us to the union headquarters at Fiftieth Street and. Sixth Avenue. As we climbed the thronged stairs a strange roaring increased in volume, and as we reached the second floor we saw that the roaring came from a tremendous mob of musicians which was swarming over an area that must have been a city block in length and about two hundred feet wide. They were closely packed in some places and in others spread out a bit. Holberg explained that different segments of the musicians' union congregated in different parts of the hall. There were the jazz musicians. These met near the rear of the hall, near Fifty-first Street, and spread towards the middle. The classical musicians met near the Fiftieth Street side. And, there were all kinds of shades in between. The recording musicians, the radio men, those who played in musical shows, those who were employed in theatres, like Radio City Music Hall, or Roxy's, and then, descending the scale, the ones who made twenty dollars on a Saturday night playing for a college dance, the ones who depended on weddings; these all had their own special cronies who met at certain parts of the hall. And of course there was no rigid demarcation. Frequently a musician from one group would join another. Finally, Holberg pointed out the permanently unemployed, whose only nostalgic contact with music was at the union.

But the startling thing about the whole affair was the deafening noise of the place. Not only was there the simultaneous conversation of a thousand voices but every minute or two a gigantic loudspeaker would blare forth, with the frightening roar of artillery, the simple announcement that some one of the members was wanted. The hubbub was terrific. My God, I thought, What infernal compulsion makes these people go through this bedlam. To get jobs? I Would sooner go on relief than come to this horrible place.

But the musicians seemed quite happy, and intensely interested in their mutual affairs. Little old men wandered to and fro selling neckties, or violin strings. The scene had the quality of a fair, and I had the curious feeling that should a stray cow wander into the hall it would excite no comment and might even bring an early sale. Holberg was grinning broadly at Otto whose face had twisted into a tortured, unbelieving expression, as though he were suffering excruciating pain. "For heaven's sake, for God's sake," he cried, "let's get out of this madhouse. The noise is killing me."

Holberg grinned even more. "That's what this place is called," he said cheerfully. "The Madhouse."

We went to the office at the back of the hall and I paid the union for the services of the orchestra. The men would collect the money later. As we left Otto uttered a huge sigh of relief. "I must come here more often," he said gratefully. "It feels so wonderful to leave."

We returned to the house and Otto joined me in looking for Thede again. It was three-thirty and soon it would be time to leave for Elizabeth. Maia and then Olga helped us search. We went through the house thoroughly but discovered only Ebbie and she hadn't seen Thede either. Damn her to hell, I thought.

Finally we got into the station wagon and left. Thede would have to take a train. She was there when we arrived, but she had succeeded in upsetting everyone, even Olga. Otto decided that something would have to be done about her. But what could we do, short of getting rid of her entirely?

The concert in Elizabeth was only moderately good.

I was awakened by a sharp, intermittent ringing. I rubbed my eyes and scratched and yawned and wished that the noise would top. Oh. It must be Lo Presti calling. He must be getting even because I had awakened him at midnight. I had told the boy to call, but—damn that noise. I reached for the telephone.

"Have you had breakfast yet," I mumbled into the transmitter.

"This is Frank Lo Presti."

"I know, I know. Have you had breakfast yet?"

"Yes, sir."

"Would you like some coffee?"

"Thank you, sir."

"I'll be down in twenty minutes." I could not recall having ever felt this way, not ever in my life. It was a terrible feeling, like a dozen hangovers. What was the matter with me? What had I done to deserve this? I couldn't imagine. For several minutes I sat on the edge of the bed, staring at my feet. Then I got up and staggered into the bathroom.

Now as I looked at the ancient face in the mirror I had the feeling that on it was written every moment of the sixty years of my life. I remembered having felt when I was young that of course it would be impossible ever to reach such a ridiculous age. Well, I had been wrong. It was not only possible to be sixty it was even possible to be dead. How soon would it happen should I change my will? Ah, the hell with it.

Now I thought of poor Lo Presti, and of Otto's brutal behavior. What a change had taken place in him, and in Olga and Maia. And even in me. And Thede. But maybe she had always been unfaithful to me. Why should it be only a temporary aberration? How could I tell?

Now it seemed to me that everything had gone to hell. I knew that the quartet would never play again as it used to play before Andrea died. An ugly acid had begun to corrode the House of Beauty. Casa Bella.

On the way downstairs I thought of Thede again. She would no doubt leave me. Better not to think about it. Anyway, how could I be sure? Maybe the way she was behaving was only temporary. Still, no doubt she had seduced Frank Lo Presti. Was I being paranoid? After all, I mustn't jump to conclusions. And I didn't want to be unfair to Frank.

I went into the library. And the young boy rose to greet me. He was darkly beautiful and shy. And guilty.

It was a silent breakfast, with only an

occasional monosyllable interjected from time to time. Still, not unpleasant. Somehow I felt warmth and sympathy for Frank rather than jealousy. As though we were fellow victims of the same disease. Well, and weren't we? And Otto too?

When we had finished eating, I said, "Mr. Otto has not scheduled the oboe quartet very often in the beginning. But he wants you to come to all the rehearsals and concerts and to study the scores for the repertoire that will be performed.

"Yes, sir."

"Did you have any trouble in cancelling your engagements?"

"I cancelled most of them, sir."

"It will be possible for us to see that you don't lose any money as a result of the tour."

"Thank you, sir."

Mrs. Bundy brought more coffee. Frank drank mechanically and without waiting for the coffee to cool. I was always mildly surprised by people who could drink hot liquids. But perhaps the lips of oboe players were not sensitive. Probably the abrasion of the reed mouthpiece toughened them. Through bleary eyes I gazed at Lo Presti's lips. Was there a stain of lipstick along their dark length?

Suddenly I came awake. But then I realized that there was nothing I could do about it. Nothing. Maybe I should go for a walk. Gruffly I said, "Do you remember where we rehearse?"

"Yes, sir."

"I'll see you later." I talked to the front door, slammed it and. left the house. Thede was incredible. Why didn't she open a bawdy house? Then she could make lots of money and have all the fun she wanted. I tried desperately to think of a solution to the problem, but could not.

Otto stood near a window, frowning at his violin. His eyes were bloodshot and it looked as though he hadn't slept well either. Now he stared moodily at his violin.

"Lo Presti is here," I said.

"I'm not deaf. I can hear him practicing."

Was it getting to him too, I wondered. But I just shrugged and followed, him to the' rehearsal room.

"Ah, Frank. Hello."

"Hello, Mr. Otto," Lo Presti said shyly.

"Frank, I wanted to talk to you. You see, it is always important to me to know the extent to which a person will take criticism.

Apparently I went a little too far with you yesterday and I apologize."

"Oh, no sir. I have been criticized more harshly. It's just that—" he was silent for a moment and confused. "It's just that I wanted to please you. I—wanted very much to please you and. I felt awful when I didn't."

"My dear fellow," Otto said expansively, "I consider you to be one of the first oboe talents of this generation. Do you think that I would consent to play with you if you were not? But it is important that you be able to accept criticism, and that you work hard. We'll get along fine. After this tour I want you to go to Europe to study. You are still a boy. I have the greatest hopes for you."

Frank was feeling pretty good now and as Olga and Maia came in he greeted them happily. Olga was surprised and looked sharply at Otto. But his cordial expression changed when he saw her. He walked stiffly to his case and it was some time before he joined the others. They began with the oboe quartet and the improvement in Frank's playing was amazing.

As I had anticipated, Thede did not come at all.

The next day was a vacant one and the Casa Belles left New York to begin the tour in earnest. Frank met us at the station. He told. Otto that he would probably see him in a few days. The oboe quartet was not scheduled for another week and he was sure that he would be free in time to play the concert. He was mistaken, for some of his engagements could not be cancelled and it was more than two weeks before he was able to leave New York.

But when the quartet arrived at the hotel in Cleveland. Otto found that Frank had registered the day before. I said, "Should I telephone him?"

"No. You'd better arrange immediately for a place in which we can rehearse."

This was a task which I loathed. Since hotels were not often willing to let musicians rehearse one usually had to beg for a room.

But it had to be done. I went to the desk clerk and said that I wanted to talk to the manager. I was asked to wait, and it was some time before I was shown into a sumptuous room. Seated at a desk was the manager, dignified, grave, even saturnine. He nodded to a chair, then busied, himself with some papers. Presently he looked up.

"And what can I do for you?"

"Our quartet would like to have a room for a few hours in which to rehearse."

"A singing quartet?"

"No, it's a piano quartet."

"You mean they'd need four pianos?"

"No, the classical piano quartet. Violin, viola, cello piano."

"Oh. Well, I'm afraid they would disturb our guests."

"I don't think they would, but just to make sure don't you have some kind of sample room? All you'd have to furnish would be four chairs. We have our own piano."

"I'm afraid all our sample rooms are taken up for the day. Generally they are reserved by salesmen who use them to display their goods. What firm does your organization represent?"

This was getting painful. "We do not represent a firm."

The manager stood, ready to end the interview. "Look, "I said desperately "Expense is not a matter of importance to me. If you can find some place that we can rehearse in for about three hours I'll be glad to pay any rental fee you care to name."

This was a different matter. "Come with me," the manager said.

At last the business was completed and the Krikelaires brought the rehearsal piano to the grand ballroom. It was a beautiful room which opened on the lake. I telephoned Otto and told him where to come and in a few minutes everyone had appeared.

"Listen, Billy," Otto said, "you'd better go Youngstown and get everything ready for the concert. I'd suggest that you tune the piano the first thing after you get there."

"I know, I know. Haven't I been doing it all right so far?"

"Of course, Only it's better to tune the piano after a trip than before. But you must know that too."

"Yes, yes. The trip jars the piano out of tune. I know. But since the piano is already in Youngstown where else *would* I tune it?" I said irritably "And *I'd* like to suggest that you do the tuning yourself, since you're so anxious to make certain of every little detail."

Otto laughed. "I know, Billy. It's an old fault of mine, worrying about details. Please don't be annoyed with me." I was irritated. In addition to everything else I was damned if I wanted to put up with Otto's nagging.

After returning from Youngstown I telephoned Jim Krikelaire and we decided to have an hour of relaxation over the chessboard. My joy in the beautiful little trap I had forced Krikelaire to fall into was spoiled when I noticed that Otto was standing nearby with a look of disapproval on his face.

"Jim should never have fallen into that one, Billy. Now look. If he had castled Queenside he would have immediately checkmated you, don't you see?"

I groaned. It was so obvious that I became furious with myself and with Otto. Why did, the little bastard have to seek out my every spare pleasure and destroy it? For a moment I fumed silently. Then I had an inspiration. "Otto," I said craftily, "how about playing us both a game of consultation chess? You know, one against two?"

"Why I'd be delighted. It's an excellent idea."

Grimly determined to put Otto in his place I began set up the chessmen.

Otto said, "You don't mind, do you, Jim?"

"No, of course not, Mr. Otto, Be glad to play with you."

"Fine" And. Otto drew up a chair. Then he check mated us in seventeen moves and smiled as I threw up my hands in despair.

I sullenly decided to miss the concert that evening. Instead I went for a walk and then ate dinner in a lonely restaurant some distance from the hotel. It seemed to me that traveling throughout the United States with the quartet was a tiresome business. The restaurants were the same, the hotels were the same the cities were the same. And now it had gotten so that even the concerts were the same. All the same, every damned one of them.

The next, morning I thought I would go for another walk. But passing through the hotel lobby I Saw Olga. She said, "The rehearsal is postponed for half an hour. Otto phoned from the fiddle maker and said that he and Maia would be a little late." She seized my arm and marched me toward the dining room. "Let's have some tea, Billy. Lo Presti is in the ballroom and he's making a new reed. I would go there to warm up but he squeaks on his reed like a mouse." She shuddered. "Thank God. I'm not an oboist."

She steered me to a table and we sat down. The waitress came and Olga said, "A cup of tea, please." She smiled at the waitress with a warmth which forgave her irregular, yellowed teeth. In the still moment of Olga's smile I wanted to kiss her. I couldn't understand this impulse. Unattractive teeth usually repelled me.

I said to the waitress, "Please bring me a glass of water and some bicarbonate of soda." And to Olga, "I ate breakfast very quickly this morning. One shouldn't at my age, I suppose."

"Age, always age," She sighed. "I will be forty years old in June, and soon I shall suffer the fate of all musicians. My life will have been spent, who knows how usefully, in the pursuit of fleeting, evanescent sound. Do you know, Billy, a way I hate music." She took a sip of tea and made a frightful face. "I hate tea, too, but what can one drink? Coffee is worse and milk! My God"

"What A thing to say. You of all people. I thought you loved music."

"Rarely, yes. Almost always, no."

"But why?"

Otto had stolen silently behind. Olga's chair. In sepulchral tones he declaimed, "Because when an art involves another than its creator the art itself is never permitted fully to materialize." Now he said briskly, sardonically, "Excuse me for the condensation, my dear, but I am ready to rehearse. Afterwards we can discuss the inferiority of Beethoven."

What a nuisance Otto could be. I determined to ask Olga to lunch and to hear her through.

Olga got slowly to her feet. "It is not the master who is inferior," she said quietly, "but we."

We left the dining room and went upstairs. As. we approached the ballroom a strange, whirling noise increased in loudness. It was like a tiny, desperate wind, imprisoned in a cave and trying madly to escape to join its fellows. It raced up and down the scale, wildly, tirelessly, and as we opened the door

Frank Lo Presti stopped playing.

"I guess I'm warmed up now," he said, looking for a handkerchief and, finally wiping his forehead with a sleeve.

"What in heaven's name were you playing boy, " Otto asked.

"Oh, just some exercises I invented. They warm you up fast."

"I should think some long, slow tones would do the trick best."

"Well, I start out with those but then I get impatient."

"Always remember, my boy, that art is patience."

"Yes, sir."

I wondered what art had to do with warning up exercises.

"Oh, Billy," Otto said. "I forgot to tell you. This is an overly reverberant room. Next time, if it is possible, try to get one that's less resonant."

"How can I tell what's resonant and what isn't? I don't know anything about acoustics."

"Just stand in the middle of the room and sing 'The Star-Spangled-Banner' or something. You'll know. If you think you're singing in the bathtub, then it's not for us."

"Oh. All right."

Otto sat down and carefully tuned his

violin. He looked inquiringly at Olga and Maia, who had already tuned. Maia nodded and Olga yawned. Then Otto gave the signal which began the oboe quartet.

Frank had tossed off the Allegro and Adagio like a wild disoriented Pan. Now, suddenly, another and weirdly different voice sang a shrill melody. Higher and higher rose the oboe's wail into a stratosphere of sound, until it seemed that the range of human hearing was at its highest threshold. I could not find this music in my score and put it down to look at Frank. The veins of his temples were bulging, his eyes shut with a quivering tightness which thrust the long lashes, outward, so that they trembled, like tiny fans. Downward he spiraled, like an exhausted bird, with a fluttering trill, to the final chord.

"Well," Otto said. "Well. I see that something new has been added."

Frank was embarrassed. "I've been thinking that I ought to write a new cadenza for this work," he said apologetically. Mozart didn't write one and—so I thought I would." He looked hesitantly at Otto. "I'd like to d-dedicate it to you, sir," he stammered.

"Thanks. You realize, of course, that an oboist of Mozart's time could never have begun to play such a difficult piece."

I sensed what was about to happen. Otto was going to throw the cadenza out. What a cruel thing to dd.

Fortunately Olga spoke up "All right. That may be very well be true. But what is important is that Frank has succeeded in capturing the spirit of the Adagio. I think Mozart himself would have approved. Yes, I am for keeping the cadenza."

"I feel exactly the same way," Maia chimed in.

For a moment Otto was silent. Then, astonishingly, he said, "What do you think, Thede?"

Olga and Maia were shocked and incredulous. That Otto should think of ignoring their wishes. And to ask the opinion of Thede! The outsider, the dilettante, the thorn in their flesh. They were so amazed that they could say nothing and only sat and stared unbelieving at each other. I wondered why Otto had, made so serious and obvious a mistake. Was it really worth so much to him to deny Frank his place in the sun? He'd better have something up his sleeve or the girls would never forgive him.

Even Thede was somewhat taken aback by the question. "Oh," she said, doubtfully "I really don't know about these things:"

"That doesn't matter. Just tell us what you think. The amateur's viewpoint is sometimes interesting."

At this Olga and. Maia relaxed a little. I was disgruntled. The clever devil had gotten out of it after all.

But still Thede hesitated. Then she said cautiously, "Well—I think the cadenza has great virtuosity. Of course the Adagio is a very slow, solemn piece. Perhaps it needs brilliance. Perhaps brilliance is out of place. Frank, honey, why don't we hear it again?

Frank saved the situation. "Never mind," he said sadly. "I'd rather not play it if Mr. Otto doesn't want me to."

It seemed that Otto had won. But I could tell that he wasn't happy with, his victory.

Olga had agreed to have lunch with me, but now she was twenty minutes late. Ah, here she came. She was wearing a business suit her bobbed hair was beginning to grey and. as I watched her striding across the lobby of the hotel I thought that she looked like John L. Lewis.

Now she seized me by the coat. "Let's go," she said. "I'm starving."

"So am I," I answered. "Let's go indeed."

Olga knew Cleveland well and insisted that we eat at a seafood house some distance away.

"Can't you think of any place closer," I pleaded. "I'm famished."

"Oh, but you'll like this restaurant. It's excellent."

I capitulated. Olga was always willing to go hungry to get exactly the kind of food she wanted and I knew that I could argue with her for an hour without changing her mind.

We went out into the raw, windy day and Olga hailed a cab.

As we crawled through the heavy traffic she began to grumble about the way Otto was treating Frank. "He's turning into a Nazi," she muttered. "If he keeps on I'll hit him with my cello."

I smiled inwardly as I imagined a splintered Montagnana cello and Otto in the hospital, the victim of twenty years of rage burst loose at last. But then I felt ashamed. I had always loved Otto as though he were my son. But Thede had ruined my love. Ah well, better not to think about it.

We drove up to the seafood house$_s$ I paid the driver and we went in.

Olga ordered a large lobster and when it arrived she attacked it furiously. In a few minutes only the empty shell remained and she looked at it unhappily. But only for a moment. Then she ordered, and ate another one.

I was busy with an excellent Alaskan King Crab. Gradually I began to feel more human. At last I said, "Olga, what were you going to say this morning when Otto interrupted you?"

"Hmph?" She swallowed. "Oh, I was going to tell you how impossible the whole art of music is. For instance—this is first rate lobster." She speared a large piece of the pink flesh and chewed it with relish. "For instance," she continued indistinctly, "while it is probably true that Beethoven is the greatest artist of them all, what is the use of him to humanity if his music cannot be performed?

Hah?"

"But Olga, you have performed his quartets for twenty years."

"Not at all. I have rarely even approximated the tremendous vision of Beethoven. Look. I'll tell you one or two things. First, what is really intolerable in music are the technical limitations which prevent the composer from finishing his own work. He writes a symphony and has to leave it to a conductor and a hundred men to perform. Are they competent? Practically never. And absolutely never are musicians ultimately competent. This includes Casa Bella, and don't let Otto tell you differently.

"Here, I will explain it to you better. You see, Billy, there are the independent arts such as painting, or sculpture, or those divisions of literature such as poetry, or prose in the form of a novel, and so on. And then there are the cooperative arts such as music, the drama, the ballet, et cetera. These require musicians, actors, dancers, others. Now let us compare the two groups. You can go to the Louvre, for instance, and spend a lifetime in wonder and awe. But tell me, Billy, how many times in your life have you seen a really first rate performance of a Shakespearean play? Four times? Five maybe? Then you are very lucky. The drama, bah! Music, fah!"

"But Olga, you cannot object to Beethoven, and is he not music? And why could he not finish his own compositions? He was an excellent pianist, wasn't he? He could play any of his thirty sonatas."

"Yes, but can he play them now? Hah? Of course not. He dead. So Is Cezanne, but you can look at his paintings. And. as he painted them, not as shown to you by some amateur copyist."

I ordered a lime lettuce salad with Roquefort dressing. "Sorry, Olga I really can't believe that you dislike music."

"Dislike it? I adore it. That very small part of it which is created by genius, of course. Most music is terrible you know. And what is especially dreadful is the undemocratic aspect of it. An orchestra, for example, means the spending of many individual lifetimes in the learning of skills to be used solely for the performances of the works of other artists. In other words, music is like a special aristocracy which grows fat on the labor of its serfs." She drank her cold tea and made a face such as only Olga could make. She belched, got up from the table and left. I sighed, and followed her.

In the taxi Olga was pensive and for a long time she sat silently and watched the sluggish traffic. Then she said, "The way of art is similar to that of sexuality. Indeed, it is as though one's entire organism, the spiritual aspect of it as well as the physical, breathes orgastically, creating, creating with its hearing, its vision, its sense of touch, its passion, giving birth to objects, to music, to human beings."

"Do the others feel as you do, Olga?"

"Not either of them," she said sadly. "And not even poor Andrea when she was alive." She sighed a vast, regretful sigh.

"There are many, many things about which we have always disagreed, of course. You should know how we can disagree."

The taxi pulled up to the hotel. "Conversation makes me hungry," Olga said. "I wonder whether it is too late to get something to eat." I paid the driver as she hurried through the revolving doors. When I entered the lobby she was standing disgustedly in front of the dining room which was plainly closed. She stalked to the cigar counter and bought six chocolate bars, then settled herself comfortably on a divan and ate them two at a time with a dreamy caloric calm. I watched four of them disappear as though by sleight of hand. I was charmed by her failure to offer me a chocolate bar, and a little envious.

Now Olga heaved a colossal, groaning yawn. "I have never spoken with a man or a woman," she continued sleepily, "without feeling, however faintly, that he or she has something special to say, and that the most important thing in his life is to say it. And that practically no one ever makes the effort, but only talks about the weather."

The last of the chocolate bars vanished and she pulled herself to her feet, stretched and yawned again. "Well," she said drowsily, "I think I'll take a short smoke and then sleep for a little. But first the mail, hey?" We went to the desk to get the mail and Olga said, "Oh, yes one more thing. It is this, and it is very important. We must encourage the least of us to say his own special, private little thing. He *must* be encouraged. He should have all the encouragement in the world. For no matter how ugly, or tawdry or even worthless our efforts are, it is our function to create. And to abandon this function is to abandon humanity."

I took her arm and she guided me to the elevator. "Of course," she continued, "when we have made our little *objet d'art* it is natural for us to rush next door to our neighbor and cry, Look! Look! See what I have done! Then, by the way, is the only time the artist should have anything to do with society. *After* the work of art is finished. Not before, never before, except in the most casual way. Advice to a good artist is seldom helpful. Of course you will tell me what works of art have been commissioned, and dictated, and instructed, and, so on. Yes, but these circumstances have nothing, less than nothing, to do with the heat of creation. And furthermore those who say that the artist has a debt to society are a pack of fools. Why has he a debt to society? Does society, except in rare instances, consider that it has a debt to the artist? Did not Schubert, one of the greatest of all artists, starve during his tragic lifetime? No, man may inspire the artist, but he has no right to demand anything of him. This is the communist theory that the artist must serve the people. When you hear your conservative friends declaiming about the duty of the artist to the public, accuse them of being communists. You should have some fun."

    She lit a small cigar. "But back to music. The terrible thing about the musician is that he must spend almost all of his creative time with the music of others. So that there have been few musicians who have ever found, sufficient time to compose. And of these few, almost none have been great composers,"

By this time we had reached Olga's room and she had her key in the lock. I said, "But if you think creation is so important then why do you not compose yourself?"

"Aargh. I just got through telling you the objections which I have to music in its present form. When they have done away with its evils by inventing an electronic machine or some other wonder of the machine age through which the composer can express himself directly and permanently, then I will try to write something." She was silent for a moment. Then she said softly, "Ah, the wonderful, unborn music of the future. It is all I can hope for, all I can believe in."

"But Olga, dear Olga, what about all the wonderful music which has already been composed?"

"Let skilled amateurs play it among themselves," she said sharply. "It is no harder to learn to play the cello than it is to learn to play golf. Away with all professional musicians, and away with all concerts. Down with them." She looked at her watch. "We'll have to stop now. I have to rehearse shortly and. I want to sleep a little first."

But I said doggedly, "All right, all right. But still you haven't told me what you do personally to create."

The blush in the cheeks of this colossal

woman was that of an embarrassed young maiden. She coughed. "I—I write poetry," she confessed looking aside shyly.

As I walked down the hall I thought about Olga's philosophy. I knew that I had, enjoyed too many gratifying moments in my years with quartet to want to see music in its present form ever done away with. And what if Olga's ideas were to come to fruition? Would the generations of the future be deprived of the immortal music of Mozart and Beethoven? And Haydn and Schubert and Brahms and Debussy? And how could the vast, wonderful literature of music be played without musicians? It was all very well to say that the music of the future could be composed on machines. But even if this were true what then of the music of the past? Few amateurs, no matter how excellent, could really do it justice. And. I began to hope Olga might be wrong.

On the way to the grand ballroom I ran into Otto. We talked for a time of various matters having to do with the quartet. But the conversation with Olga was still running through my mind and at last I interrupted Otto to say, "I got the impression this morning that you don't entirely agree with Olga. You know, about the impossibility of really playing music well."

"Oh, nuts. She should really not talk to you. You will only get confused."

"She rarely does talk to me, you know, but today she did."

Otto sighed heavily. "All right, all right. Now I'll tell you something, Billy. The true nature of music is something which even Olga does not understand. And just between ourselves I try to keep it that way. Playing string quartets is a tricky business and I've found that the best way with Olga is to manage her. Without her knowing it, of course."

"You see, the responsibility of the true musician, and God knows there are few enough of them, is to represent the composer in all his dimensions. And the most important of these is the subconscious dimension. It is not enough to play in tune, to underline the important voices, to understand the form the general feeling and mood of the music, and so forth. One has also to be kind of psychiatrist. Is Mozart, for instance, the composer of lightness and gaiety and joy? As nearly everybody thinks he is? Of course not. Far from it. He is a composer of the most tragic seriousness. One has to delve far beneath the surface of his music to find its true meaning. And of this he himself was not aware.

"And. the same thing is true of all the great composers. Every blessed one. They do not themselves know what they have *really* written. They cannot know. It remains for the musician, who must also be a composer, and a musicologist, and a. psychiatrist, to reveal the meanings of the great musical compositions in all their dimensions.

"You see, usually the composer has a relatively simple, spontaneous job. He only shows a flash of the incredibly complicated structure of his subconscious universe. It remains for us, the musicians, to divine the true story and to bring it alive. And in so doing we perform a task which the composer could never begin to do.

"In this way music is the greatest of the arts because it is the only art in which there is even a remote chance that the true story can be told."

"What about the drama and the ballet? They are also cooperative arts."

"Too many people involved. Of course this is true of the symphony orchestra, the opera, and so on."

"Hmm." I considered this for a moment. Then I said, "One more thing. I am curious about how you can manage Olga. Isn't she something of a problem? How in the world can you get her to do what you want her to do?"

"It's really not difficult. Olga is extraordinarily sensitive, you know. I don't actually *tell* her to do anything, heaven forbid. But when I *play*, she immediately understands on a subconscious level, which is after all the level on which music needs to be understood, what has to be done."

"What about Maia?"

"Same thing."

Then I blurted out the fatal question. Afterwards I felt like a fool, but at the moment I could not restrain myself and I said, "And — and what of Andrea?"

A look of pain wrinkled Otto's features and he did not answer immediately. After a time he said, "Andrea always understood. She understood everything." Then he turned and went into the grand ballroom.

That night I could not sleep. At last I sat up in bed and switched on the light. Should I take a sleeping pill? No, better not, I had been taking them every night and was getting to be an addict. Perhaps there was something to read.

I got out of bed, stretched and yawned. Then I noticed several letters and a package on the desk and remembered that I had not yet finished reading my mail. I went to the desk, picked up the mail and sat down in an easy chair.

The first letter was unimportant, but the second one was from. Teresa Dante. I remembered her clearly, a charming child. I began to read with interest.

>Dear Mr. Esca,
>
>You will be surprised to hear from me. I must ask your help, but please let my asking be between ourselves. My mother has been ill since Andrea's death and I must stay home and care for her. The estate which Andrea left was not large.
>
>I guess she couldn't support the family and. manage to save much.
>
>It has occurred to me that since Andrea was a famous artist we might possibly realize some money if we

could sell her journal. I am sending it to you under separate cover.

This must have been what Gino—no Antonio had spoken of that night after the funeral. The journal must be in the package. I unwrapped several sheets of brown paper and uncovered a small book, bound in red leather. On the title page was printed "A. Dante."' Strange that the package had arrived at the same time as the letter. I skimmed through the book and saw that it was written in Italian. Well, it wouldn't take me very long to get the language back. I had spoken nothing else in early childhood. I returned to the letter.

> Do you think the idea is possible? I think the journal is very beautiful, and I would like to keep it for ourselves always. But first Andrea wrote it with the idea of eventual publication in mind and we would like to carry out her wishes And, too, we need money.
> The trouble is that the journal is not quite finished and the person who translates it will have to somehow complete another chapter or so. In any case, please let me know whether you

think my idea is feasible.
>Most respectfully yours,
>Teresa Dante

A precocious letter. I turned again to the journal, and again felt the old loss of Andrea. But as I opened the red book I suddenly felt an alarming faintness. My head swam and I felt weak. What in the world could be the matter with me? What could possibly be wrong?

No use getting alarmed, for hadn't I successfully passed a thorough medical examination only a few weeks ago? Of course. I felt a twinge now and then, but didn't everyone? Wasn't this the normal creaking of the body going through its numberless daily tasks? After all what machine does not complain a little now and then?

But wait a moment. While reading my electrocardiogram the doctor had paused for a tiny instant to frown. I remembered it clearly now. Why had he frowned? Was he concealing something? I decided that the only thing to do if I was not to worry myself to death was to get another medical opinion. But I must go to someone unknown to my New York doctor or I would never be sure they were not getting together to deceive me.

I was feeling better now and reached for the telephone.

But what was I thinking of. It was the middle of the night. My nerves were tangled and confused, like crossed wires. I went into the bathroom and took two Dormital tablets. Wearily I climbed, into bed and after a time I fell asleep.

In the morning I felt much better. But I am not a man to take chances and I telephoned a friend who suggested that I consult a Dr. Ordby, supposed to be one of the leading cardiologists in the country.

I telephoned Dr. Ordby's office and found that I could not get an appointment until the next day. What if it was my heart? Well, it would be no good to worry about it. I took Andrea's Manuscript to the writing desk where there was a straight-backed chair.

But now I put the little red book aside. For some reason it seemed distasteful to me. Anyhow it was more important to answer Teresa's letter first. I wrote a rather large check and made it payable to Pietro Dante. Then I wrote to Teresa that I was sure the journal could be published and that the Dantes were to consider the check an advance against future royalties.

After mailing the letter I went with the Krikelaires to the concert hall in Akron. We moved the piano onto the stage and I tuned it. Then we returned to Cleveland. I decided not to go to the concert but to spend the rest of the day reading the journal. I was missing too many concerts. Well, they would have to get used to my not going. I was an old man and couldn't keep up with young affairs. I grimaced at the irony.

After we got back to the hotel I went up my room. But after fifty miles of fresh, bracing air the room seemed unbearably close. I stuck the journal into an overcoat pocket and went outside again. Perhaps a slow little stroll in the park. It was very cold but I was warmly dressed, even to fur earmuffs. The park was strewn with the carcasses of bare and exhausted trees, looking human in their deadness, with here the knothole of a whited eye, there a crag of snowy jaw, or a limb extended in impotent threatening. The silent cemetery of the park was overhung with desolation, except that here and there a tuft of hopeful, silly green thrust itself through the snow. I got out the journal and began to read, my thick gloves turning the pages with surprising ease.

I opened my eyes. Above me a man looked down with concern. I must have fainted. And now I was really scared. The damned doctor had deceived me after all. I could have broken a hip. Half a dozen of my friends had broken their hips and were now dead. Old people were always breaking their hips, and was I not old? I must see Ordby today, tomorrow might be too—

"Lucky thing ya missed, that rock, mister. How ya feel?" The man helped me to my feet. Never move an accident victim. Never—

"Ya feel okay, mister?"

"Fine, fine thank you. I must have slipped and fallen, I—

"Streets oughtta be sanded," the man said, and brushed his coat energetically. The lake stared like a flat, grinning skull as he turned to leave. The trees extended their branches in a threadbare canopy. The hotel seemed impossibly distant. I thanked my benefactor and began the long, stumbling journey back.

Entering the lobby, I walked slowly, wearily to the cigar case. But then, with a strong effort of will, I turned away. Couldn't I have just one? One of the small size? No, I mustn't.

A new elevator girl was on duty. She smiled at me. I smiled back feebly and said, "Seven, please," and "Thank you," when we had arrived. I felt weak and the room seemed far away. I fumbled with the key and opened the door. I took off my shoes and lay down on the bed. It was good to lie so. When I awoke it was night.

The next morning I was fluoroscoped and had a blood count taken and an electrocardiogram. Then the stupid, lying mal practitioner told me that there was nothing the matter with my sixty-year-old heart. That these things sometimes happened inexplicably. That I might have had a mild stroke. Then I was told to stop smoking and given a diet to follow because "You are over-weight" which was perfectly obvious to anyone who could see. No, no. Nothing else wrong. *Take* it easy and you'll be *all*—special, long bedside "all"—right.

Liar. Or nincompoop, I had found out the truth about the so-called science of medicine. Blind men in a dark room at night looking for a black cat which wasn't there in the first place.

Suddenly I felt a hatred for my body. What had I to do with bones, blood, teeth, excreta? What had they to do with me? My arm was a foreign, busy country whose laws were unknown and unknowable to me. I was imprisoned within an animal who could only be watched from a distance, without understanding or affection.

My body was an idiot beast, obsessed with its torrent of furious blood, with its stomachic destruction of dead animals, with the imbecile insistence of its heartbeat. I saw with contempt the trillion people who had been, the thousands I had personally known. I saw the myriad excretions, the mountains of dung, the seas of sloshing urine, the multitude of jiggling reproductions, the skeleton swarms of the dead. I saw the chomping eaters, with scabs and boils, sweating, scratching animals, all of them.

That evening I went down to the hotel restaurant for supper. My vision unfocused in fantasy, came sharply into focus again. I saw a tremendous woman shoveling determined mouthfuls of food into a baby, willing, obese, greasy.

I sat down and ordered a steak dinner, and ate it with gusto.

DELIRANDO

Thede leaned against the railing, far below my hotel room window. Cleveland. How many more concerts would there be? Forty? Fifty?

I thought of the brutal schedule. They had rehearsed steadily throughout the vacant morning. Piecemeal, like links in a stubborn chain, the tiresome duties fell reluctantly away until only the ugly string trio remained. But the sawing and scratching were left far behind as I noticed Frank wander toward her across the lawn to the lake edge.

He knelt on the concrete embankment, almost at her feet, holding onto the iron railing with one hand and with the other tempting a duck with a bit of something. The scene was shattered by a paroxysm of quacking as the duck demanded its bread. Thede considered the bird thoughtfully as Frank threw it several crumbs.

High above, the fiddles screamed. The fiddle of Otto spat and crackled, the fiddle of Maia sobbed and moaned the big fiddle of Olga roared and raged and fought violently with the others.

I thought of her father, of her father and the squirrels.

He was always trying to catch a

squirrel or a rabbit. On Sundays they went to the park, except in winter when they went to zoo. What a strange man, her father. Sunday lover of animals, weekday butcher of them: their bones, brains, flesh, sweetbreads, kidneys, livers. Ugly things all. I remembered Thede telling me of her childhood. She, daughter of the butcher, playing the upright piano on the floor above the shop, and the faint accompaniment of cleaver striking bone, and the frightening knowledge of it, and how loudly she played, a thunderous requiem drowning the horrible noise. But sometimes, oh, sometimes in a moment of silence, exploding through the thin, cracked flooring it would lash out at her again, thud, thud, thwack, with a crackling as of murder, and how though she played, with fury she heard it still. Until the meat, wrapped and quiet, vanished through the doorway with a final tinkling of gay little bells. Somehow the memory reminded me of Andrea, and, briefly, I shuddered.

A faint burst of the dreadful music came through an open window somewhere and I paused in my reverie. They were like tortured, snarling animals, I thought, the three of them. They were always tortured. Even Andrea, especially Andrea. For as long as I had known her, she had been one of the tortured ones. Was she glad to be dead?

Screaming imprecations the music came at me. Damn the crazy shrieks. It made me think of a human being in the last stages of torture. Or—or of unbearably painful insanity, or *hara-kiri*, or any torment infinitely monstrous and vile.

The muffled cacophony of Starch fought through the obstruction of glass and wood. It ravaged the air, which stood innocent and helpless, and crashed to a violent inhuman end.

Suddenly I felt faint. I looked down toward the lake, but Frank and Thede had gone. I turned and went to the bed. How would it all end I wondered. How would it end?

The duck yammered.

Otto frowned at his violin as he plucked a string. He stood finally, his mouth open in routine astonishment. It always opened when he listened very carefully. He plucked again and again. To his sensitive ear not one but several clashing tomes could be discerned shivering against each other like a cheap, tinny piano. "The strings they make these days," he said despairingly. "My God, I've tried half a dozen 'A's today and now the only true one in the lot has turned false."

"Do as I do," Olga said contemptuously. "Make your own." Her tone condescending, she continued, "It's very simple. You take the intestines of a sheep—"

Otto groaned. He plucked the string several vehement times and at each confirmation he winced. Maia, rummaging through her lot of strings, finally held one aloft, waving the twisted coil of gut triumphantly, like a victorious flag. "Here, look, I've found one you can use." She sang the words joyfully to a little impromptu melody of her own invention. "I took it off yesterday because it was somewhat too thin for the viola. It is surely not false." And the word "false" ended tragically on her deepest note.

Otto ran his finger along the roughened yellow gut. In contrast to his own fastidious habits Maia sometimes used the same string for many weeks. "Not false perhaps," he said doubtfully "but a trifle hairy." He straightened the misshapen, maze-like undulation of the gut, bending and, manipulating it. "Still, I'd rather have them old and true than new and false." Maia made knotty lassoes out of her old strings. They reminded me of hangman's knots. "I'd like to put some weights on it," Otto said. "That would take the kinks out. Maybe tonight."

"What a fool," said Olga venomously. She had run out of patience with Otto. Him and his Storch.

He ignored her. "A" strings were difficult to mount even when new. He tried to insinuate the end of the old string into the tiny recess which was buried deep within the interior of the scroll, but the worn twisted gut would not quite reach it. He bent and straightened and manipulated while the others practiced.

Finally the job was done. The string uttered a long, rising moan as it yielded again to the old slavery. Otto opened his great case and returned the violin to its tailored chamber, which, molded like a cast to the instrument's peculiar dimensions, held it in a gentle vise, firm and inescapable. He plucked the newly tuned string several times. It seemed to be true. How good.

"Come, ladies, let us have a small intermission."

Olga lurched to her feet like an ungainly camel. Leaning her cello against a chair she walked toward the door, stopping a moment to wait for Maia who was putting her viola away. Otto plucked the string once more, triumphantly resoundingly. The dying tone followed us as arm in arm we strolled out of the room.

Maia's new avocation was golf. She prepared for ten minutes of putting, unfolding a collapsible golfing kit and setting up a miniature practice range. She selected half a dozen golf balls, carefully examining their white, pocked surfaces before arranging them in a neat row. As she addressed the first ball the serenity of perfect absorption stole over her face.

Otto took two curious cigars, rounded at the narrow peak but triangular at the base, from a small complicated, humidor. He offered them both to Olga who grumpily accepted the brown, elongated pyramids. After a moment of examination she chose the larger cigar. A flame, shot from the glinting cylinder of the humidor and they inhaled fragrant poisons while little balls clinked unerringly into a mechanical hole.

Otto seated himself on the step below Olga, who, after an hour of the hated Storch trio, sat muttering with volcanic promise. Suddenly a thick spurt of smoke shot from the twin Craters of her nostrils. It swirled above Otto's head like an angry nimbus. He drew deeply on his cigar and sent forth an answering cloud of smoke, white and massive, which pursued and mingled with the disappearing vapors of Olga's cloud, the expanding, conflicting pattern finally dashing themselves to nothingness against the infinite horizon. I inhaled and envied them.

I thought with many anxieties, of the vanishing day, of the complicated structure of the Storch, of my troubling situation. The vision of Andrea flashed across my mind and a tiny pain familiarly stabbed my heart.

Otto yawned a tremendous, tired, groaning yawn, his eyes wet and smarting with smoky tears. Olga gazed at Otto with the malfocus of speculation. She blew a cloud of smoke at him, a small experimental cloud. He coughed. "Stop it, Olga, please."

Maia attacked the little spheres with precision and futility. Naked in their dimpled whiteness they returned faithfully, again and like some cultivated boomerang, transplanted and modernized.

Not a trio really, I was thinking, the

many doublings made it almost a sextet. And one of the great contemporary works, according to Otto. But how far they were from a really first rate performance of it. What was the trouble? One couldn't quite isolate it. Thede, after all, couldn't ruin a string trio with her playing. Still, she was at the root of it all.

Another cloud of smoke made Otto cough and sneeze. Maia looked up disapprovingly as he moved down several steps. Olga followed him, moving within firing range. And Otto was struck by a vicious gust of smoke. "Olga, will you please stop—" he turned angrily only to receive another acrid blast which sent him into a fit of violent coughing.

As Otto staggered to his feet Olga and Maia began to beat him, pounding his back now with vengeance and now with concern. Blows of joy and anxiety they were, mighty buffets which drove the breath from his body as soon as he could gain a little.

There came a time when he tore himself away. The tears were streaming from his red, swollen eyes, and a look of anguish was on his face. "Stop it," he gasped, "stop it." Then more slowly, almost to himself, "Stop it." He shook himself free of Maia's timid hand and staggered back into the hall still coughing deeply.

Olga was examining the leaf of the cigar. "*Ex*cellent smoke," she said in a tone of high satisfaction. Placing a good two inches of the weed inside her mouth she began to puff at it with pleasure.

But Maia, her face a dull red which obscured the cherried disfigurement of her neck so that only a scar appeared against the vise of her jaw, turned violently to face Olga. She stamped her foot. "Why do you bait him so?" Her voice was high and shrill. "Why do you bait him so?"

"Let's wait a moment. He'll be all right."

"But why do you bait him? Will you tell me?"

Olga hesitated. Then, "Why do you think?"

"After twenty years I do not think. I—" Maia was breathing passionately. For a moment she did not continue. Then regaining control of herself she said softly, "I do not think, Olga, I feel. "She sighed. "But it will pass away."

"I have always been against Otto, little one."

"But you have also been for him. More than you know you are for him still." She was silent for a moment. Then she said slowly, in a voice of steel, "I do not wish you to bait him again."

Olga's eyes were almost entirely closed, her face tilted back in an expression at once dreaming and ominous. The cigar was still clenched between the teeth of the bulking jaws. From beneath the long grey ash of it fumes leaked lazily. They permeated the slitted eyelids and seemed to be expelled by them as Olga murmured quietly, threateningly, seemingly without moving the muscles of her face, "You are brave today, my friend."

"Perhaps it is because I have nothing to lose," Maia answered coldly. She was startled by the sudden awareness of Otto standing in the doorway. Embarrassed she crept past him, eyes lowered, shrinking a little, as though to avoid his notice. He smiled at the small retreating figure. Then he turned to Olga and regarded her calmly. "After you my dear."

With a regretful savoring of the remains of her cigar, Olga threw it into the sanded cemetery of an urn, littered already with the headstones of many stubs. She spat absently and squaring her shoulders marched heavily through the doors.

For the rest of the rehearsal little was said. Only the moaning of the fiddles was eloquent and sometimes a deep premonitory groan. The shadows of the afternoon admonished as they lengthened, like warning fingers, black and cynical.

The rehearsal ended finally, unbelievably, and they adjourned until the next day. Instinctively they separated and charged with the friction of weariness and hostility they sought new places in the deeps of the city, places of rest and comfort and the nourishment of surcease.

My turmoil was a visible thing as, shaving, I looked at myself in the mirror. And I wondered if it could be so obvious to the others. On the other hand, however, how could it not?

I decided to go for a walk, but the elevator was broken. Well I'd walk downstairs, I could use the exercise. I lit a cigarette and inhaled deeply. I held the smoke for a long moment but it did not calm me and I opened the door leading to the fire stairs. On the floor was a small sign. "Not here," it read. What could it mean? Well, I'd ask someone. The stairs were dark, lit only by an occasional red bulb.

Things were thoroughly bad. Of

course. It could not be expected to be otherwise. It was bound to happen. It was even deserved. I stopped short on the landing and began to mutter in a savage, almost inaudible treble. "What can you expect of Thede? Not much. What could you have hoped for? You're old enough to be her father. Stop fooling yourself, Esca, stop fooling yourself. That is the worst. "

I leaned over the banister and peered hopelessly into the black hole of the stairwell. "And in the end for what?" I asked myself "For what?" Then I continued slowly down the stairs, my coat flapping in a ridiculous farewell. Tottering on the stairs like a drunk I paused for a moment.

"Even now she is with Frank. You will never know her again. Forget her. Don't be a fool, forget her." But how to forget a woman like that. How to forget. And immersed in thought I nearly broke my neck as I stumbled down the last few stairs. "Not here" the sign shouted in the red gloom. I wiped my forehead and cautiously opened the door to the lobby. No one was in sight except a passing bellboy. "Young man," I said, "what do these 'Not here' signs on the fire stairs mean?"

The boy looked curiously at me. I was breathing heavily from my long uncertain journey and my bad stumble. "They mean, 'Don't put the ash stands here.'"

"Oh. Thanks very much." I continued into the lobby. Still no one. Good. The shook of the lizard toe left me breathless. She was reclining, lost in the deep armchair so that from the rear only the toe was visible. With a great effort I calmed myself. One, two, three. I sauntered slowly by, lost in thought, only noticing her at the last moment.

"Thede." How agreeably surprised I seemed. "Waiting for someone?"

She hesitated. "No, Billy." And echoing came the whispered endearment softly, as though it were an afterthought, "Honey." I touched her silken arms, then helped her from the chair prolonging the clumsy pleasure of embracing the fragrant, imprisoned body.

Slowly we walked through the revolving doors to a Waiting taxi Briefly I wondered who she had been waiting for Otto? Frank?

We were to leave in the early afternoon. Only three more concerts in Cincinnati, Dayton and Indianapolis then on to Chicago, our new headquarters, where five concerts were scheduled. Olga and Otto were to appear as soloists with the New Chicago Orchestra in the double concerto for violin and cello by Johannes Brahms. This was to be their final Chicago appearance and would take place at the Academy of Music on March 18th. They had played this concerto many times together but it was very difficult and always required the most diligent review. And so the last rehearsal in Cleveland was to be spent on the Brahms. Then the train for Cincinnati.

Little time was left and Olga's temper was short. She had forgotten the disagreeable episode of the day before, and her fault in it, and she attacked Otto energetically. "Don't slide on your damned fiddle. It makes me want to vomit on the floor."

But Otto had awakened with a headache and was not in a conciliatory mood. Thede was nowhere to be found and it developed that she had left with the Krikelaires for Cincinnati. "My dear," he began with great sarcasm, "I...".

"I'm not your dear. And don't slide so much."

He shook his head, impatient at the interruption.

"Look. If one has to move a finger from one note to another, how is it accomplished? Through the fourth dimension? There must be a slight evidence of the journey."'

"You can't get out through the fourth dimension," she rasped, "If I can do it on the cello you can do it on the fiddle." He wanted to speak, but she said, contemptuously, "Journey. Don't you realize how far my journeys are? The cello is huge. To reach an octave you move only a few inches. For me it's at least twice as far. But I don't slide." She made a retching sound. "Furthermore"'

Otto looked to the heavens. "But you stop the bow," he cried. "In that moment of silence you accomplish all sorts of skullduggery." His voice rose in exasperation. "If I allowed myself such a privilege I could make ten inaudible glides and have time left over for a cup of coffee. Now enough of this. You've given me quite a headache. Once more, if you please." And immediately, even while he spoke, he began to play, his exquisite phrase stifling her angry retort.

And so it went, on and on, two razors of perfectionism sharpening each other with an interminable honing from which flew sparks, incendiary and dangerous.

On the far side of the room Maia was practicing inaudible strokes on her miniature golfing range. Olga finally shouted at her, "Quiet, Maia, quiet, for God's sake."

Maia took careful aim. "If I can't hear it," she muttered, "you can't hear it."

"Go somewhere else, please. We do not like to work in the middle of a frivolous activity. It is insulting and distracting."

Otto was opening doors and windows. The weather had become warm and humid almost overnight. "No, Maia," he snarled. "You had better stay. She will murder me one of these days and the state will require a witness."

Slowly the ball trickled across the strip of cloth and failed to roll to its appointed place. Maia straightened herself tiredly, stretching her arms and seeming all at once to become aware of her surroundings. She sighed deeply and shook her head. "No," she murmured, "neither of you understands." She touched the red disfigurement of her throat. "It has nothing to do with your stupid playing, of course. When has either of you become upset by objective criticism? At the most Olga has to be handled gently. But for twenty years, if I am polite, I can say anything to her. Suddenly not. Why? When, until now, has either of you been bitter and nasty about trifles? I don't remember an instance. The highest standards are possible without this terrible anger against each other. And this anger, like a cancer, can well destroy us all unless you can understand and root out what is at the bottom of it."

We were leaving soon, and rolling up the long strip with the lonely hole at the end, of it Maia began to pack the materials of the practice range until only the club remained, and a solitary ball.

Otto had turned and walked to his case. He opened various compartments, apparently looking for something which he could not find. This disturbed him and as Mala talked he became increasingly upset and looked feverishly and fruitlessly among the recesses of the case. His eyebrows wriggled with anxiety. The individual hairs seemed anarchically to fan out in surprise and concern as though like centipedes, upended and frantic, they wanted desperately to come right again.

Even Olga was apprehensive. "What on earth, Maia. What are you thinking of?"

"Andrea," Maia whispered across the empty reaches of the room.

"What? What? Speak up, girl," Olga demanded.

"Andrea! Andrea!" Maia shouted. She

began to swing the club violently. After a time she gathered her belongings together walked over to Olga and put them on a chair. "Andrea," She said again softly now, and her voice was filled with sadness.

The silence was portentous in the reverberant room. But slowly the noises began to gather. For there are certain rooms which by their very nature are filled with the shadows of sound. Now the echoes of Andrea's name magnified themselves until the room seemed, roaring in its silence. Like a thudding heartbeat it pounded at each of us, Andrea, Andrea, Andrea. And some of the roaring came from the room which was alive, and some of it came from within ourselves.

And in the center of it stood. Maia, idly swinging a stick, and back and forth, back and forth, her face calm, yet filled with weariness. "Andrea is the source. What is killing us is nothing more nor less than she. Tit for tat" She swung her club rhythmically with the words. "Tit for tat. Poetic justice, hey? What do you think?"

Otto carefully blew a speck of white dust from his violin. And with his fingernail he plucked a faint inquiring note. He frowned and plucking very softly he returned the instrument, the tiny tones at once exclamation and protest.

"What do you think?" Maia asked again "Olga? Otto?"

Olga spread the cello across the plateau of her lap. She folded her yellow flannel several times into a sandwich-like face, wrinkled and evil, the pursed lips of it flapping silently as she polished the cello. Cleanliness is next to Godliness, I thought vacantly.

"The idea," Maia went on, almost to herself, "the abhorrent idea that one could replace Andrea. Andrea. As though she were a worn bridge or an old string. Or a faithless mate."

The tiny plucking sounds did not waver, nor Otto's frown. He cocked his head the better to hear, his mouth gaping, his ear close to the strings, his attitude one of oblique deference as he looked unseeing into the distance of the lake.

Olga turned her cello downward and polished its back with a slow, tender rhythm. As her obscuring hand swept by, the sparkling red varnish revealed a grotesque of Olga, the curved surface distorting the light into strange reflections as it rocked and swayed under the polishing.

"Let's stop Let's not go on with this patched-up farce. The quartet is dead. Let it remain dead. Decently dead. Oh, how strongly I feel that we should start anew." And slicing viciously at the little ball Maia sent it sailing through the opened doors. "Anew or not at all."

Far away the wild white mote wheeling and whistling bounded down and down in a hysterical dance of joy and freedom. Bouncing gaily now in sprightly and diminishing leaps it skipped and hopped and dribbled away the remainder of its unexpected voyage, rolling slowly and soberly then to the edge of the infinite lake.

The huge auditorium had certainly not been designed for chamber music, I thought. It would be a terrible task to get the group seated correctly in a hall this size. Recently built, too. These new ones were always the worst. Christ look at the size of the damned thing, I thought. Life in America never seemed to be intimate.

I regarded the Krikelaires as they sweated and groaned to get the piano on stage. For some reason I was close to them. We often played chess together in the afternoon and we would sometimes talk and drink beer.

The piano was in place now and the Krikelaires disappeared through the wings. Now I started to tune the piano. The little red lights flashed discord merrily, since every long trip got the pianos badly out of tune.

Maia and Olga and. Otto came into the auditorium. "Ready in a few minutes," I called. Olga, scorning the stairs, hauled herself onto the stage with a flash of elephantine thigh. Maia chose the long way and presently her blond head widened the slit in the curtain. "Frank does not wish to return to New York," she announced. "He wants to come along with us even after his contract is up. If nobody minds, that is, he—"

"Later." Olga interrupted. "We'll talk

later. Let's rehearse."

The music racks went up with a small clatter. Thede came in with Frank. Otto played a final chord, on the piano and stood up with a sigh of relief. "Let's start off with the Schubert B flat," he said. He handed Maia his violin and walked down into the hall to listen.

They began to play and I wandered friendlessly about the auditorium, pausing now and then to listen. I climbed the stairs to the balcony. A voice in the dark startled me. It was Frank.

"This is the only spot in the balcony where it sounds good, Mr. Esca. Right here."

I listened for a moment. Apparently Frank had, discovered a point of resonance. "It will always sound better in this place, my boy. Now let's move the trio around a bit." We experimented until the balance was fairly satisfactory. But there was still a dead, area in the back of the orchestra. Frank suggested that everyone move forward as far as possible. The Krikelaires were called, the change effected, and Otto was pleased to discover that the dead area was greatly reduced.

Now Otto got his fiddle from Maia and they began the Schumann quartet. In a few minutes Frank called out, "The sound is about as good as you can get it in a place like this." And Otto decided to stop experimenting.

The night's concert was unusual in that it was to be broadcast, and now the radio crew arrived to determine the number and placement of the microphones.

"Let's have a balance test," Otto suggested. "But only one mike. It's all you need if you can get it in the right place. Not too far away now or you'll pick up room noise."

They played the softest and, loudest parts of the Schumann, the dynamic extremes. Next they recorded a short passage and listened to it. Then Otto said reluctantly, "See you all tonight, I guess." And to Frank, "Know of a good place to eat around here?"

The newspapers the next day were enthusiastic about Thede. And even her colleagues were pleased. Olga said, grudgingly, "Not too bad. It's the first time I've heard anything like a pianissimo from you. Now you can start to learn about music and, who knows, you might possibly make a pianist yet."

Maia was thankful that there could be a little harmony. "I thought you played well too, Thede," she said.

Otto looked immensely gratified, but

he contained himself. "Now, now," he smiled. "Not too much praise or you'll give her a swelled head."

There was a rapping at the door and Krikelaire entered. "Did we buy this or did the radio crew leave it behind? I found it in the piano." He held up a very small microphone. "It's ours," Otto said swiftly and took the microphone.

After Krikelaire had left Otto threw the microphone on the floor. I turned around to look at Thede and saw that she had grown very red. A new experience, I thought. I had never seen her embarrassed before.

Olga and Maia were staring at Thede remorselessly. "I wonder who put that microphone in the piano," she stammered weakly. Olga got up and walked out and. Maia followed her.

I felt depressed and discouraged by the discovery of the microphone. No wonder she had played so softly. She needed only to touch the keys to drown out everyone else. I wondered how she had managed in so short a time to get an accomplice among the radio men. Perhaps she had convinced them that the pianist was the soloist and the others merely accompanists. Or maybe she had slept with one of them. Who could tell and now I became utterly disgusted with her. "Thede,"

Otto said bitterly, "you ought to be ashamed of yourself. I shouldn't be at all surprised if we dispensed with your services." Then he left, slamming the door behind him.

We were speaking of Thede. "Throw her the hell out," Olga grumbled. "What do you say, Otto?"

"I'll wait until I hear what Maia has to say."

"I'd like nothing better than to see the last of her," Maia said gloomily. "There's only one thing holding me back and that's Billy."

"Please," I said. "Don't even think of me as a factor in all this."

"There's only one thing I can think of," Otto said. Olga, if you could tell her in your most ferocious tones that this is absolutely her last chance it might do some good. Try to convince her that if she gets out of line once more she's through. And if the rest of us don't go along with you that you'll resign. .She must realize that if it's a choice between you and her she cannot win. Will you do this?"

"So happy to," Olga hissed.

And she had delivered a succinct but vitriolic lecture to Thede. But in return Thede was to infuriate Olga almost past endurance. It so happened, that Olga was extremely sensitive about her cello. She refused to let anyone go near it, not excepting Otto or Maia. If someone touched it, even accidentally she became very angry.

But one day she saw Thede wearing as a turban the yellow flannel which she used to polish her cello. Not only was the flannel, as were all accessories to the cello, sacrosanct, but in order to get to it Thede would have had to open the case and remove the instrument. It is fair to say that Olga turned purple. She was shaking with an emotion so violent that it is known only to murderers and to the insane.

"Take off my flannel," she screamed.

"This isn't your flannel, Olga," Thede replied sweetly. "I bought it at the five and ten cent store. Attractive isn't it?"

Olga choked with frustration. She had been fairly set to strangle Thede and now she could do nothing. From that moment on she never forgave Thede, but was her bitter, remorseless enemy.

We were in Chicago at last. And now the minds and hearts of Otto and Olga were concentrated with a passionate intensity on the Brahms double concerto. For this was to be played on March 18th, a day which was all too near. The remaining time was a fever which the mighty concerto absorbed like a vast, insatiable sponge. But this fever was heightened by the frightening disappearance of the intervening concerts, whose number diminished relentlessly with the passing of each day.

And with every rehearsal they became more isolated from the rest of us. To appreciate this isolation is difficult for the uninitiated. But compare the task of the ensemble with that of the orchestra. Who is as saucy as the thirteenth second violinist? On the humblest level, that of simply playing the music, if our violinist misses a note is it not played by a dozen others? What security.

But this, of course, is not the case in a string quartet. A missed note brings about not only the humiliation of the player and the outrage of his colleagues, but the tortures of his conscience. One is alone, always alone. How much more isolated then is the trio? And the duo?

For although in the trio there is a frightening feeling of nakedness, a lurching uncertainty as though a leg of one's chair has been snatched, away, it cannot be compared to the duo. This is worse than the concert artist who is entirely alone, for the members of the duo are like two mountain climbers whose lives depend on a single rope. Let one of the climbers drop the rope and. the life of the other is endangered.

And so the two seized hungrily at each passing moment as it slipped irresistibly into the reservoir of time. The daily rehearsals included preparation for the other Chicago concerts, and there was an irreducible amount of traveling about which little could be done. Otto and Olga studied scores of the concerto at every possible opportunity, even while traveling to and from the daily concerts in the station wagon. With the few hours remaining to them they rehearsed Brahms desperately, until they were tired and, vacuous.

Most exhausting of all were the after-concert receptions. Such an occasion was frequently a social evening which had as its sluggish reason for being the presence of the quartet. But the round of introductions accomplished and the dutiful praise dutifully accepted, lines were usually drawn and like scattered quicksilver, clusters of people were likely to congregate and talk among themselves.

Thede was attractive to the these clusters and frequently they would form and reform about her. At such times she was a queen and reigned with dignity, with a nod here, a syllable of acknowledgment there, or the merest hint of a smile, queenly in its gracious reserve. She was respectful to the dowagers, demure with their husbands, and discreet with the younger men, preferring their wives and sweethearts. Her regal acceptance of an invitation to play was a largess which delighted her subjects and offended her colleagues. The Casa Bellas never offered their services at receptions.

"I don't see how I can *stand* to play with her," Olga said. "One is supposed to have some kind of feeling for one's colleagues."

"No, my love" Maia replied "That is only necessary to play well. We do not play well."

Next they would be asked to play. The business of playing at parties was for amateurs. Not that Thede wasn't an amateur, but—

"I think I'll leave," said Olga with determination. "It's the only thing to do."

"No, Olga. Please." Maia, in the course

of twenty years, had learned to expect trouble from Olga. But this year she had managed to keep her from leaving a single reception so far. An unusual year altogether.

As Thede sat down at the piano I noticed Frank making his way toward us with an exaggerated stealth. He was rubbing his hands together excitedly and his face was flushed and enthusiastic with a cherubic naiveté. Then noticing the melancholy on Olga's face he too became grave. As Thede began to play he whispered conspiratorially in my ear, "I think Chopin's great, don't you?"

The day was so crisp and biting that one's eyeballs ached in the lake wind. It was a fresh, energetic wind, and did not pity weaklings. I shivered but was grateful for the dry cold. There had been several stagnant, humid days and the wind was refreshing.

God in heaven I felt tired. As I walked to the concert hall a sense of absolute weariness overcame me and my spirit was enfolded by a gloom which insulated me finally with a sense of profoundest discouragement. The depressing thought occurred to me that I had completely lost my resilience, like an old elastic stretched taut over the years. The walk from the hotel to the concert hall was a short one, but look how Otto's violin case already weighed me down. How could violins be so heavy? Like—like gravestones they were. Like gravestones. The damned, boy. He would be right back and—well, to hell with him.

A hulking mound of slag loomed funereally in the grey morning. It was the auditorium. Otto would be there. And Olga, too. I shivered at the cold and hurried on.

Now I went through the hallway and dragged myself up the winding stairs. Unusual for me to be so tired. The winter, I thought hopefully, it is only the long winter.

As I walked toward the artists' room I

was startled by a shocking burst of sound. Olga was warming up and she was angry. I could always tell. The flood of roaring bass recalled to me vividly the time when the power of Olga's anger had broken the thick rope of her "C" string. I remembered the tiny streamers of silver, unraveling flying every which way, and the white bleached gut, split and torn.

As I entered the room, Olga glared at me and exploded into a new paroxysm, a frenetic passage on a higher string, shrill and murderous. Clouds of dust flew from her bow speckling the cello's red bosom with a strident pointillism. Otto stood cautiously rubbing his hands while the sentient cello crackled and rumbled. I noticed a tiny lake of sweat on the outthrust upper lip. She was never cold, I thought enviously.

There were two pianos in the room and I placed Otto's case carefully on the nearest. Taking out a bow he began to rosin it. Then, very softly, he tuned his violin. "Thank God for a clear day," he said tentatively, and played a soft arpeggio. The gentle chord was drowned by a wave of furious sound. He tried again, with a nervous jocularity, "I couldn't stand another squeak really not. Why don't we announce to the newspapers that any squeaks are due to the local weather?" Olga growled and looked away. He had tried, since Maia's warning, really tried, to get along with Olga. And she had tried too, one could tell. But it was no use. He had lost his old ability to manage her. He could not even manage himself these days it seemed. Often he would stand staring blankly ahead and appear shocked when someone spoke to him. He returned the violin to its black vault and began uneasily to file his nails. Soon the orchestra rehearsal would begin. The idea was unpleasant to me. Who was this conductor? Rieger? We hadn't even met him let alone worked with him. Otto didn't trust him. They said it was a wonderful orchestra, but did it matter if the conductor couldn't be trusted?

Otto seemed unusually agitated. It was exceptional for the touch of his violin not to soothe him. Now it seemed to increase his anxiety. He continued to complain about the weather. Still muttering he took his other violin from the oblong chamber and looked underneath it. He opened the drawer and began to search through its many compartments and hiding places.

Olga stopped practicing and watched his bumbling exploration, watched him open each little repository, look inside and close it again. With increasing heat and disgruntlement he swore softly in several languages. Her gravel voice frightened him, swiveled him around. "What are you looking for? Breakfast? A change of clothes?"

"You startled me," he said reproachfully and resumed his search.

But she was impatient, anxious to spend the remaining time in rehearsal. "Maybe a bicycle in that warehouse of yours? Come on, we have at the most two hours."

"Just a moment," he said. He placed the heavy case on a table, sitting down the better to search. After a few minutes the table began to look like a small junkyard. "Ah!" he stood up triumphantly. He had found a small square of sandpaper and he began to brush it against the fingertips of his left hand.

Olga grunted in amazement. "Sandpaper. My God, sandpaper. The oh, so sensitive pinky." She shook her head in exaggerated wonderment.

He ignored her. Too much practice thickened the skin. Calluses were for cellists. He continued the mild abrasion, carefully rubbing the paper across his fingertips. Now and then he would lean back with raised eyebrows to admire his handiwork.

The mild whisking sound infuriated Olga. "You bring your humidity with you," she snarled. "As the Americans say, you are all wet." She leaned her cello carefully against a chair, then began to pace furiously back and forth, back and forth, stopping now and then to glare at Otto.

But in the ensuing silence, broken only by the small crackling of the sandpaper, her words came back to her and she started to snicker and then to laugh loudly at her joke. "Hu-hu," she began tentatively. Like a wheezy engine at first, the sound grew gradually in volume and energy. There was something bloodcurdling about Olga's laugh, it was a kind of war-whoop. Hu-hu-hu. The laughter increased until Otto said sharply, "Stop it. You will be heard." Too late, damn it to hell, she was well underway now.

Olga's laughter was rare but memorable. As Otto stood watching her disgustedly I was amused by his anger. Yet her howling really was frightful. She rocked back and forth on her feet and screamed, "You are all wet!" Then another gale of laughter, "Hu-hu, hu-hu-hu." And one had the feeling that such a sound could only come from a giant resonating chamber, that within Olga a huge cavity, hollow and reverberant and extending throughout her body like some malignant wind tunnel, had been set into an uncontrollable vibration.

"You are all wet," she screamed again,

and Otto's face tightened up like an overwound clock. "Shut up," he whispered, "shut up, shut up." The famous Otto crescendo had its effect. "Shut up," he yelled.

Quite suddenly she was silent. But her face, convulsed in laughter and now deprived of it, froze its wild identical contours into, through some mysterious endocrine, a look of the most desperate hatred.

I was amazed by the ferocity of her look. I turned away to escape it but when I looked again the eye was glazed and a feeling of horror came over me. I had the crazy conviction that staring at me was the dead face of Andrea, her death mask, its final, changeless, convulsion. The frozen features held Otto spellbound. For an impossibly long moment the spastic grimace maintained, its rigid outlines. Only gradually did it relax, And with the passing of the awful tension I felt my blood begin to flow again.

Slowly, tiredly, the distorted face recovered itself. Olga sat down at last and with a savage thrust of the sharpened steel cello peg impaled the rug against the floor. The blow loosened one of the strings with a groaning twang and she began slowly to retune.

The shock of the sharp sound was like a slap in the face to Otto and he became fully alert. What could he do, what could he say? I knew that if he mishandled the situation this schism between them might well become fixed, permanent, even enlarged as time went on.

Hesitantly I began to talk to her, attempting through conversation to restore and normalize. "Olga," I said cautiously, "you will ruin your cello's adjustment with these violent, jarring blows." She ignored me and for a moment I was at a loss. I noticed myself in a mirror on the wall. My face looked old and lined, the hair scanty and receding at the temples

Now I looked deeper into the mirror. She was sitting dejectedly, arm on cello, leaning on a wrist. Otto was across the room. Her face was lifted up by the pressure, revealing a single fang through the loose cavity of the mouth. Otto took out a comb and began to run it through his hair. "The years pass," he ventured, "and suddenly we are old." I stole a glance into the mirror. She had not moved. Otto tried, again. "No Indian is as stealthy as time," he continued, "and one day time, very like an Indian, pounces upon us." He combed his hair again. "An effective scalping after all. Generous to leave a little." He sighed. No matter which way he combed there was a definite bald spot.

I looked at Olga again. She was still motionless. Was she dead? The thought left me strangely unmoved. Otto looked at her for a long time and then shrugged his shoulders and resumed tuning.

Again, I thought of Andrea. Poor Andrea. If she were only alive. Then I wouldn't be so terribly, terribly tired. Tired of the quartet, of the weeks of traveling, of the lousy receptions, of Thede, of Otto, of all of them. And I felt that the others were tired, too. Even Olga, despite her immense strength was weary. Ah, well. Tomorrow at least the-concerto would be over.

"Come on," the voice was an impatient snarl, gravelly and contemptuous. "Pretty yourself after the concert for the ladies. Strike the tuning fork."

The simple daily request, in the context of weeks and months of increasing irritation, of mounting hostility and defiance of Otto's authority, suddenly seemed to have only one possible meaning—it meant that the end of the quartet was only a matter of time.

But it was *not* sudden, it only appeared to be. How could anyone objectively have been unaware of our degeneration? And there was no doubt about it. In my mind, I reviewed, summarized evaluated the vindictiveness of Olga, the slur upon barb, the sneering hatred. And the downcast negation of Maia, her reluctance, her outright desire to abandon the others. Was that not what she had meant when she said, "let us start anew, or not at all." Yet it may have been only my natural unwillingness to believe in the end of Casa Bella, but even now I didn't want to believe, to accept what seemed to be the truth. Hopefully my mind searched the past, but found, only bitter, confirming evidence.

"Come *on!*" The gritty monotone was a flickering fuse.

There was nothing else to do for the moment. The soft one with its four hundred and forty tiny shudders for each passing second stole into the troubled air. Olga grunted while she matched her "A" string to the limpid sound submitting noisily to the merciless canopy of the octaves, while Otto, with quick little taps of the bow, adjusted his violin in a rapid arpeggio.

Then by common consent they began to practice the great Brahms Andante, the colossal piece which like a mountain range divides the concerto into three parts. Slowly they tested and retested, the double notes of the melody until a single voice emerged, newly born of the long labor, differing from the parent voices and yet more wonderful than either.

"You see," said Olga with a victorious leer, "I knew it could be done without smearing and sliding. I'll buy you a roll of sandpaper."

Otto was abruptly furious. "Look, you idiot," he shouted, "look and see how I do it. For your sake I have invented a whole new kind of playing. I do not slide but neither do I stop the bow. Look, will you?" he cried, almost sobbing with the violence of his anger as he stretched his fingers to cover the huge distance which encompassed the entire melody.

And Olga looked at the ivory cage of human statuary, the tiny Parthenon within whose vibrating frame the tones of the melody awaited the bow's release.

Otto managed to gain control of himself. "Look," he said again, panting a little. "Can you do as much?"

The ivory cage gave bitterly against the strain, crumpled, collapse, huddled tiredly within itself. As they fell away from the string the fingers plucked the melody faintly in reverse. And Otto, owner of the cage, he whom in turn it owned, laid his violin with an angry love to rest with its sleeping mate. Prisoner's all. Like a furious archer he dismantled the tense bow. Then, nursing his hand, he marched out without a backward, glance.

And Olga and I awaited the call to rehearsal alone.

Soon the murmurings of the orchestra crept up the stairs, a cello first, a bassoon, the horns, a stray violin. Slowly they grew in complexity and volume until the opening door did not increase the sound but only organized it into the thematic material of "The Flying Dutchman." The rehearsal had begun.

Otto stood in the doorway for a moment. Then, his face expressionless, he moved woodenly to his case. Olga watched him anxiously as he opened the alloyed lid. Without thinking, it seemed, he chose the Lunot. He carried, it with him always, although it was not his best instrument nor even his most beautiful one. But like an oriflamme a red gold continent raised itself in bas-relief from the yellow carved surface. He gazed as if in a daydream at the violin, plucking the strings absently, contemplating the design, voyaging along its mysterious outlines.

Olga was in a state of indecision and conflict. She had spent twenty years with this man. A lifetime. Still for her there was the matter of pride. And so she waited and waited for what seemed hours. But finally she could wait no longer. "Otto, my dear," she said hesitantly, "I—I am sorry to have offended you."

Otto was silent and continued to regard his instrument. "Really, my dear, I had not the intention to hurt." Otto remained silent, thinking.

"Maia was right, you know," Olga ventured timidly.

My head began to ache. The tension of the situation was becoming unbearable. I looked from Olga's pleading face to Otto and then back to Olga.

"Yes, Maia is right," he replied, at length.

"But what, after all, can we do?"

He did not answer immediately. My throat was dry. A pitcher of water waited on the table. I drank several glassfuls of it and my throat still seemed dry. Otto opened the drawer of his case and again withdrew the long-legged mannikin of the tuning fork. "Yes," he said savagely, "what can we do. What can we do but obey our symbol to the end." He held the tuning fork aloft. "This is our symbol, you know, this blind little pea-headed statue." He struck it with all his strength against his knee and it sprang into painful vibration. He touched it to the bridge of Olga's cello with a mocking bow. A clear tone issued from the point of contact. "With the long obedient legs. At its signal we also are beaten, we jump and cavort and follow a monotone. *Look* at him, will you?" His voice rose against the orchestral din, a din so thunderous now that its vibration could be felt through the floor. Six crashing chords and then complete silence.

The tone of the fork was subsiding. How it could hardly be heard. There was a timid rapping and the door opened upon us. Annoyed, Otto turned to see who had knocked. It was a musician. He was tall, taller than the frame of the door, and he carried a flute. He smiled and made an apologetic little bow which carried him forward into the room

"Mr. Rieger is ready now, please."

Otto nodded. "We shall come down directly." Some of us even look like tuning forks, I thought. The musician bowed again and left. But they did not follow immediately. Otto walked to the window. The day was lowering and cold and outside was the howling wind. "Whither do we tend," he murmured.

"We'd better go," said Olga quietly.

They descended the spiral staircase into the world of applause. They bowed, Olga sat, the rehearsal began.

Klaus Rieger was happy. Like many conductors he enjoyed the business of conducting, which like any art can be so simple on some levels and so complicated on others. The tall waving arms, thin to emaciation from shoulder to elbow where they thickened suddenly into heavy clubs, swung with a threatening rhythm over the great docile orchestra, covering with their careening reach huge unpredictable areas. Now he leaned forward tenderly, his eyes closed in calm dreamy pleasure behind the tri-focal lenses. Or lurched back suddenly, the thick lips parted as he breathed an adenoidal passion. Up down, up down, he thought himself a man of power. He was one of that school of conducting which believes in no baton, the naked hands are more expressive, and his curled little finger was a work of art. The cheeks puffed, the stranded fringe which covered the large bald skull was distributed with a gardener's care.

My apprehension turned to dismay. The quality of this group was excellent but even a Stradivarius in the hands of an amateur—eurythmic ox! Give a cue to the horns, the *horns* now, the bassoon! My *God*, what could Otto do? The Holberg method? Not sufficient, not ever, not with this dolt. I looked at Olga. She was perspiring, a lock of grey hair plastered, across an eye, and muttering, I could tell, an inaudible profanity.

The concerto limped painfully toward its dismal end. "And have you any suggestions, my dear Mr. Otto? Miss Hallant?"

Klaus Rieger was brimming over with happiness and good will.

"I think not." Otto had made up his mind. He would try the musicians. They loved, to get through rehearsal early. It made them feel kindly disposed and that at least was something. It was useless without a good deal of overtime, and the cost of every minute, multiplied by a hundred, men — Rieger would never grant it. My head ached terribly now. I placed a hand against my eyes.

"Although," he sighed, "the orchestra could remain slightly, ever so slightly more in the background. Of course the empty hall multiplies and distorts everything, so one can't really tell. There are one or two other things, now that I think of it—"

Olga looked around at the men while Otto talked with Rieger. She recognized several old acquaintances and waved to them. They waved back enthusiastically, then were still, fearful of arousing Rieger's anger. But Olga, her cello a broom, swept through the scattering orchestra until she reached and shook hands with each of several embarrassed players.

A small revolution seemed to be taking place among the cellos. Several of the younger players approached Olga.

"Mademoiselle, you are wonderful."

"Well, you are not wonderful. If you only want to listen to the work get a recording of it. You are supposed to be with me not as an audience but as colleagues. I have this trouble with the cellos always." Then seeing their faces she spoke kindly, "Never fear. Together we can do something. Only join with me, do not listen from afar."

Rieger was annoyed. Such a breach of discipline. And Otto was impatient. "Olga," he called, "we want to rehearse the beginning."

"That's what I'm doing now," she called back." The orchestra surged around her. "You are one hundred and seventeen when you enter. I am only one. Let us see who can be more virile, you or I. The beginning is no place to be polite."

Rieger turned to Otto. "You know of the reception after the concert, my dear Mr. Otto."

"On second thought, —oh yes, of course—on second thought I guess we might as well stop now. There's practically no time left, anyway and Olga apparently wants to say something to the cellos. Will you join me for lunch?" It was the only thing to do.

By all means," said Rieger with dignity. He called, "Rehearsal over," and left the podium majestically.

The men had not heard him. Olga was now the center of a throng of musicians. Otto hesitated. "Coming, Olga?" He spoke clearly, penetratingly. She looked up, startled. "Not yet, Otto," she said. "I'll see you later." And to the musicians, "Where is a place to sit. I'll show you."

We sat in the golden stall. Like a muted engine the orchestra muttered and rumbled in the distance. The timpanist came on stage and began to tune the large metal drums. After a time he was joined by the harpist who sat tinkling endlessly. As the giant orchestra trickled in by twos and threes Frank said, "Good to see somebody else working for a change." He chuckled at the 'somber faces of the battery section, caretakers of the timpani, bass drum, snare drum, xylophone, triangle, chimes, glockenspiel. "No fun waiting through a whole concert to go boom once," he said. "And, if you came in wrong! Golly."

Thede said, "Yes."

The orchestra sat tuning and improvising in pleasant disharmony. The little cadenzas of the flutes, the batrachian grumpings of the contrabassoon, the twitterings of the piccolo gave me the mysterious impression of a strange, articulate forest, growing randomly, the fiddlesticks tiny willows waving every which way, the troop of bass viols ancient centaurs, half man and half tree, another bassoon joining the first, twin bamboo, varnished and manacled, the tuba a bronze, Brobdingnagian tulip, the kettle drums toadstools, dead white with a poisonous muttering. And now the stage shook with the tumult as the forest shouted its eerie cry.

And the concertmaster strode on stilts to the center of the stage and bowed deeply to the scattered applause, remaining so for a time, bent somewhat at the knees, a curious question mark. The legs gave way even more and I began to be afraid that he might fall. But suddenly he straightened his body, wheeled and uttered a piercing hiss. S-s-s-st, and the surly jungle retreated until only the "A" of the oboe remained, a sad, lonely compass. The concertmaster paused for a treasured moment looking sadly at the audience. Then he sat reluctantly down and at this signal the orchestra leaped into a hundred agreements while the oboe, drowned by the anarchy of "A", spat and crowed defiantly. Until at another signal the sound vanished.

"Boy, a hundred and seventeen guys. Gee." Frank whistled a small wondering whistle. Then hastily, as though he had not meant to condemn, "Boston only has a hundred and four, I mean, —you'd think if more were necessary,—" he began to stammer, "I m-mean, so does Philadelphia—"

Maia broke in swiftly, "Strange things happen in Chicago, I'm told. What takes them so long, I wonder. Isn't it time yet? No," she said looking at her wrist. The old, old story, the years flash by but the seconds crawl. The harpist plucks a hundred strings. All are the same.

Thede said, "Only a hundred and fourteen."

"There are two women's observed Maia "The harpists."

"Even with the women harpists. A hundred and fourteen. I counted them."

Maia looked at her watch again. She seemed increasingly nervous. In recent months she had not always played. Sometimes the viola was not required and she listened. Performing herself she had never a moment's doubt. But removed from the immediate scene, helpless to influence the course of events, she felt a pre-concert anxiety. Now again she was apprehensive. What takes them so long, I wondered. And for the twentieth time I read, the program. Brahms first, then Weber, Schumann, Respighi, Wagner and an unknown American composer, one Richards. Not an inspired arrangement.

It was eight forty-seven. A stray peep from the orchestra protested the delay. A partly opening door revealed only blackness. Three thousand necks craned, in military curiosity.

And, the majesty of Olga marched,

slowly, inexorably across the roar of applause. The cello held casually in one hand, the bow depending from the other like a proud and unused walking stick, she swayed forward with an ever so slightly rocking, cocky gait, as though going for a lazy stroll in the country. Nothing could hurry her.

The small man, first on the stage for so many years, found it difficult to walk so slowly and there was almost a collision as the huge woman paused and turned to the noisy orchestra, to the snaredrum of the fiddlesticks applauding against the metal racks so that the music tottered. She bowed to the enthusiastic musicians and Otto was compelled to follow her example. Grinning with satisfaction she waved and blew a kiss, then continued, bowing now to the audience, nodding, smiling. The three reached, the middle of the stage and Rieger retired to the podium and joined daintily in the applause. The avalanche of noise riveted the bowed heads with its thunder. Finally, it subsided.

Rieger signaled to the oboe as Olga sat at last, gently and powerfully forcing the needle-sharp end pin deep into the floor so that the cello could never slip. The victorious oboe crowed again as Otto tuned his violin with a series of swift, useless little tapings of the bow and Olga submitted to the iron tradition with an indifferent plucking of the strings.

Then Otto nodded to Rieger who immediately glared to the left, to the right, became an agitated scarecrow, arms lifted high for a fearful frozen moment.

A violent burst of sound seemed almost to blow him from the podium. He staggered to and fro on his little island beating helplessly against the invisible enemy. The elements over-whelmed him and his long frame flapped convulsively as he reeled like a man about to lose his balance and trying to catch himself.

Suddenly, impossibly, a larger voice, deep and authoritative, commanded the silence of the tremendous ensemble. The deepest bass of Olga's cello began the sinister warning notes of the long cadenza. Head leaning against the scroll, whose black pegs were buried like nails in the greying hair, eyes shut and blind with an inner staring, she struggled with the demon of each passing note, her face alternately suffering, sneering, indignant. Until she finished the mighty cadenza and leaned back, exhausted for the moment.

The chastened orchestra was silent then, except for the prayer of the woodwind choir. Olga listened without hearing, as one looks without seeing, to the tentative wavering notes of Otto, notes of sweetest inquiry, until suddenly, passionately she displaced his melody only to give way to the shrill power of the fiddle. And round and round they went pursuing the fleeing elusive melody in increasingly tight knit circles.

Rieger had recovered from his momentary lapse and he prepared to conduct as the end of the cadenza appeared with the turning of the page. He raised his arm in a noble attitude and as the soloists finished he brought it down majestically. He was totally unprepared for the ferocity with which the throng of instruments assaulted him. With the precision of a lightning bolt, with the anger of the chained, they attacked, him again and yet again. What had happened to his orchestra, the thought crept numbly across his mind, they were so loud. Like driftwood he tossed on the roiling tide making desperate puny gestures of protest. But the orchestra, frantic in its new dimension of strange angularities, and terrible interdicts, of weird gravities and intoxicating atmospheres, ignored the puppet at the helm who like an impurity was washed away by the flood of sound.

I was entranced and yet fearful as though, huddled in our tiny shelter, I had, been caught in a brilliant electrical storm. Sparks flew everywhere, but mainly between the two protagonists, the two swaying lightning rods, who attracted and dispersed the energy of a hundred players. The intricate dialectic was transmuted into thrilling waves of sound as the shrill passion of the fiddle fought the roar of the cello. Maia's eyes were closed. But her face betrayed an acute sensitivity to the music.

And now they were in the hush of the Andante. The lovely tranquil tones of the orchestra became a velvet canvas upon which the dual sound of Otto and Olga painted itself. Now each gently superseded the other in a tender, endless melody until I felt the hypnotic calm of a daydream so deep that even the dance of the final movement seemed to me to move with the slow pulse of a prayer.

I looked closely at Otto and Olga. Yes, one could tell, one could always tell. They felt well toward each other again. It was plain to see. And Maia suddenly sat upright and joined the mood of the dance. I looked at the others. Frank was wide-eyed and open-mouthed. But Thede—strange, I thought, how easy it is to read that face which never changes. She is bored to distraction. Well, no matter. The concerto would be over in a few minutes and we could rejoice again together and somehow the group would survive.

The flying dance approached the end of the concerto with the speed of an arrow, hurrying with a headlong velocity toward the moment, of climax. The vacuum of three thousand somnolent faces had long been dissolved and increasing masses of excitement appeared among them.

Suddenly Maia sat bolt upright in the blackened box. 'For one frightful moment the music of the violin staggered, faltered and was silent. The intricate passagework and interplay robbed of its guiding melody left Olga holding the stage alone, her face red, contorted, unbelieving, the bald bewildered accompaniment see-sawing back and forth, back and forth, helplessly and without meaning. And when Otto resumed his melody, it was with a subtle change of inflection which suggested that the silence after all was intentional and part of the concerto.

But in his second of silence he had missed five notes. Neither the unhurried grace, nor the accretion of assurance which comes from twenty years on the concert stage, nor the imperturbability of the devil himself could erase that damnable, helpless fact.

In all of the audience only a few could have known of his minute error. Another violinist, perhaps the assistant conductor. A critic? Unlikely.

Rieger was completely absorbed in making delicate pincer-like movements with thumb and forefinger. He bowed gracefully from side to side as he conducted. Since the beginning of the dance he had recovered himself and was on firm ground again. He performed a tiny two-step, unnoticeably, humming a private tune. Things seemed to be going better now, he thought, and wondered at his temporary lapse. He seemed completely unaware of the fatal stutter, still less of its consequences.

Olga's face, still blotched with spots of anger, reflected the enormous effort she was making to concentrate. Still, the music took into its natural friendly charm an implacable, ugly rhythm, relentless and unforgiving.

But Maia now, and for the remainder of the concerto, leaned forward desperately, head bowed in an attitude of prayer as though she were trying to will the duo back together. It was she who had initially recognized the sickness of the quartet and now she tried to eradicate the fatal mistake. For she knew that otherwise they would all live with the fear of its happening again.

And Frank. To Frank it was as though he had been startled by a broken lamp, brilliant with a sudden darkness. But the music continuing he cautiously relaxed.

And Thede. To Thede nothing had happened. She had closed her eyes and was dozing lightly.

The ovation which followed seemed interminable and yet I wished it might be prolonged. Let the fools beat their hands bloody. What difference did it make to them if Otto missed five notes or five hundred? Or if, as usual, he had missed none? I reflected upon the idiocy of artists having to rely upon fools for their livelihood and wondered how they continued to do it. And afterward. Open house it would be, the eternal open house no matter how ill the host. A thousand well wishers and backslappers and hangers-on would torment Otto with their stupid comments. Now and then an old friend, with a knowing wink and smile, an old friend — better his enemy, who would be there never fear, wishing him hearty, wishing him well. I went to wait for them in the artists' room.

The applause subsided, a few hands scattered and, sore still beating in a last vain attempt to make the soloists come out for still more applause. The vicious circle. The door of the artists' room was slightly ajar as I entered. And Olga was polishing her cello with savage flagellant strokes. The color of it was red, always red, like sick blood. Otto crept in silently like a thief without looking at either of us. He did not try to speak to her but sat with his violin and, one by one he began to replace its strings. He changed them every week and although it was not yet time, changing them now gave him something to do.

He disengaged the "G" string. He busied himself cleaning, dissolving the pattern of the old rosin which lay spread upon the fingerboard like a sneering mask, exposed by the loosened string. It seemed incredible that so tiny an incident should father such pain. Why should he feel guilty for God's sake? To have missed five notes in perhaps five thousand concerts was nothing to be ashamed of. And yet his shame pervaded the air and even forced me to avoid the eyes of the others. What madness, I thought to myself.

Now the shining silver of the string attracted, his attention. It was almost new. The cry of the string was raucous as he tore it completely loose. Now the cleansing poison on the black length of the fingerboard. The stench of it wrinkled and burned his nostrils, but since Andrea's death he could no longer use alcohol.

He had never made an error like this before. The five notes were indelibly graven on his memory, I knew. Ah, another chance? No, he would never play this work again. But why? Why? Damn perfectionism, I thought, and remembered the lapses of other artists, great artists.

No, it was not the same. But why not, I wondered. And one part of my mind tried, laughingly to dismiss the five notes while to the other the tiny error seemed tragically symbolic. Had he never before made such an error? Never? He was not a machine, after all and, ironically, I thought of Olga's machines that would compose the music of the future.

Obsessed by the idea I tried to remember, searching back, back through the years, the sounding board of my memory seeming to vibrate with the roar of a thousand past audiences, a thousand past concerts. Was there nothing, not the comfort of a childhood slip to remember?

Otto had told me once, I recalled, of his beginnings in music. The first teacher — what was it? Yes. To learn fast, practice slow. He had found it to be true, he said, and he always practiced, at a killingly slow pace, memorizing not only with his ear, but with his eye, his fingers, and most of all his brain, that was the most important, the brain.

But the Brahms had not been prepared differently. He could write the entire score, from the flute to the contra-bass, from memory. He could do this with everything and until now the system had never failed. Never? Otto looked miserable. Olga had gone. He tried to replace the "A" string, his face working in nervous spasms. It was difficult. The black cavity was hidden in the secret scroll of the violin, like a tiny empty period. Neither of us spoke. We didn't even look at each other. I tried again to remember, wishing for an innocent little mistake, somewhere, something I could mention to comfort him. But I could think of nothing.

Angrily I wondered what was wrong with his orientation toward failure that he should react so to a simple mistake. Inwardly I cursed Otto and worried, for him. He continued to replace his strings with the greatest concentration.

Maia was delayed by a guard until just before the crush of admirers made their way backstage. She was the first to reach us, but there was time for no more than an embrace and a passing word of comfort before the mob swarmed into the room. Now its thousand fingers probed the wound relentlessly. It chattered at him with a tireless cruelty. Like a Star Chamber it dismissed Otto's condition and demanded its just reward—an audience with the soloists.

Let him turn this way or that, it was hopeless. They were upon him with their questions, or worse their praise. Let him try to hide in stubborn conversation with an old friend, the smiles of the idiots sneered at him. And the questions, always the same stupid ones, seemed tonight to have undertones of subtle ugliness.

"*Mis*ter Otto. Do you always play from memory, *Miss*ter Otto?"

"How long does it *take*, *Mis*ter Otto? To learn..."

Take, *mistake*, *mistake*...the words repeated themselves, again and again, beating a tattoo against the smirk, always the sneering smirk.

And Rieger joined the idiots. One more. "Oh, Rieger, at last! About the reception. Olga and I both have splitting headaches. We do these things in pairs, you know." It was too much, he couldn't stand it.

Rieger was crestfallen. "How too bad."

"Olga has already left, you see." Bad, bad...

"Well, if you really can't..." Really can't,

really can't...

I broke in, "Klaus, I'm sure you can understand, we really can't do it tonight, I m sorry." And I turned toward. Otto His eyes were closed now and he suffered visibly, breathing in short, painful gasps, his forehead dewy with droplets of sweat.

Maia had been watching him. She detached herself from Hellmut Schmidt who was developing a new theory of vibration. "I will take him to the hotel," she said. "Billy, bring his things, will you?" And gently taking Otto's arm she led him to safety.

Olga was in a vile mood. The concert that afternoon in Gary, Indiana, had delayed them so that a plane trip was necessary. And Olga hated nothing so much as air travel. But to make matters worse she had slipped and fallen badly on the way to the airport and her cello had suffered a tiny, inconsequential injury. I suspected that the injury had happened at an earlier time, for how could the cello be hurt, surrounded *as* it was by steel?

Nevertheless it took us all nearly half an hour to comfort her. She had taken the cello out of its case and nursed it like a grieving mother. I began to suspect that subconsciously she wanted to miss the plane. "Olga," Otto said gently. "We must absolutely go now." She gave him a nasty look, but got reluctantly to her feet.

The plane was a huge caricature of flight, the four tiny propellers ludicrous, impotent. Olga was an ill-natured demarcation among the passengers who climbed the little flight of stairs. Her armored cello careless of the bruised knees of others she was swathed in a cautious space. Her colleagues mingled more casually with the others who were traveling to St. Louis.

Seated, Olga and Otto, as if by a

common signal, twisted small cylinders of wax into their ears and began to read scores. A moment later the motor roared into life as though furious with the victorious wax. The mute lips of the smiling hostess commanded the fastening of seat belts. I seemed to remember her from somewhere, seemed to remember her painfully. Where could we have met? But as the plane began a slow crazy dance, maneuvering for the takeoff position, my attention has diverted from the stewardess. Soon I began to read.

I sat with Otto As his eyes roved over the deaf score of Beethoven. Opus 131. The opening bars had terrified Hector Berlioz. Perhaps the greatest of all music. For here Beethoven had descended to the underground of the human spirit and there he had found and torn open a drain leading downward still, into an immense cavern, till then unlighted. And Opus 131 revealed the grisly city. No wonder Berlioz was terrified. Suddenly Otto tore the wax from his ears and returned to the comparative sanity of the motor.

Thede and Frank were sitting together. She gazed blankly out of the window at the milky clouds while he seemed deep in thought. Otto had asked Frank to play a solo. Since his memory slip he wanted to get away from everything for a few days and rest. Of course Frank would oblige. And Maia could play the violin and they would do some piano trios for violin, cello and piano. But was it good for Otto to run away like this? Wouldn't it be harder for him to come back? Wouldn't there be a mental hazard, or something? I didn't know.

Olga, after a brief struggle with the stewardess, sat in the center of the plane, ruler of her domain. Her subjects were a utility, merely, there to transport her and her cello to their destination. And the combination of Olga's obstinate expression, the wax in her ears, and the roar of the motor discouraged any superfluous conversation.

She was studying the Photostat of an ancient score sent to her by a friend in Paris. The composer was unknown. With some difficulty she had identified the period. Sixteenth century, it seemed, a Sarabande. But not very interesting, she had told me. People always assumed that music if old was good.

For some time I watched: her. I wandered if she thought often of Otto's lapse. And how she explained it. Early senility perhaps? Or the antics of an unfaithful lover trying in this oblique way to confess his infidelity?

The plane landed with several little

bumps.

"Olga, I'm afraid," Mala said nervously.

"There's nothing to be afraid of. What makes you afraid? Otto? Don't be silly. There's nothing wrong with him. What are we rehearsing today?"

"The 'C' minor."

"All right. Sound your 'C'."

"I left the 'C' tuning fork at the hotel," Maia said sharply. "Use the 'A' for now. You can't have a tuning fork for every piece. What if we play something in the key of F sharp minor? Want an F sharp tuning fork?"

It was so unlike Maia to speak with heat that Olga was puzzled rather than angry. It must be Otto, I thought, and Olga said, "There's nothing the matter with Otto."

"Then why are we playing new things suddenly? Things that we don't know at all? Is it not because he is afraid to play from memory? Is it not because he wants some excuse to use the music? Hasn't he been eaten up with worry since the time of his memory slip? And not only that, but doesn't his playing get worse every day?" The mannikin of the tuning fork hummed dolefully. "And look at little things. Strange little things. He carries a cane. He's growing a moustache. He goes to the movies frequently. His whole way of life is different. You know," she said thoughtfully, "it may not seem to be related to the ways in which he's changed, but I think he's never gotten over Andrea."

"Have any of us?"

"No, but I think Otto is having a kind of nervous breakdown. Strange, in the beginning he seemed to recover from Andrea's death. Although he was sick in bed for a few days even then. Remember? All right, he got well. But since then things have gone from bad to worse. It is unthinkable that he should at last have had a memory slip. He is the most infallible player I have ever known. More than infallible. He has a photographic memory. It should be impossible for him to forget. Now he forgets thy? Is there not something wrong with his brain? And now all these crazy little changes. Perhaps a medical diagnosis...

Maia stopped in mid-sentence as the door burst widely open and slammed against the wall. It was Otto. He was sporting a moustache, a cane, a Homburg hat and a wide grin. "Well," he said, "are we ready? We don't have much time." And the rehearsal began.

We arrived in Colorado Springs late at night. The next morning Otto awoke feeling refreshed. It was a break with the habit of twenty years, but for some time now he had given up resting on the day of a concert. Indeed, he was likely to engage in strenuous activity. So he and Frank and I decided to go mountain climbing. We left young Krikelaire and the station wagon at the first likely looking trail and struck out across the hilly countryside.

    We had walked in silence for some time when Otto said, "You know, Frank, I was never cut out to be a violinist. I studied the instrument, of course, but my primary interest was in languages, and I was once considered to be quite an expert in Chaldean. At another time mathematics was my first love, and one of my dearest avocations was painting. My portrait of Olga is quite famous in Europe, you know, even though she hates it.

    "Anything but the fiddle, you see. In the beginning it was even doubtful whether I would play first violin in the quartet. At the time Maia was so obviously better than I was. But she didn't want to be first and at last I was persuaded to lead the group. And so now I am a violinist. Who would have thought it. Perhaps it is only a gigantic delusion and I was never meant to be a musician at all. Certainly I had the chance at everything else. I have been thinking I should give the whole thing up. You reproach me for wasting twenty years? But certainly because one has been a fool for twenty years is no reason why one should be a fool for twenty years and fifteen minutes."

Frank was horrified. "Gee, Mr. Otto, you're wrong, all wrong."

We had been climbing now for almost half an hour and Otto stopped at last and looked down on the surrounding countryside. "A false feeling of superiority one gets from this height, eh?" he said. "No, let us not deceive ourselves. It has taken a long time to catch up with me, but I can no longer play the violin. I shall give it up."

Frank was almost at the point of tears. "Gee, Mr. Otto" he cried. "You don't know what you're saying. You're the greatest. There's no one like you. It's only that you made that mistake. Jesus Christ! Anybody can make a mistake."

We continued our climb. Otto was silent for so long that. I began to feel relieved. Perhaps Frank had convinced him. But now Otto said, "No, my boy. It is you who are wrong. The error which was after all a small one has nothing to do with it. What time is it getting to be?"

"It's about eleven-thirty," Frank said miserably.

"Time to return. On the first day one has not much stamina." Otto was breathing heavily. And so was I. "Take hold of my hand he said to Frank, "and we will go down now." And arm in arm we descended. His grizzled hair glinted in the rays of the brilliant morning, sun. A stubbornly retreating red for many years it was turning white rapidly now, as though in sudden surrender. You're becoming an old man, my son, I thought. Suddenly with a clattering of loose rock. Otto slipped and almost fell. Frank's hold tightened instantly and Otto clambered back to safety. He turned toward us with shining eyes. For a moment he could not speak. Then he whispered, "I almost fell to my death. And in that frightful second. I saw into the abyss. And I had a feeling of the most extraordinary happiness. Haw strange it was. How unbelievable."

"Gee, Mr. Otto," Frank said anxiously, "are you all right?"

Otto drew a long breath. "I am all right," he answered. "I *am* all right."

And that night he played with something of his old fire. But his recovery did not last long and in a day or two he was playing as miserably as ever.

A few days later we arrived in Salt

Lake City. We were having breakfast in Maia's room when Otto stopped eating, pushed his plate aside, and said, "I understand someone succeeded in drowning in the Salt Lake. Apparently he was a powerful swimmer and swam to the bottom of a pier and tied himself to it. Must have been an exhibitionist. As are people who climb to a high, dangerous place and swallow poison. Or who slash their wrists superficially and, don't die at all." He fumbled for a cigarette. "Of the serious ones, of course, there are those who dive into steel furnaces, or who tear their throats on barbed wire, or who drown themselves in vats of lye—"

Maia was horrified. "Otto," she cried, "don't speak this way. Please. You frighten me."

"Open discussion is a catharsis, Maia." His voice rose. "It is high time we had an open discussion. Enough of hiding it." He stood and began to pace the floor, muttering to himself. Then continuing his wild declamation he began almost to shout. "They strangle themselves with wigs, the women, or use their own hair. The shepherds kill themselves with wool cutting shears, the glass blowers by plunging into vats of molten glass. They throw themselves into snowdrifts if they want to freeze, or volcanoes if they want to boil, or—" he paused with a wild glee, "they swallow dynamite and press the plunger, getting rid of the torment inside by exploding it, you see? You see?" Suddenly he was calm. "How terrible of me, Maia I didn't mean it, of course. It is only that I haven't been playing well, you know." He sighed. "And that is really too, too difficult for me to bear."

"You know, Otto dear," Maia said cautiously, "I have never dared to tell you, because I hoped it would never be necessary, but you really don't play quite right."

He stared at her. "How do you mean," he said suspiciously.

"Well, one can manage to play holding the bow any which way, of course. But there is only one right way, like so." And Maia demonstrated. "Try it, darling," she said, handing him her instrument.

He frowned, and drew the bow across the strings.

"Do you hear how pure the tone sounds?"

"It seems better." He frowned again. "But why should. I miss notes with my left hand if I don't hold the bow correctly with my right?"

"Everything is related, sweetheart. There are nerves which control the muscles connecting both shoulders. There was a slight awkwardness in the way you held the bow which threw the other hand out of kilter. Through the years the pressure built up until one day you started to miss notes."

"There may be something in it," he said doubtfully.

"Of course you can't get rid of in a day what it has taken years to build up. But if you will practice holding the bow in this way you will start to build a much more infallible technique."

"You may be right. I hope you are. I'll try it."

That night Otto attempted to commit suicide by slashing his wrists.

It was the earliest part of the morning. I had awakened with an inexplicable feeling of uneasiness. Of late I could not sleep through the night. Whether it was Thede or advancing age or the general situation with quartet, or all three, I do not know, but I seldom slept soundly anymore.

The maid had found him in the bathroom, his eyes glassy, his wrists bleeding and when I arrived Maia was already with him. Helplessly she applied tourniquets. She did not know what to do and a doctor had been called.

The doctor came, washed his wounds and put Otto to bed. As he applied the tape to the wounds I could not help but notice their extreme shallowness.

Now sleep was impossible and I sat thinking and in a state of high nervousness. That stupid story about the bow. How Could Maia possibly have thought he would accept it? But I had not dreamed it would come to this. Could the tour continue? Better cancel it and get treatment for Otto's mental condition.

Oddly, Otto's suicide attempt turned Maia against him. She had always leaned so on Otto. He was terribly sensitive and high-strung, but he was the only man in her life. She had always depended on him, only on him. And now she grew very angry, as though he had betrayed a trust. The habit of a lifetime had been rudely shattered and she began to avoid him.

Thus, Otto became almost entirely isolated within the quartet. Maia and Olga were hardly civil, to him and he had almost no one to talk to except Frank and me.

During the last twenty years Otto had seldom escaped his sedentary way of life, but now he began to be much more active than ever before. He was able to take Frank with him on daily walking trips because Thede no longer interfered with the boy's hero worship. Now she spent most of her time with the younger Krikelaire. She never ceased to amaze me with her imagination.

Otto and Frank left Salt Lake City early each morning. Nearby there were many mountain trails and along these trails they would wander. Frank was becoming, if possible, even thinner. The daily walking trips were taking a great deal of his strength and endurance and now his haggard young face constantly wore a look of distress and anxiety.

Olga and. I took him aside one day. "What is it, Frank," I asked. "What is the matter? You look like a ghost half the time."

"It's only these walks with Mr. Otto," he said. "He finds these steep hills to climb and he takes awful chances." The sensitive face suffered in remembering. "He almost fell from a cliff yesterday." The dark brown pools of the eyes mirrored the awfulness of a sudden, crashing death. "I caught him just in time. He's so careless, so careless. And do you know he actually enjoyed that terrible second? He enjoyed it. He wants to kill himself." Frank wiped his forehead. "I really can't go on with it much longer."

Olga was disturbed at this news. She hadn't thought it was so serious. "Don't tell

Otto," she said, "but Billy and. I will come with you tomorrow." And Olga visited several stores in the downtown area of Salt Lake City and bought at random a walking outfit. This costume included an alpenstock, a black derby hat, a large feather, polo trousers, boots, a smoking jacket and earmuffs.

The next day Olga had difficulty in getting into her absurd clothes and by the time she arrived at the hotel parking lot we had gone.

Otto put his arm around Frank's shoulder and leaned on him lightly as we walked. In the beginning the trail was level, but soon we ascended a slight rise and various little signs of spring began to dot the landscape.

I looked at Otto now and noticed his haggard face. Around his lips there played a small artificial smile. It occurred to me that Frank did, not know Otto as I did at all. To me, Otto was an utterly charming, warm, friendly, generous human being. But to Frank no doubt he was tense, desperate, grimly unhappy. But I was sure he loved him anyway. His devotion to Otto was obvious. No doubt he felt that here at last he had found a great man. A man daily victorious over self-destruction or some such. To me it all seemed a mad charade that someday might become tragic reality.

Now Otto slipped and almost fell into a mighty crevasse. His face had assumed an increasingly wild expression and now it had the crazy freedom of a lunatic orator, the lips spittled and the eyes staring in a horrible independence. He screamed. Frank grabbed at him frantically and caught him by the sleeve. And at the moment of his rescue Otto's face became calm. "I almost fell," he said, and in his voice there was a strange undertone of gladness. He leaned against Frank's shoulder.

"You sure did," Frank cried despairingly. "You almost fell to the bottom of that cliff."

"Do you know," Otto said dreamily, "that in the moment of falling I had the most wonderful feeling of clarity, of release, of a happiness I have not known since tiny childhood."

Frank looked helplessly and without understanding into Otto's face, and then into mine not knowing what to do. But I didn't know either.

"Do you know what a tricon is," Otto asked. "A tricon means three cards of the same kind. I used to be a magician. Well. A tricon, a tricon—" now he hesitated. "Let us analyze the cards. The first card symbolizes, for me, the superfice of one's life. All, *all* one's time is spent riding a rocking eggshell, and in its moist, humid quagmire we are stuck, tiny ants, trying to disengage ourselves from the white glue. We pull loose a foot and count it a triumph, when all unsuspected another foot kicks and clamors to be set free. If one of us performs the miracle of complete freedom, even for a moment, terrible things happen. The cartwheel of death appears and there we are, helpless, squirming, flat on our backs, lost in a small eternity."

"Are you feeling well, Mr. Otto?" Frank asked anxiously.

"But if we succeed in climbing to the top, oh, the top, the skeetering, skittering rim of the shell, the shell madly yawing, careening, we fall into the deepest non-return of the chasm, or, who knows, into the bottomless ocean, or, who knows, into a hell so burning bright that it is not possible to die therein, only to long for the flypaper of the lost eggshell, the eggshell forever gone, our fellow ants, abandoned, and we, crying oh, oh, abandoned—"

As he raved on, Otto had begun to climb again. He leaned against Frank and his eyes were shut tight and I was sure that any minute he would take both of them to their deaths. He was talking without being consciously aware of the meaning of his wards for his syllables seemed now to run together and make nonsense of what had not been clear in the first place.

"Circles?" he postulated, "Then we must go straight, straight up. Circles?" he ridiculed his phantom opponent, "No, straight on is the thing, straight onward and upward. It would be too terrible to go on forever in circles. It is the one thing I have avoided. The great danger."

Now Otto stumbled again but immediately righted himself and said to Frank, "That's it, the solution! The extraordinary happiness—the end of all things—it is in sight—the three of them—but Andrea firs—she—but Olga too—" He hurried on. "The music—" He painted with eagerness and walked so fast that I had to stop and Frank had to run to catch up with him. My heart was pounding and I knew if Otto was intent on killing himself I was unable to stop him.

He was raving on like a lunatic about Maia and Olga and Thede and Beethoven. The sight of him taking great leaps up the mountainside followed by his gaunt disciple put me in mind of a dadaist nonsense play and I felt inclined to laugh. Ants? Eggshells? Jesus, what the hell was he talking about?

He gasped for breath and, sweat poured from him. His face was transfigured as though he had seen a vision. "Maia" he cried, "Maia." He began to weep violently "Oh, Maia," he sobbed. "I am so sorry. Ah, what have I done. But now they will never know. They—"

Suddenly I heard, a shriek, a terrible piercing shriek of laughter. Turning around I saw Olga in caricature, alpenstock aimed, and, screaming hilariously. She swept down on Otto, each dislocated jump, each rock another gale of howling merriment. Otto fainted, his legs slowly melting beneath him until he lay on the ground, his head thrown back, saliva dribbling from his lips as Olga stood over him, her laughter abruptly stifled. "What's the matter with him, Billy?" she asked.

"I don't know," I said. I was almost out of breath but relieved that Olga had come. "I think he's seriously ill. You should have seen him a minute ago."

"Shouldn't we maybe get some help or something," Frank said.

"No, I'll carry him," Olga answered and hoisted. Otto to her shoulder as though he were a child.

"But why were you laughing, Miss Hallant?"

"Well, isn't it obvious? Otto is just too funny in that ridiculous walking outfit of his."

"Oh."

"He has never walked much, you see. Of course, to tell you the truth I haven't either. But I have better taste than he, don't you think?" She shifted Otto to another shoulder. "I would have caught up with you sooner but you were terribly slow. I climbed straight up the hillside and I only happened to look down and there you were. I wonder what's wrong with Otto."

After a time we came to the roadside. A truck was approaching. Olga waved to the driver and the truck stopped. We were given a ride into town. Otto did not awaken.

The doctor suggested that Otto be taken to the hospital. Apparently he was completely exhausted. In the ambulance he regained consciousness and sat up in alarm, but relaxed when he was told what had happened.

In the hospital he was carefully examined, but the doctors could find nothing seriously wrong with him. Still they thought that he should rest for several days. Otto was quite rational and agreed to everything. Hurried plans were made, programs changed and Olga and Maia were thankful that the tour was far enough along so that repertoire was not a problem.

Now we began to discuss what had happened. Apparently a number of things had combined to bring about a breakdown, surely temporary. He could remember little of what had taken place on the hillside. It seemed that he had been thinking of Andrea when he received a violent shock of some kind. It was understandable, I supposed. For me to think of her even now was a thing of anguish. And, he had tried to bury, to somehow bypass, the whole question. But he was a sensitive man and he could not so easily escape a feeling of guilt. He felt that if he were not very careful, if he did not analyze it thoroughly, this guilt might well pursue him for the rest of his days. He must think the whole thing through, think it through as carefully as he could.

And what to do now. Ordinarily he would never spend, several days in bed in the middle of a concert tour. The "Show must go on" tradition was too much in his blood for anything less than the most severe illness to stop him from playing.

But he had been badly scared. The concerts were relatively unimportant, one in a small college and one in a private home. And he was very tired. And above all he must think this thing through, he thought. He slept.

I went with Olga and Maia to visit Otto. "How do you feel, Otto dear," Maia asked anxiously.

"First rate."

"What a relief to hear it. We have all been terribly worried about you."

"No need. I'm fine."

"How soon do you think you'll be able to play?" asked Olga. "No hurry, you understand."

"Very soon."

"We have just finished a. concert at a private home," Maia said swiftly. "At an afternoon tea. It was really terrible. You were lucky to be sick. This woman who engaged the quartet, a Mrs. Stongey, is fabulously rich. She is a hideous creature with a huge paunch. And the affectedness of her accent has to be heard to be believed. Here we were the four of us, herded like cattle at a prize show. 'And now, my dears, allow me to present Mrs. Gwathmy.'" Maia's tones were thin and fluted. "'Mrs. Gwathmy, you know, is chairman of our 'Bundles for Borneo group. And this is Mrs. Throught. Mrs. Throught, don't you know, is leader of our local choir. She loves music, don't you, Mrs. Throught? And this is Mrs. Peelper. Mrs. Peelper has just returned from a tour of Mexico.' And Mrs. Peelper said, in measured dignified tones, a single word!" Maia's voice dropped an octave, "'Popocatapetl.' She has a limited vocabulary. Popocatepetl was the only word. I heard her say all afternoon. She said it several times, apropos of nothing."

Next to Andrea, Maia had been the mimic in the quartet. Otto knew the type of Mrs. Stongey all too well. He had suffered her for twenty years.

"When do you think you'll be able to leave the hospital?"

"Tomorrow."

"Do you think you ought, Otto dear?" Maia said doubtfully.

"You were sick as hell," I said.

"I'll be all right. Where's Frank?"

"We wouldn't let him come," Maia explained. "Nor Thede. We didn't want to surround the invalid with too much company at first."

The nurse came in. "I'm afraid you'll have to leave now."

"Goodbye, Otto darling," Maia said.
"Goodbye."
"Will you play the concert tomorrow?"
"Yes."
"Well goodbye."
"Goodbye."

"Goodbye," said Olga.

"Physically he seems to have recovered," Maia said as we walked down the hall. "But the only way of preventing him from going off the deep end again is for him to consult a psychiatrist. And you can't do that while touring the United States.

Disconsolately, shoulders hunched hands stuck deep into their pockets, the pygmy and the giantess walked to the hotel to report to the others.

Despite Otto's optimism he did, not feel able to play the next day, or the next. But now it was the first rehearsal after his illness. "There are only twelve concerts left," he said "Our repertoire has long ago caught up with the demand. There remains only the business of getting to play better. Particularly where recording for the Hollywood cinema is concerned. It's a special kind of playing."

"Why?" Thede asked.

"Because everything must be perfect," Olga retorted. "Records are for always."

"Oh," Thede said thoughtfully.

Maia broke in quickly. "Shall we begin with the Brahms 'A' major? We know it the least well."

And the rehearsal proper began. Otto's

playing was bad and it grew steadily worse throughout the morning. Finally his bow shook so that he almost dropped it. And all the time his face was serene in an unknowingness that was frightening. Soon Maia asked that they stop for the day. "I've a headache," she said.

Later Maia and Olga and I were seated at a table in the hotel restaurant. "It is the second time I have known him to be really sick," Olga said nervously. "And both times within a few months of each other. He must be going downhill."

Maia picked disconsolately at her food. "What is discouraging," she said gloomily, "is that his illness was more or less the same both times. That is, it seemed to be emotional. This is nothing to be laughed at. People have died from emotional illness." Her anger with Otto had changed to dismay. How could she reject him after all these years. "It might happen again," she said unhappily, "and what then?"

"Well, what can we *do*?" Olga asked anxiously.

"I don't think we should go to doctors, for one thing," I said "They can't cure him. They don't even know what's wrong. It is up to Otto himself, I think."

"His playing is terrible. I've never

heard anyone go to pieces so fast."

"He's still obsessed with Andrea," Maia brooded. "I was talking with him only today. I'm sure that's part of it. Perhaps most of it."

Olga bit her lip. Now she was badly worried. This apprehension was not her style. She was a violent woman and in life, as in art, she dealt in conflict. Apprehension was intolerable to her and she suffered because of it.

Maia continued, "I think he is very ill," she said despondently. "Perhaps a longer rest would help him? He's no good to us the way he is anyway. He might as well rest."

Otto had not entirely recovered from his illness. To add to his troubles he had contracted a palsy of the face, and his left cheek was twisted into an impossible grimace, a grotesque, inhuman mask. It was Bell's palsy, he explained to me. "I've had it before," he said. "Not so severely. It goes away spontaneously, in only a few days. I must get some grease paint. It's the lucky side. The audience will see nothing."

Since leaving the hospital Otto had become even more detached from the others. His apparent response to the concern of Olga and Mala was to abandon them completely.

And strangely his playing recovered entirely. He was an even better violinist now than he had ever been before. And, thank God, he was no longer afraid of his memory.

The first concert which Otto was to play after his illness was a difficult one, including the Beethoven "Ghost" trio, the Starch, and the Chausson piano quartet. But he seemed to have no fear of it and walked boldly onto the stage. The miracle of his stage presence did indeed hide his damaged features from the audience. The concealing violin held high, near the ear, and plucked with the masking left hand as though he was tuning, he strode with a deceptive speed to his chair, bowing slightly, curtly, perfunctorily, not to the audience but looking straight ahead, letting the girls do it. They had rehearsed their entrance and now appearing from opposite sides of the stage, sitting quickly so that Otto could sit they smiled and nodded to the enthusiastic crowd.

They began the Beethoven and Otto became a different being with ten times the energy of old. Although his playing had recovered, somehow it was changed. As though his worldview of music had shifted in orientation, his tone was covered now with a fury. The softest pianissimo were sharpened so that they had an edge, and at the slightest chance his violin leaped and gnarled as though he wished to enforce his will with a whiplash of sound. He had been unusually silent since his illness. But the training of years ground out an automatic relentlessness of procedure, and the rehearsals, well worn through the passage of thousands of repetitions, had effortlessly and mechanically accomplished their task.

The concert was a brilliant success.

The tour was over except for the movie which they were to make in Hollywood. We had sat up late the night before. After the concert in San Diego we were invited to the home of Konrad Mertzenauer, an old friend of Otto's, who had indeed been responsible for the San Diego engagement. Mertzenauer spoke about his plans for a new type of chamber music organization. The project was so interesting that Otto seemed to come out of his shell and even began to talk with some animation about the idea.

It was midnight when Thede became concerned about the persistent thunder and the heavy rain. She suggested that we leave soon. The rain was coming down in torrents and even now the streets would be difficult to travel.

But Mertzenauer shrugged the idea away. Rain was not a problem in San Diego. And he talked so intensely that the others were reluctant to leave. His project dealt with chamber music societies throughout the entire state school system. He said that there were few fiddlers today in the schools, but many wind players. All right, then. Let the young people play classical music for woodwind and brass ensemble.

Thede was insistent. "Can you put us all up for the night, Mr. Mertzenauer?

Because if we don't leave right now we'll have to stay over."

"How I regret that I cannot. But the shower will not last long. We have little rain, only around ten inches a year, and in your winter, not in May. However, I'll call a taxi for you."

Otto shot a look of hatred at Thede as Mertzenauer left. "Really, Mrs. Esca, you don't need to break everything up simply because of your stupid boredom." His voice was harsh. It was the first time he had spoken so to Thede in front of the rest of us. And now he became violently angry. "Why-don't- you-just-shut-up," he gritted.

Thede ignored him. He became white with rage. "I have played seventy-one concerts on this tour," he snarled. "In no case was there an after-the-concert reception nearly so interesting as this one. You—"

Mertzenauer returned. "The taxi cannot be here for another hour. We're not prepared for heavy rain here, you see, and there is a great demand for the taxis." He smiled. "And now I am afraid that we will be forced to continue our discussion."

Otto never forgave Thede. He had not been intimate with her for a long time now, I knew. But this finished whatever friendship there was left between them. He became bitter and angry and even vindictive toward her.

But the morning was glorious. Everyone's spirits were high and even Otto emerged somewhat. Krikelaire said, "There's some wonderful scenery around here. Shall we detour?"

The reminding angered Olga. "Thanks then," she said curtly and went to sit in the station wagon. Young Krikelaire, Maia and Otto sat in the front, the rest of us in the rear.

The countryside was revived by the sudden, unexpected rain of the previous night. A few patches of still-wet road glittered in the morning sunshine and were soon replaced by the larger shimmering of mirages on the pavement ahead. Far off the land looked as dry as before, but as we climbed toward the foothills, small gullies still ran strings of grey, unaccustomed water, and farther up in one place we heard what seemed a hundred lascivious burblings grow and grow and then join and burst into an increasingly widening torrent, sibilant and powerful.

Olga was moved to speak. "It is a wonderful sound," she said dreamily, "It is the promise of life and fulfillment and yet like every truly significant wound it has many undercurrents, many implications. I wish I could know their meaning."

"Truly it is an opera," Maia breathed, "an opera without heroines or—"

At this Otto could contain himself no longer. "You realize, do you not," he snarled, "that you are joining hands with the imbeciles who maintain that nature is art? That the song of the lark is greater than Beethoven? Next you will say we should stay at home and leave art to the nightingale." Then he grumbled, in an undertone, "Perhaps it might be best after all."

Thede said, "Yes, Mark honey."

But already we were past the narrow path of the rain. The van led the way through a mighty panorama of quilted farmland, lush, sometimes cut by orderly little channels of water. A man with a white flag stopped us while a dozen cows crossed the road. A woman came out of the farmhouse to open the gate.

"Look, look." Maia was happy as a child. "The little one following the big mama. Aren't they charming" And. irrationally, "I must drink more milk."

The white flag was lowered as the last cow ambled through the gate. "How many cows have you?" called Maia. She smiled at the surly farmer.

"Forty-six lady. One got run over last week by some college boys Speeding." He spat and walked through the gate, casting a look toward something plainly more important, the mooning clouds over the mountains.

Young Krikelaire honked his horn. There seemed, to be some delay. The elder Krikelaire got out of the van and lifted its hood. He did something to the motor, spread a road map to the wind and then climbed back into the driver's seat. The small procession moved on into a branch road that led upward.

The countryside grew wilder as the cars climbed along the flank of the mountains, the clouds around their dark granite heads piled high and rolling higher and higher, white-topped. But they were black and fearsome underneath, and cut by steady flashes of lightning, with a far thunderous roaring that was unbroken

"Never rains here," Thede said pleasantly, and was answered by an angry silence.

We crossed toward some sunny mountain ridges that spread upward like fingers of an eager outstretched hand, just below where the canyons between these ridges joined, a clear stream escaped through

a deep, narrow gap and then dove under a bridge that was lean and weathered as a bleached, old log. Krikelaire slowed the van down the grade and stopped. He glanced toward the thundering roar of the storm looming over them as he went to inspect the long narrow bridge, to measure its width. "Eleven inches to spare," he smiled, to Olga. "And iron guard rails. No chance, none at all, of anything happening." And seeing her expression still doubtful, "Even if I were to drop dead, the cello would still be safe.
There is even a ten-ton limit marked on it, and we weigh less than eight tons," Krikelaire added in a reassuring tone.

"But it looks old and worn—" Olga complained, shouting over the storming roar from up the mountain side.

"Don't worry, Miss Hallant, it'll hold me up. Your car will wait until I get off the other side." He climbed back into the van and started very slowly across the trembling bridge. Krikelaire was an expert driver and we could see the perfect precision with which he split the available space in two.

The truck crawled across the unsteady plank way some thirty yards in length, the eyes of the little group concentrated on the perfect driving of Krikelaire, the van's movement silent as a bug's in the growing roar of the canyon. Then suddenly one of them caught a shadow, and cried, out. The gap above them was filled with a wall of water and rolling timber and rock a hundred feet high. Grey and foaming and terrible it swept upon the bridge and like' a frightened animal the van shot ahead as the flood struck, exploding the bridge into a thousand matchsticks in a conflagration of water that shot high into the air, uprooted trees flying among the planks, and with them the van, flung up and to the side, and then gone, as a second, a higher wall of water rolled over all the canyon bottom, drenching even our car.

Helpless, silent, for none could yet say what was lost under the great thundering of the flood, we sat and watched it, saw it rise higher and higher until finally it swept heedlessly past us and downstream.

It was a dispirited quintet that arrived, in Hollywood. Young Krikelaire had stayed with the search party. We did not see him again. Tired, discouraged, we scattered to our hotel rooms.

Olga was stricken, chastened silent. For she knew that an irreclaimable part of her life was lost. Frank took her into the shop of a dealer in stringed instruments and she bought a cello without trying it. She looked old and the flesh hung from her arms in unhealthy ropes. Her grey hair was bleached and scraggly with not caring. She was weak from loss of sleep, from not eating.

She tried the new cello for the first time at the recording studio. The blunt end pin slipped and the cello clattered on the floor. Olga looked at it stupidly for a moment, then burst into tears. Maia put her arm around the sobbing giantess and tried to soothe and console her while Otto picked up the new cello. He handed it to Olga but she shook her head pathetically and wept, "My cello never slipped before."

We canceled the recording for the day and Otto ground the new end pin to a fine, sharp point. It took several days to complete the recording and by the end of the week Olga had recovered sufficiently to be photographed. Here Thede stole the show.

Hands lifted above her head in a new flamboyance she thundered, pedal down, head tossing, to new heights of glory. It was impossible not to feel that she was deliberately trying to create the impression that she was the leader of the quartet. Otto and even Maia felt compelled to speak sharply to her about her posturing. But Thede had taken up with one of the cameramen and retorted that Herbert knew best about motion pictures and she only did what he advised.

For the actual photographing of the group they all bought cheap new fiddles. If the grease paint slopped over and ruined the new varnish it wouldn't matter. Even Olga bought an inexpensive cello. The records had already been made and good instruments were not needed for the film synchronization. But the end pin of the newest cello slipped too, and Olga again burst into tears.

When I returned to my room, I found a message from Teresa waiting. It seemed that Mama was seriously ill with a heart condition and they needed money for her treatment. I immediately wired Teresa five hundred dollars and made reservations on the evening flight to New York. It was a good time to get away from the quartet. They could finish their work here without me.

The others all agreed with me, Thede a bit eagerly it seemed, and we decided to continue to support the Dantes financially.

"Trouble seems to stalk the Dante's," Olga said. Yes, I thought. And Casa Bella too.

LE STREGHE

I never return to New York without a sense of excitement. I breathe the stink of the big city and it is like a breath of fresh, pungent air. Threading my way happily through the crowd of people I followed the porter to a taxi.

We took the West Side Highway and Henry Hudson Parkway all the way to the George Washington Bridge and it seemed to me that the trip was over almost before it had begun. Surely New York taxi drivers cannot be equaled anywhere in the world.

The morning after my arrival, after I had bathed, shaved and eaten, I started busily pecking away at my typewriter. But then it occurred to me that I ought to call Teresa Dante. I rang the Dante's number and she answered the phone.

She was surprised that I had arrived in New York so soon. Yes, she would be delighted to see me but she could not leave the house because her mother was ill. I assured her that I only wanted to know whether I could come to see her to see the family. If it was all right I would be there that afternoon. She said it would be fine; and. then she thanked me for the money. They were most grateful for it but they suspected that it was only a charitable gift. I manufactured a good-deal of indignation, certainly it was not a gift, the book could easily be published, it was sure of publication.

I said good-bye, sat down at my desk again and read through the translation. I was dissatisfied, and I began to realize the difficulty which faces every translator. Achieving the effect of the original must always be a delicate, perhaps impossible task. I was tempted, to read a little of the translation again. It might be that a second reading would improve it. I rearranged the manuscript and started at the beginning.

My name is Andrea Louisa Dante. I was born in 1912 and was destined in only a few short years to begin the study of music. At the age of seven I received my first lessons on the viola, an instrument which I have continued to play all through the rest of my life. I have five brothers and one sister none of whom are at all interested in music.

I began to study music because my father wanted me to. I chose the viola because it was his instrument and of course as a small child. I wanted very much to be like him. I never had a chance to play with little girls because I always tried to play as well as I could, and, this took all my time.

When I grew older my parents became concerned because I could, not speak. I have been to many doctors, but still I cannot speak.

But my personal life is not very interesting, and this book will be not so much about myself as about the quartet, the famous Casa Bella Quartet, and about quartet playing in general.

To begin with, I should say that rehearsals will proceed much more rapidly and efficiently if all the players use scores instead of parts. There are no performing editions made of scores, so it will be necessary for each player to make his own edition.

The procedure is as follows: one procures two scores of the composition to be played and tears them apart into separate pages. The next step is to take two large sheets of stiff paper and to attach them to each other with hinge tape. Then, with rubber cement, glue the first page of the first score to the upper left hand corner of the first sheet of stiff paper. Then glue the second page of the second score to the space directly beneath the first page. Then glue the third page of the first score to the space directly to the right of page one. Continue until all the pages of both scores have been used up. Each player should stop attaching the, pages when there are a few measures of silence for him. This will be a good place to turn while playing. Continue to attach the pages of the scores to the other side of the large sheet of stiff paper. Add more sheets of stiff paper as necessary.

It was really a technical treatise. Come to think of it, maybe that was the reason I was dissatisfied with it, maybe it just wasn't possible to translate it any better. I skimmed through the remainder of the journal but found only material which might interest another expert, certainly not the general public.
Well, enough of the translation for today. It occurred to me that Thede did not know of my safe arrival and I called Western Union and sent her a telegram. Not that she'd care, but one had to keep an eye out for form, I supposed. Then I decided to go for a walk and went outside.
Now I felt a sharp twinge in the region

of my heart. I began to think that the twinges might be psychosomatic and associated with the journal for every time I had tried to read it, as far back as I could remember, I had gotten a physical reaction of some kind. I decided to test this theory by giving up the translation for a few days. If the pains vanished only to reappear when I began work on the translation again, then I would know.

When I got back to the house I telephoned for Tony Sforza, my favorite taxi driver. Tony would arrive in an hour so I decided to have lunch.

I ate slowly and thoroughly. There was plenty of time. Mrs. Bundy watched me with, relentless satisfaction. But suddenly the taxi honked, and I swallowed, my coffee hurriedly and fled.

"Hello, Sforza," I panted as I closed the door.

"Hollo, Mist' Esca. Howsa t'ings? How you been?"

But I knew from experience that Tony Sforza was not in the least interested in me. As I had expected Tony immediately launched into a frightening description of his family life. As we left the George Washington Bridge I interrupted him and asked him to stop at Rockefeller Center. Then I sank back in my seat and listened to his lurid tale.

We turned onto Sixth Avenue and I said "When we get there, Tony, you go around the block a few times and I'll stop in at the Center and buy a few things. Let me out at Fifty-first Street."

"Hokay, Mist' Esca."

I walked, rapidly to Rockefeller Center and bought an orchid for Teresa, a shawl for Mama and a meerschaum pipe for old Pietro. Then I went outside. Tony was waiting out in front of the building, risking a ticket for illegal parking. "I go rounna block t'ree times," he said disgustedly. "Anyway, never mind. So I says to her, I says," he continued with great rapidity, "wotcha t'ink? I'ma gonna worka my balls off a for you all a day an' I'ma coming home late inna night an' you sittin' on you fat ass like a goddam queen an' I no gotta my dinner?" Tony continued in this vein all the way to Brooklyn while I rested and even took a little nap.

Sforza was almost at the climax of one of the more sensational of his recent adventures when the cab rolled up to the home of the Dante's.

"Later, Tony," I said. "On the way

home. You can finish it then."

"But itsa only a little more," Tony pleaded.

"I must really go now. I'll probably call for you in an hour."

Tony was disgruntled. "Alla right," he growled.

I climbed out of the cab, straightened myself and walked toward the house. As I approached the door it opened and Teresa stood in its oak frame. She seemed to have grown in these last few months. Her hair fell about her shy maturity in a cascade which reached below her shoulders. She extended a serious little hand, and said, "I am so glad you are here, Mister Esca. Please come in,"

She was wearing a cross descending from a golden chain and a short skirt and blouse of navy blue. I followed her into the dark interior of the house. Teresa took my hat and coat and went into the next room. When she had returned and we were seated I gave her my few gifts. She thanked me with a charming astonishment as I pinned the purple flower to her blouse.

"Oh, Mr. Esca, I've always wanted to have an orchid. Since I've been grown, that is." She gazed raptly at the flower for a moment then turned to me with shining eyes. "I—wait for me a moment please. I'll see whether Mama has awakened." And she took the shawl and hurried upstairs.

I looked around the room and wondered why the house was always so dark. As far back as I could remember the Dantes never turned, on the lights except at night. Even when Andrea was alive the house had always reminded, me of a tomb.

Teresa came down the stairs. "Mama is still asleep," she said, "but Papa should be home soon. He just went to buy some tobacco."

I fished the journal from my pocket. "I wanted to talk to you about one or two things," I said. "Perhaps now would be the time."

"Yes, of course. Let's get a desk and some paper."

She led the way into the room, darker still, where Andrea had lain. Suddenly a blacker darkness flashed before my eyes and I felt a moment of panic. The room reeled and I clutched at Teresa's shoulder.

"What is the matter, Mr. Esca? Are you ill," she cried in alarm.

"No, no, my dear. I have had these spells for twenty years," I lied. "My doctor says they amount to nothing and that I will have them as long as I live. Pay no attention to it." It was Andrea again, no doubt. I would have to be careful of Andrea.

"Very well," Teresa said doubtfully. She went to the desk and fumbled with the lamp. Suddenly a brilliant light shot onto a blue circle of blotter. Rays streamed upward to a mirror above the desk and I saw, with hurting eyes, two half-ghosts of youth and age.

Now a pungent perfume stole into the room. I looked up and saw Papa Pietro standing in the doorway, a halo of smoke wreathing his white hair. He chortled gleefully and hurried forward, extending his hand. I shook it and we embraced, leaning forward over mutual paunches.

"Minter Esca, Mister Esca, what a surprise! How are you, my friend?" Teresa brought his present and he said, "What? What is this?" He unwrapped the package. "A meerschaum," he cried, "a meerschaum! Just what I always wanted. Thank you, my friend, thank you." He was delighted with the pipe, took it apart examined its amber stem. At last he said, "Mama has awakened. Come, you must see her now. Come."

I followed Papa Pietro's broad and shifting bottom up stairs which, indignant at our combined weight, protested with a treble squeal as Teresa followed us.

We entered the bedroom. Mama Karla, wearing her new shawl, regarded me with unblinking eyes for several minutes, then motioned me to a chair. As she looked down from the high perch of her bed I wondered what to say. Somehow it did not seem like a time for social trivialities.

Mama said, "Thank you for the fine present, my friend." She fingered the shawl. There was something hypnotic in the way the staring, eyes looked at me. I became a little uneasy. Wasn't it necessary to blink? Something about the wink reflex? The aged brawn eyelids closed slowly, then opened again as I said, "It is a very small thing, Mama Maria. I am glad it pleases you."

She cleared her throat. "Now the book. Is it another of Teresa's dreams?"

Old Pietro threw up his hands. "Mama, Mama," he said petulantly. "You were too sick when we wrote the letter to Mister Esca so we did not ask you. Now you are angry. Do not be angry."

It was as if Mama hadn't heard. She continued to stare at me, waiting for my answer. "I have just begun to work with the book," I explained. "But frankly it seems to be mostly about things which are not likely to interest many people. Its subject matter is much too complicated ever to attract a great audience, dealing as it does with such difficult musical questions.

"Now if we were to write a biography about Andrea, it might be very successful. She was a famous artist and the story of her Life would have a universal appeal. We might also include some material from her journal. Of course, I may not be able to write such a book, but if I cannot do it we could get a professional writer to help me. What do you think?"

Mama sank back with an exhausted sigh, the sleeve of her nightgown moving up to expose a skinny brown bone. "Mister Esca,'" she said slowly, "if you want to make such a book we would be glad for your help. But I think we do not want someone else. No. No one. It would be pain to us and I do not want it." She drew a tired little breath. "But come to me again," she whispered. "And bring this secret book." Papa Pietro opened his mouth to protest, but Mama had closed her eyes.

We left silently.

In the gloomy sitting room we sat and sipped burgundy wine. Teresa said, "If you want to write a biography of Andrea perhaps you would like to look at her letters and papers. I think she also had a diary."

"An excellent idea."

We went to the second floor and. Teresa led the way to Andrea's room. She opened a window to get rid of the musty smell, then raised the window blind. I looked about the room. The morning light revealed a daybed, an old desk, a table, a chair and a large chifforobe. On the floor near the window lay a viola case. A closet was filled to overflowing with clothes.

As I looked about the room I saw that the walls were covered from ceiling to floor with canvases done in oil, except for a few watercolors and sketches. None of them had a title or signature. Everything seemed to be of the non-objective school, filled with violence in form and color, a series of little explosions. Near the window stood a large stack of manuscript music. There was one piece of sculpture, a huge black monstrosity. Its title, the only title to be seen, was "Beethoven." Old Pietro was staring open-mouthed at the paintings and the sculpture and I thought it strange that he had apparently never seen them before.

Teresa was looking through Andrea's antique, many-drawered desk. "There's an awful lot of stuff here," she said. "Papa will you get a suitcase for Mr. Esca so he can take what he needs?"

Old Pietro, called suddenly back to reality, blinked and said, "Sure, sure, right away," and made haste with his slow Italian trot.

"Nothing but letters, mostly bills," Teresa said. She continued to explore the ancient correspondence, pausing now and then to examine a letter more closely. "A friend from Trieste one from Germany. Can you understand German?"

"No, English and Italian are my limit."

Papa returned with a large valise and Teresa began to stuff it with mail. Soon the desk was almost empty. The bottom drawer was a secret one, small, narrow, almost unnoticeable because it blended with the surrounding, decorated wood. Only oblique cracks revealed its presence. Teresa slid her hand under it and pulled. It squeaked protestingly but wouldn't come out. "Darn it," she said, "the thing is stuck." She yanked viciously at the drawer and at last, squealing raucously, it came free. It was empty except for a very small red volume. "Oh, it looks like the diary I was telling you about." She riffled through the pages and then, reluctantly, *she* handed it to me. I hesitated, but Teresa said, "Go on, take it. I guess she'd rather have you read it than any of us."

For a moment I remained, undecided. Then I shrugged and tossed the diary into the valise which was now rather full. We went: downstairs and I telephoned for Tony. And during the hour which it took Tony to arrive I ate some delicious clam soup.

On the trip home. I thought about Thede. I had not heard from her since leaving Hollywood, damn her soul to hell. I knew that she was having a gay old time with the cameraman. Or someone else. The thought made me writhe. How long had she been deceiving me? I would never, know. I only knew that she was deceiving me now with a vengeance. How curious it was that in the beginning her affair with Otto had not been nearly so painful to me. Now the pain worsened, became more intense every day. It must be that the shock of initial discovery had left me numb, and that this protective numbness was only now melting away. And of course I had been busy on the tour. Now I was relatively idle, and scarcely an hour passed that I didn't think of Thede and her infidelities. She was like a canker in my soul, and with the passage of time the canker flourished and grew larger and larger and more agonizing until it became unbearable. Why, why didn't she telephone? Why couldn't she give just a little effort to preserving the fiction that she loved me? I was damned, if I would call her. But why not? Well, I just wouldn't. A shred of pride remained in me even after the tour and I wouldn't. It was incredible that I had agreed to go on the damned tour. How could. I have ever thought that I would be able to tolerate the daily spectacle of my cuckoldry? I couldn't understand it. I didn't see how I could have thought I would be able to endure it. For recently there had been times when I thought I would go mad with jealousy, and the thought of killing her had occurred to me. And, yet I had endured the tour. Quite well, in fact, all things considered. Until now, that is. If only I could get my hands on her, I thought.

Tony's furious voice broke in on me. I interrupted him to ask, "Did you ever think of just letting her have one?"

"She'sa gotta big brother."

"Oh." And that day I listened to Tony's adventures with a fascinated absorption.

It was night before I found time to look through the contents of the valise. The Italian letters were from relatives and not very interesting. Most of the other letters were from the city of Murcia, in Spain, but there were several from Germany, France and other countries. The rest of the papers were bills, some of them dating back to 1946. All of them were marked "Paid in Full."

I opened one of the Spanish letters. No good. It was written in Spanish, of course. Having looked superficially at everything I turned now to the small red volume. Teresa was right. It was a diary. I felt a sharp pain in the region of my heart as I opened the little book but clenched my teeth and began to read.

During the rest of the day I was paralyzed by terror. And then, in the night of Tommasso, they urged me to play. Four old men and a ravished child. Did automatic fingers obey forgotten teachings? I remember nothing. For when I was only twelve my brother forced me to the ground and taught me the mysteries of love. Could I scream for help? Tommasso was my brother. My brother! What an awful fear he instilled into me, what a dreadful fear. "Don't make a sound," he snarled. "Don't make a sound." It has been almost seven years, but I have not spoken since.

October 7, 1930
I thought Vienna would be my escape but Tommasso has followed me. How uselessly I have been chaperoned by my loving family. Since that dreadful day seven years ago he has had an ingenuity in capturing me alone which is no less than genius. And now all this time, a fantastic thought has come into my mind. Can it be that I am in love with Tommasso?

March 18, 1931
Otto is a fascinating man, Marcus Otto. Two women will join us. A quartet but my mind is for Otto. He is very gentle, and I think Of him when I am with Tommasso.

September 11, 1931
I have been here a year. In the beginning I hoped that something new and exciting would unfold in Vienna, a new city, new faces, the conservatory.

But I found teachers who are only experts in pomposity. Almost all the students are frivolous, except for the new quartet. How glad. I am to leave this dismal city, even though the debut in Berlin terrifies me. But we shall return soon. Perhaps it will not be so bad.

And then the monotonous plagiarism of the days will begin again, like a boring roulette in which one can never win.

November 4, 1931

We are on tour God in heaven we are on tour! Freedom at last, but I still think of Tommasso, half in fear, half in hatred.

Last night I made love to myself thinking of Tommasso.

I shut the diary with a snap. I was angry with myself. I felt that I couldn't go on with it. What right did I have, what right could anyone have, to read anything so intimate as another's diary? As if in confirmation I felt a sharp twinge, then another.

I looked through the letters once more and sorted out and reread the ones in Italian, but was unable to find anything of value in them. Mama didn't want me to ask the advice of anyone else, so I couldn't get help to translate the other letters. In effect the valise was filled with useless data.

I looked, at the diary again. No, I didn't want to touch it. Some other solution would have to be found. For the present I thought that I would continue with the translation of the journal and hope that it could be published eventually. It might be useful to a small segment of the musical world.

But I didn't want to do it immediately. Let it wait. Maybe it would be a good idea to begin the study of chess seriously. What a delight it would be to defeat Otto when he returned!

And I acquired the works of Alekhine, Znosko-Borowski and Capablanca, I played regularly with my friend Phil Burton, who had once been champion of Manhattan, and lost just as regularly. But Phil said I was improving, I began to study chess openings and was impressed by the immense research which had gone into the game.

But one day I had a twinge of conscience. I hadn't gone near the journal for two weeks now. Worse, I had been neglecting the Dantes shamefully and decided I must go out to Brooklyn immediately and see how they were. I telephoned for Tony and while waiting for him I got out the journal.

I read: "At the speed of ♩=100 there is no difference in duration between a sixteenth note and a triplet eighth note, for the quarter note lasting one one-hundredth of a minute the triplet eighth note lasts one three-hundredth and the sixteenth note one four-hundredth of a minute. The common denominator is twelve hundred and so we see that the triplet eighth note lasts four twelve-hundredths and the sixteenth note three twelve-hundredths of a minute, the difference in time being one twelve-hundredth of a Minute, or one twentieth of a second. Since it is impossible to consciously make a difference so small as one twentieth of a second in the relative durations of the two notes, they must, for all practical intents and purposes, be regarded as having identical lengths of time."

A bit esoteric, I thought, and it was with a sense of relief that I heard the honking of Tony Sforza's horn. But on my way to the taxi I felt, for the first time in weeks, a sharp, confirming pain in the region of my heart.

I rang the doorbell and waited for several minutes but there was no answer. Then I rang it again and several times more. I peered through the window but saw only an empty room. I was about to leave when Teresa came to the door. Her eyes were red with weeping, her young face suddenly old. She looked at me wearily. "Mama is dead," she said dully.

I was thunderstruck. "My God! When did it happen? How—"

"In her sleep," Teresa said hopelessly. "In her sleep" She passed a hand over her eyes and sighed. "I have to go now," she whispered. "I do not feel well." She was about to close the door when old Pietro crept behind her and croaked, "Come in, Mister Esca. Come in and drink wine." He looked ghastly. Since Mama's death he had aged twenty years. The thick, white stubble of his beard framed the face of a haggard, ancient cherub. Again he said blearily, "Come in, Esca. Drink wine."

"No, no thanks. I think I'll go along now. I'm terribly sorry for both of you." Holding on to the bannister I climbed down the steps into the street. I felt numb. How typically cruel of life to let her die. She had seemed to be getting better, and now—

I wandered aimlessly for a time. A taxi passed, I hailed it and we began the long trip back. The brilliant sunlight blinded me and I covered my eyes. Life was disintegrating, crumbling into a meaningless welter. The calm, unhurried, unworried years were no more. Now in only a few months, the bottom had dropped out of everything. Andrea had died. Thede, with the aid of my best friend, had deceived me. The quartet had deteriorated, the state of my health was, well, doubtful and now Mama had died.

When we arrived, I paid the driver and got out of the cab. For a few minutes I hesitated, then walked slowly to the bridge, It was almost noon but I felt no hunger. It must have been the first time in my life that noon had arrived and I was without hunger.

For a long time I stood and watched the river. I thought about Thede and tried to imagine what she was doing. Sounds of thunder awakened me from my fantasy and I saw a flash of lightning that seemed very near. A few seconds passed and there was a tremendous crash of thunder. It must be dangerous to stand on the bridge. Now I saw that a change had come over the sky and that angry clouds had gathered. A fresh wind made my coat cling to my body. The black horizon was sundered by lightning and again I heard the rumble of thunder. How dark the river was how symbolic the heavens. A fit of acrophobia came over me and I was suddenly afraid that I might fail into the churning water. As the first drops of rain began to fall I walked slowly back to the House of Casa Bella.

The morning was wild and frantic, but at last everything was packed and all the last minute errands done and I was on my way to the Maine estate with Mrs. Bundy.

The train arrived in Bangor late at night and we hired a cab to take us to the estate, some thirty miles away. On the train I had played casino with Hrs. Bundy. She was a demon casino player and we had played steadily all the way from New York to Bangor.

But now I would have a little respite. I gazed out of the window and the black eternity of the night inevitably reminded me of Thede. Maybe I should divorce her. It would be intolerable to give her up, but if I didn't I would never have a moment's peace again. Always I would be eaten by jealousy. Always. No, at my age marriage was no longer for me, not with a sexual firebrand like Thede. She had not always been like this. No, during the early days of our marriage I knew she had been contented. But now it didn't seem possible for her to meet a new man without jumping into bed with him.

And again I was consumed by jealousy and hatred. As the taxi sped, through the night I found it difficult not to beat my head against the walls, Mrs. Bundy or no.

In the morning I worked with Mrs. Bundy, unpacking and straightening up the house. But in the afternoon I continued with the translation of Andrea's journal. It was painful, but I clenched my teeth and ignored the twinges.

Toward evening I decided to stop and leaving my desk I sank into an easy chair. It was too bad. There was no doubt that the journal was bare of anything that might conceivably interest the public. Only the most accomplished of professional musicians could possibly find it profitable to read about such technical matters. If the book were published in its present form it might realize a few hundred dollars. But if I were able to write the fascinating biography which could be written about Andrea's life, it might earn a great deal more. And old Pietro could get started in some little business of his own, and Teresa would be taken care of until she could support herself. I sat thinking for a long time.

At last I decided to have another look at the diary. As I leafed idly through the little book I was strongly tempted, to read it. No doubt it contained a great deal of useful information, perhaps even enough to help me write a complete biography apart from the journal. Now that Mama was dead the professionals could attend to that anyway. I riffled through the pages of the diary for what seemed the thousandth time. What would Andrea have wanted me to do?

I found myself at the place where. I had stopped the translation.

> January 29, 1932
>
> Tommasso has become so natural an obsession with me that he affects the simplest happenings of my life. I noticed it again today. The newspapers fill in extra bits of space with little pieces of useless information. The misguided belief that knowledge in itself is of value. I read these stray bits as I read everything, even the advertising of the soap labels. I am for all the world a vacuum cleaner.
>
> But Tommasso. When I read, "The Dead Sea is ten miles wide and forty-six miles long," the thought, "What a lovely large area in which to drown Tommasso," occurs to me

automatically, and the disappointing realization that one can't sink in the Dead Sea comes only later. The newspaper didn't print *this* information. It just goes about getting people's hopes up.

The next one, though, is better. "In ancient Druid ceremonies men were placed in straw cages made in the shape of animals. They became religious sacrifices when the cages were set on fire and they died in the flames." The idea is not practical, but the principle is sound. I must think how to apply it.

March 16, 1932

Tommasso came again today. Oh, for the joys of a nun.

(There appear several blank pages. — W.E.)

September 26, 1935

Oh, Otto—do not, do not insist that we play from memory. It frightens me so. It is so difficult to remember a viola part, the counterpoint, the harmony. No melody, rarely any melody. And the crazy disharmonies of the modern music! What relation does one note have to another? None, none at all. Thirty-nine quartets have I memorized so far, and fear seeps into my being with every one. I do not know what it is to live without a score, when I eat, when I sleep. I take my scores almost onto the stage before relinquishing them, and then with the fear, always with the shivering fear, that I will forget. So far it has never happened, but it will, I know it will

January 14, 1936

Frequently I Pray. Not of the things of God, whom I have forgotten for many years, as He has forgotten me, but with a kind of Passion and longing. The Jews at their wall of wailing might have prayed so if they too had abandoned God. I pray as I play. It is the same.

April 7, 1936

The flattery. I cannot abide the disgusting flattery. After every concert repulsive men with their fleshy wives surround me. First they slobber over my splendid performance. Then they envy the great joy I must feel when I play. It is perhaps fortunate that I cannot speak my thoughts.

Sometimes I overhear them. "Isn't it too *bad* that she cannot speak" "I feel *so* sorry for her" "If she were only *attractive*, you know—"

Let them die, let all them die.

May 23, 1936

A decision today! After a long time of thinking about the uselessness of music, the terrible, toil, the agony, the fear, always the constant fear, I have decided that the sacrifice is useless, that it is made for people to whom art means nothing. And so I shall never play again. In any case, who can tell how long the quartet will last? Already I think the seeds of, its own destruction are visible. No, I shall never play again. Instead I shall marry, it does not matter whom, and if I can, which I doubt, I shall have children, little tiny babies like Teresina was. Ah, how immediately happy I am.

* * *

But can I really give up music?

May 29, 1936.

Yet another concert. Day after

day they come and they come. What a way to live. I fear all the concerts, but today especially. For the Queen of Belgium, a command performance!

* * *

I was paralyzed with terror, I felt the urine beginning to wet my clothes. When we came into her majesty's presence I wanted to shriek with fear. For the first time in my life I was thankful that I could utter no sound, no sound at all.

August 7, 1936

Oh, he is so beautiful in his ugliness. We sat, tentative partners. Slowly our hands touched, then our lips. He looked at me startled, like a fawn. How clumsy he was. Poor, poor Otto. How I love him.

September 30, 1936

In only two months! He is wonderful! And how happy he is. And for me!!! What a thrilling experience. I feel so superior to the others. He has chosen me, after all. The darting touch of him, the delicacy of his caress, the power of his thrust. And all, all mine.

Shall we marry, ever? I feel that I should regain my voice.

November 18, 1936
    Today completed trio for piccolo, double bass and kettledrum.

February 6, 1937
    Today completed quintet for four horns and viola.

June 29, 1937
    Today completed octette for flute, oboe, English horn, Contrabassoon, trumpet, viola, harp and glockenspiel.

November 30, 1937
    Today completed first symphony.

December 22, 1937
    Home for the holidays. And Tommasso with his evil leer. I have thought of horrible, sadistic things such as having his eyes put out. I read trashy fiction sometimes in which spies are captured and tortured, and my mind *leaps* to Tommasso, hungrily, avidly.
    But it is really a pleasure to

think of him so. Exquisite. And today I found the perfect punishment for him. I happened to see, with Teresa, one of those old, serial movies. Teresina squealed with excitement as the heroine, strapped with thongs to the log conveyor, approached the crosscut saw, the whizzing crosscut saw.

Now here is my idea! Why not have Tommasso, similarly strapped, approach *very slowly*, a huge, rapidly revolving disk to which I fastened a circular piece of the coarsest sandpaper? Eh?

Of course there are certain details to be settled, such as whether he is to be sandpapered away standing up or lying prone. But these are after all only details.

May 16, 1938

A marionette show! What a spectacle! Teresina danced with joy. And how I envied Renard. That entire aplomb! Was the tail more perpendicular? Or Renard? And what a tail! So powerful and assured. Oh, if only I had, such a tail, such a nose, so hairy and splendid a countenance, such-flashing eyes! The attitude so magnificent, the furred, features so rich and wise. Ah to be so sure that one is adored.

May 18, 1938
    I stole two dozen handkerchiefs today, little brown and red ones, some with lace. Pretty things. I shall keep the plain Ones. The others I shall give to Teresina.

October 6, 1938
    Today a frightful thing happened. It seemed to me that a sharp knife threatened to stab me to death. No one wielding the knife, it was quite sufficient in itself. And all day it has pursued me, no matter which way I turned. But I have become accustomed to it. It doesn't actually kill, it only terrifies.
    These cutting weapons are horrible. A few minutes ago I was looking at the veins in my left hand, when a knife appeared and threatened to sever them. The bulging blue worms of the back of the hand, like thick blue strings, monstrous and slack, and the sharp bow, and the red tune.

October 8, 1938

And to the Psychologist and his ink splotch. The ink has dried randomly on the paper and the patient is supposed to tell what the haphazard blotch suggests. I saw tortured, dying animals, everything seemed tormented beyond endurance, rabbits with torn and dangling entrails, or foxes in a steel trap. Always suffering, always in agony.

Didn't the fool know I was suffering? Without the damned test? He need only have asked me.

* * *

For that matter everyone suffers.

November 3, 1938

I have not been able to eat anything since the beginning of the tour and know that I am eating food. It tastes like sawdust. It is this way on every tour. It must be that my tasting mechanism is ruined by constant fear of the days and the nights.

* * *

I think Otto is beginning to lose interest in me.

December 22, 1938

    To be lonely since childhood. It is difficult to understand. Have I not a sufficiently large family? Have I ever since I was born been able to be by myself? I can only think that I am somehow to blame. For surely my little sister loves me, and my brothers too, except Tommasso. Lost among the chatterers, I think, even before my voice was taken. I was a shy child and could not fight for Mama, surrounded as she was by noise and activity.

    And when Papa taught me the viola I was so anxious to please him. I practiced many hours each day while my brothers played their rough games, and this too isolated me. And suddenly I was almost grown, and there was Tommasso to steal my voice. How would my woman's voice sound now? Curious never to have heard it.

    And Teresina was born. She was like a child of my own, and I could whisper into her baby ear, sweet endearments. And once years ago while holding her close, so close, the dream of a lullaby enfolded us. I still remember it, a beautiful murmuring of sound, enfolding us both.

August 15, 1939

Today I must practice. For two months. I have been idle and my playing is beginning to suffer seriously. Soon the winter concerts will begin. Already Otto's tongue is growing sharp with the shortness of the remaining time.

I take my viola from the blue plush lined skin of a dead alligator. The bow hair's sharp invisible teeth demand their own dentifrice and I scrape them with powdery rosin. As I begin to play, the instrument protests. Buried, beneath the opulent tone I hear the faint mechanical hiss which, has tormented me for a quarter of a century. I do not attend to my playing, of course. Instead I glance out the window, about the room anywhere. My gloves lie on the floor where I have thrown them. Like shorn black hands they lie, wrinkled and sleeping. I imagine their dreams.

Finally I finish. As I return the instrument to its case I think of the suffering I have endured because of it. I look at its muddy smugness. The silent arrogance of the beast. How *sweet* it would be to seize its sneering cheeks and tear it asunder.

September 30, 1939

What a terrible struggle today. Olga can be so mistaken about music. I want to give in, but I am an artist and cannot. With my feeble energy I fought her. The wrong powerful tigress. And the others, sitting judicially by with creased brow and pursed lip. At last they decide for Olga. How I hate them. The stupid fools. And how terrified. I was. And, what a tremendous coward I am. Olga frightened me so that I could not even whisper.

April 3, 1940

Today it is beautiful. Little cirrus clouds float in a sapphire sky. The wind is fierce and frightening, the day suddenly hot.

In the afternoon I walk to the river. Little whitecaps on a bed of deepest blue. It is enough to excite the spirit of the dead. My heart leaps, my mind Is turbulent. But far, far in its background is the rhythm of a funeral march.

I have noted this duality often. I

think of a rushing Beethoven scherzo. What joy! What a frenetic burst of sound! What a tremendous conviviality! And my deeper thoughts are of suicide.

April 9, 1940

Three students stood grinning and chortling. They did not seem to have the grace and flair of youth, but stood arms akimbo or hands scratching, with a kind of devilish awkwardness, faces distorted one might say with a Dickens malnourishment, noses running and generally unpleasant. The kind of people you need only to look at to know their breath is foul.

April 16, 1940

Tonight in the concert I broke a string! It was near the end of Opus 131. And to finish that mighty work with but three strings! My God, how did I do it. I only missed a few notes but they were important ones.

And what sympathy did I get from the others? None, only angry scowls. Except dear, sweet Maia, bless her. She comforted me.

Everything happens to me. Last week I was seized with the horrible fear that I would lose my ability to play. And how this fear has haunted me! To lose my only voice. How terrible it would be. Ah, everything is against me.

June 10, 1940

We record today. Forever, forever, and ever descending generations will hear me. Over and over they will play the records, over and over with scores in their hands to check every note. School children will learn to play music through the records. Amateurs will sit side by side studying the records and if I miss a note, or play it badly, or even a little badly, or even a tiny bit badly, they will know and sneer. And who can play everything perfectly? With the last ounce of perfection? No matter how many times the record is remade? No one, certainly not I. And I am afraid. Dear, dear God, I am afraid.

July 29, 1940

I remember the earliest years of my childhood. The day I lost a tooth, but no one noticed because a new sister was born. But she had no teeth. Anyway she died.

I remember the lovely lake where we swam in the summertime. It was called *di Massaciuccoli*. It was not far away and on Sundays we would, sometimes have a picnic there and swim in the warm waters. The splashings of five children! I am still wet.

And. I remember Tommasso. How I loved him then.

August 28, 1940

Over and over, and over and over, and over and over. Endlessly. Each note is a fiery syllable engraved in my brain. My eyelids droop with exhaustion, little anvils hammered by the notes. Until I think I can stand it no longer. But there comes a day or a month or a year or some crumbled boulder of time vast and gone, when the rehearsal ends. The others leave. I sit for a while, tired and stupid. I walk to the door, leaving my instrument. We rehearse again tomorrow, the same place, the same music, the same cruel obstacles. I leave everything. Perhaps some kindred beasts will gnaw at night.

The door resists me and for a moment. I feel panic. But then it gives way and I stumble into the hall. On the wall hangs a mirror. I do not see it but I remember it as its sheen steals beneath the shades of my wounded eyes. I try to open them, but I cannot. In desperation I lift an eyelid with my hand. God help me! What do I see? Is it I? Can it be I? This nightmare of a face, the scarecrowed arm, horror written over the wretched, paralyzed unbelieving features? Can it indeed be I? I who so soon ago was alive and had hope? I lift the other eyelid.

Nothing changes. It is I, never fear, it is I indeed.

September 2, 1940.

For me the memories are clearest with alcohol. Then it seems that I am there, the past is alive, and now and then I return, without knowing how, to a time of happiness — but more often to a time of the last despair.

I remember when as a child. I would speak occasionally, but not enough, not nearly enough. How terribly silent I was my birth cry was A whisper. And I feel sometimes that I shall speak loudest from the grave.

May 30, 1943

The lightning disappearance! It seems that the last chord is hardly finished, when, "See you tomorrow at ten," and they are marching off in unison, even Olga with her cello packed, the music racks collapsed, the littered studio cleared as though by some magic wrecking crew. And there sit I alone, sole clue to the ruined day, alone and unmourned.

Save for the Escas. They leave more slowly, and now and then they ask me, very politely, to dine with them. Now and then. One day I must accept. Perhaps one day when I am not so lonely.

July 19, 1943

As I look at the enormous head of Beethoven I can only think, there am I, ugly, grotesque, but I, indeed I. For did not I make the head? Is it not of my hands? Of my soul? There it stands, torn from the murky depths of myself. Is this what my soul is like? This black monstrous thing? Then I should not be terrified rather I should terrify.

July 21, 1943

I have showed the head to Maia. She could not understand how I was able to do it, never having attempted sculpture before. I wrote to her that the strength of the genie comes from its being confined in the bottle, that when I succeed in opening the bottle only a little, nothing is too difficult for me. That if I could speak then I could not even play. Such are the laws of the bottle.

After a time she left. The head frightens her, she says.

May 11, 1944

The odors of myself are unbearable. Playing for a long time leaves me damp with a strange sweat, faintly poisonous and foul. After every rehearsal we all stink badly. Even Maia gives off a wry smell. Hers I somehow like, an acrid tickling little smell.

Odors in themselves interest me. The angry disharmony of an

Italian outhouse is not unpleasant to me. One of the worst is Esca. Surely nothing is stronger than the rankness of his aged breath. But I find it quite easy to tolerate him.

No, I think it must be the association with ugly aching things which I find hard to bear. I suffer when I smell the rubber doormat outside the rehearsal room. I smell it far away. And once inside! Olga is indeed a great garbage scow. And Otto! He masks himself only through smoking, and unsuccessfully. What a mélange! And is it ever possible to get them to open a window? Never. None has ever died of stinks, they say, only pneumonia.

And there sit the Escas, serene and unknowing. Do they have a deafness of the nose? Ah, it is intolerable. At Theodora's odor I shudder. Through the innocuous cologne I smell something faintly dreadful, something having to do with early decay and death.

July 5, 1945

There are times when I must doubt my own worth. For after all who am I? An ignorant Italian peasant woman. Do I have the marvelous training of the others? Did I study with Storch? At the *Akademie der Tonkunst* for more than a pitifully short and inadequate time? Of course not. Perhaps they are right to sneer at me. I am nothing and nothing I shall always remain.

July 6, 1945

But it is not true. It is only Otto who tries to convince me of it. I do not need to have studied with Storch or anyone else. I am better than he is! I am better than all of them! I know it, I know it! Did. Beethoven study with anyone in particular? Anyone that he would call his master? Did. Schönberg? Were they not self-taught? Then can I not be?

Oh, with anger I can see the truth. They are envious of me, all of them, even Maia! It is not, before God, that I think well of myself, but the others, are amateurs compared to me. There is only one who is my peer, Van Clausteyn of Holland, who has arthritis of the shoulder. It is a crushing handicap which helps one to achieve. Why is Beethoven the greatest of all composers? Is it not that he was deaf? As I am mute?

December 1, 1945

A soldier on the USO tour. He wanted terribly to get to know me better. Attractive too. But although Otto comes to see me seldom now I must be faithful to him.

May 31, 1948.

Read an excellent biography of Erik Satie by Rollo Myers, the Englishman. Crazy Satie and his white meals! He, says, "An artist must regulate his life." And his schedule includes: "I rise at 7:18; am inspired from 10:23 to 11:47. I lunch at 12:11 and leave the table at 12:14 ... Once a week (on Tuesdays) I awake with a start at 3:14 A.M ... My only nourishment consists of food that is white: eggs, sugar, shredded bones, the fat of dead animals, chicken cooked in white water, mouldy fruit, rice, sausages in camphor, cotton salad, cheese (white varieties). I breathe carefully (a little at a time). Every hour a servant takes my temperature.

Crazy Satie. Ha!

June 10, 1948
A poltroon! A little poltroon! Sandy ugly hair, a mouth with no lips, slitted eyes, a false grimace of friendliness, ears at a horrible protruding angle as though to escape from the pointed brainless skull. Teresa's new squire!!!

June 17, 1948
He has come again!

June 24, 1948
It is quite intolerable! Not so much that the disgusting creature has come a third time as that my little pigeon, my sweetling, seems to *like* him! She thinks him clever. Clever! I must write her' a long note. I should have already. He is an idiot! An *IDIOT*!!!
(There appear several blank pages. — W.E.)

June 30, 1948
Oh, I have many friends now! How good it is how exciting! The school for mute people, and the deaf

ones! We study the language of the hands and I have been appointed a leader in the class because I can hear!

The loss of Teresa is difficult to bear still. And to the idiot. He is only sixteen years old but does that matter? He has long ago reached the age of manhood. And if not he, will not someone else steal her from me? I shall not make the mistake of Beethoven with his nephew. For now I have so many friends. Now I am wealthy! I shall learn quickly, and my new friends and I will have many intimate conversations. How wonderful it will be to speak.

There is one elderly lady who looks so wise. A took to each other immediately. And everyone is so *kind*. How poor are the others, who are strangers to the happiness of misfortune.

Now I shall be very superior to Olga, even to Maia! Even to Otto!! And I shall not tell *anyone*, not anyone at *all*, of my secret. It will only be mine, greedy mine. Little *tete á tetes* I shall have now with one, now with another of my friends. Sometimes two at once! But never more than two, for then the speaking will be too much divided. I must choose those who are not too talkative. To more shall I be the last to leave!!!

August 21, 1948

The mute school is over as quickly as it began. Irrational hope. Although I learned to speak with my hands, and to understand the others — what did they have to *say*? What do they *talk* about? Nothing, nothing at all, only recipes and the condition of aging bowels.

And after all these many years. *How* isolated I have been. Is it not inconceivable that with six hours of rehearsal daily, with concerts several times a week, with hardly a moment to myself that I should be so alone? And I have found with greater certainty as each year passes that I am not alone in my loneliness, that the others are lonely too. For to whom may they speak? Are they not also mute? Who is able even to listen or to understand? The forbidden ones, we, each other ourselves alone.

August 23, 1948.

How wealthy are the dead.

March 1949

No one knows the real Otto. Is he an expert in kindness? With a skillful twist he becomes the cruelest of men. His face changes the mask is dropped, and there he stands, sadistic and powerful. His sexuality offers him no pleasure except in dominance. I can see that he waits only for my climactic moments. It is in these moments of all my life that I want most to cry out, to shriek, but I cannot. Ah how cruel he looks. But one day I shall, I must shriek. And what then, Otto? What then?

December 6, 1949

Otto says that if I could speak I could not play. He is right, of course, he is always right. And only imagine, he found it out in less than twenty years.

April 8, 1950

I have begun today a book of the quartet. Twenty wasted years. Perhaps they will not seem quite so futile if I write of them. Is it possible for a string quartet to exist? I cannot be really sure. It does not seem probable, but I cannot know. And so I shall write this book which may be of some help to other groups which gather to fight, and to die.

June 16, 1950

Five chapters of the new book are finished. It does not seem like a grateful task.

July, 18 1950

I am even afraid of the breath of the wind. It rushes against me and I am taken aback and frightened. The invisible antagonist and today I had a terrible fear. The thought struck me that my breasts would be cut off. Not that Otto comes any more.

July 24, 1950

Otto's attitude toward Theodora (I hate that stupid, coy nickname of hers, although she is both stupid and coy) has been in a state a doubtful flux, of unconscious hope for ten years. I really think, whether he knows it or not, that is why he chose Esca to be the manager. So he could be near

Theodora. It is finally beginning to affect his relationship with me seriously. He has now not visited me for seven months. He only makes a moveless, hopeless, silent love to her, makes love as he lives, as he breathes. Only I can hear the change in his way of playing when she enters the room, the speed of his hand—even the imperceptible rise in the pitch of his voice.

But gradually she has begun to realize it too. And grad-ually he comes to see me less. He does not explain. He knows it is useless. He must love her so that other women are impossible for him.

And, now what shall I do? The fleeting comfort that once made life barely possible for me is gone. But perhaps it was wrong anyway. I do not love Otto any more.

July 29, 1950

I had a dream last night. I could not only speak in the dream but I could sing. I was a wonderful singer, and very beautiful. Men sought after me and were willing to die for my hand. It was at the opera, *La Scala*, the opening night of the season, and I was to be Isolde. As I approached the stage entrance hundreds of men lined the walks, with flowers, and diamonds, and all kinds of wonderful presents. But I haughtily passed them by. I have only room in my heart for Otto. The press wishes to interview me, but I tell them in a beautiful, well-modulated voice, later, please. Later, and sweep proudly into the building. My dresser makes me look especially beautiful on this, the first night of the season. I walk onto the stage to a roar of applause, and begin my first aria. Never have I sung so well. The conductor of the orchestra is in tears. And as the evening progresses I feel that this is to be the summit of a brilliant and eventful career. I am especially brilliant tonight. I surprise myself with my brilliance. The mighty opera comes to its mighty finale and I come to take my bows.

But nothing happens, nothing at all. The huge audience is absolutely silent. But why? And suddenly I see the terrible reason. They are all deaf, every one of them. They have not heard a word of the entire, wonderful evening. Even the conductor has grown deaf, and cups his hand, pathetically to his ear. I shout, I scream, but no one hears me. I go out into the deaf world, and I am the only one who can hear. How lonely I am how terribly lonely.

But there is one to whom I can turn, and I run to him as fast as I can. "Otto, Otto," I cry "Otto." But he does not answer me, for he is deaf too.

August 6, 1950

The medium! Madame Sarah! A dank, cobwebbed dungeon in Haarlem—a toothless Negress with silver brows in a leprous face. Frail, formidable, she looked at me with a hatred and suspicion of such intensity that I wondered why she had granted me the interview. Ebbie, fearful and apologetic, showed me in. The savage nod at once dismissed her and summoned me.

The ceiling was very low and I had to crouch as I followed Madame Sarah through a tattered curtain. Now we were in a small room, quite bare and lit only by a glass of tallow, grave of a hundred candles. There was a bitter fragrance in the air which made me think of rotted flowers. And as my vision became accustomed to the gloom I saw the flowers, wilted and depending brokenly from a cracked vase. In a far corner was a small crystal sphere. Otherwise nothing in the room as I looked, around.

Madame Sarah sat down. Another ferocious nod and abruptly I sat too, amazed at this woman's powerful personality. Her eyes were closed now as she moaned and swayed. I waited for what seemed an age.

All at once I heard a lightning stream of Italian invective, beginning from nowhere, as though one had suddenly tuned in a foreign broadcast. Then I heard my name mentioned, and blasphemous oaths, and dire predictions. I would suffer greatly, I would die soon. I would be condemned, to eternal damnation.

These mediums are clever. I offered Madame Sarah what I thought was a fairly high fee, hoping to lessen her hatred of me, but she refused to accept it. Instead she drew the curtain aside and ejected me with a final nod of dismissal. Strange. It seemed a kindlier nod—

Suddenly I heard the sound of an automobile coming up the drive. Its screeching brakes grated horribly on my nerves and I was torn away from the diary with a sense of pain and outrage. How deeply engrossed I had been. But who could it be this late at night?

For a moment I thought it must be the quartet, then realized that they weren't due until tomorrow. Still, it could be the quartet. The thought that they might have arrived so soon disturbed me. Why didn't they come tomorrow? When they said they would come?

I walked to the window and looked out. It was a starless, moonless night and the world was black. The huge bug of the automobile distended its jaws. Yes there was Olga, carrying a suitcase under one arm and, her cello under another. And Otto and Maia. Where was—here she came.

I turned, away from the window and went downstairs and outside. Thede kissed me on the cheek. Then we all greeted each other with muted joyfulness and went into the house. Thede got some milk and cheese. Everyone seemed to be utterly tired.

They toyed with the food.
"How have things been," I asked.
"So—so," Otto said wearily.

"And the Hollywood filming?"

"Never again." He yawned. "It's a disgusting business."

I saw that he was exhausted. Better wait until tomorrow.

Olga asked, "How are you feeling, Billy?"

"Fine, fine."

Maia said, "What about Andrea's diary, Billy? Did you find out anything revealing?"

"Oh, yes. But you'll have to read it yourself, I can't tell you about it."

"Why not? Why can't you tell about it?"

"Because it's too complicated. You get a much better idea by reading it

She pouted. "You can't tell an anything about it?"

"You'd better read it."

"We'll see. But how are the Dantes getting along?"

"Mama's death was a terrible blow to the whole family. Old Pietro was shattered, and it was awful for little Teresa. It's not only that she loved Mama but that she needed her too. She's only a child, you know."

Thede said, "I'm going to bed."

Otto stood and stretched. "We've had a long, hard journey. I'm going to bed too. We can talk tomorrow." He yawned prodigiously.

I felt very tired. I had been working on the diary for more hours that I could remember. There were about eight pages left and I had been determined to finish the translation tonight, but now I felt an overwhelming weariness. Otto was leaving the room and I decided to join him. The onward rush of the diary had been broken and I couldn't summon the energy to return to it. But as Thede took my arm I had a curious feeling. Certainly I wanted to go to bed with her, but my desire was mixed with distaste, and I almost pushed her hand away.

But I controlled myself. I wasn't ready to let her know my true feelings. I said, "I don't think I'll go to bed quite yet. I want to do some more work on the diary. It's a fascinating thing and there are about eight pages left to be translated. If I didn't finish them now I doubt that I could get to sleep tonight wondering what was going to happen next." Let her have the bedroom. There was a couch in the study. To hell with her.

I did not feel like working the next morning. Instead I walked to the large Window of the rehearsal room and gazed out over the desolate Maine landscape. Far and wide it spread, a huge blanket of oppression.

Bleak it was, and bleak was my mood.

There was a long, vertical crack in the window. I fingered it idly and decided, for the hundredth time, that I must get it fixed soon, This was one of the unpleasant little details which cluttered up everyone's days. Life's garbage I called it.

I took the diary from my pocket. Poor Andrea. If only I had been aware of what had been going on in her poor, mute mind. But what could have been done to help her? Nothing. She had done what she could for herself, and had even gone to a psychologist. Life is sometimes too complex.

I walked, slowly to my study and sat down with the diary again. I riffled its pages idly, reluctant to begin the work of translation. I wasn't feeling well, damn it. My abdomen hurt and my head was beginning to throb, and when. Mrs. Bundy came to the door with a breakfast tray I gave her a note to Thede saying that I was ill, that I would not see her until later in the day.

The inevitable orange juice, bacon, eggs, toast, coffee did not appeal to me and for some time I sat and looked at it disapprovingly. At last I decided that it was impossible to eat breakfast today and I pushed the food away. Mrs. Bundy would be angry. Well, she would get over it.

I had been working on the diary for only a few minutes when I heard the beginning tunings of the strings and preparatory arpeggios rippling from the piano. There was a tiny knocking at the door. The wonderful, mysterious strains of Beethoven's "Ghost" Trio told me, by the simple process of subtraction, that it must be Maia.

I opened the door and she came into the room, the inevitable neckpiece awry. We embraced, and. I kissed her cheek gently. Then she sat down with an exhausted little sigh. She seemed to be older, her face was newly lined and, here and there a grey hair mixed discreetly with the blonde.

For a time the silence of our reunion was filled with the music. Then I said, "Tell me, Maia, how things have really been?"

"Not—well. Things have—not been going too well with us. It has been an unusual tour, you know. Quite unusual. But what of yourself? How has your health been?"

"Top notch. I guess I'm nothing but a big baby."

"Nonsense. Anyone could tell you were ill. But tell me now about the diary."

"Would you like to read, what I have translated of it?"

"I—really I would rather you told me about it," she said nervously. "Please."

"Wouldn't know how to begin, Maia. Here, read it yourself." And I handed her the sheaf of typed paper.

"I am afraid," she cried. "I don't want to." She leaned back, her head angled sidewise over the chair arm as though she wanted to escape. "There must be important things, things that you can tell me."

"It is much too complicated, my dear. Eventually you will read it, you know, and you might as well do it now." But she drew back even farther. "Maia," I said patiently, "you have nothing to be afraid of. In the diary you are Andrea's favorite!" I smiled at her. "Here take it and see for yourself."

She did not move. She could go no farther into her frozen retreat and only stared helplessly at the manuscript. The sound of the "Ghost" rose and fell. At last Maia drew a deep, unhappy breath and said, "All right, I'll read it. But before I do, you must tell me something of what is in it. I am so frightened."

"It is mainly the story of her tragic life, of course. And the quartet was one of the most tragic aspects of it. Because of the quartet she was a tortured woman, Maia. Curious. I knew her for ten years, and although I never thought she was a happy person I didn't suspect that she was the most miserable of human beings. You had better read the diary, Maia. Then you will know Andrea, the real Andrea." Again I handed her the translation and this time she took it reluctantly.

"Now, Maia, I want you to tell me about the tour. All about it."

She seemed to be embarrassed, and, for some time she said nothing. I looked at her curiously, but she turned away, looking out the window, about the room, anywhere to avoid my inquiring gaze. At last, slowly, haltingly, she began to talk.

"Billy," she said, "when you left us In Hollywood, the situation became impossible. I will never know how the movie managed to get itself made."

"Why do you think things got so bad?"

"Thede," Maia burst out. "Thede. Don't you know? Can't you realize what must have happened? She was hopeless. She could not even be depended upon to come to rehearsals! She would simply *not show up*!! She *never* practiced," Maia said bitterly, "making up for this deficiency by playing so loudly that the balance was completely destroyed. Of course the movie people thought she was wonderful, and this fed her vanity. I'm not trying to upset you, Billy, but that's how it was. It is true that she was treated shamefully by Olga, and it may be that she was only trying to get even. And Otto—for some reason he became much less tolerant of her faults. You remember how in the beginning he used to defend her? But toward the end he began to make life miserable for her too." With an impatient gesture she arose, and walking to the window gazed morosely at the desolate view. "And I mustn't get carried away by Thede either," she muttered. "Although God knows she gave us plenty of trouble. But do you know, Billy, I think none of us ever got over Andrea. All through the tour, and especially after you left, she was like—like an evil spirit, watching over us, watching malignantly never giving us surcease. The frictions between the three of us got worse and worse, and this would have happened even without the complication of Thede. Yes, it was the shadow of Andrea which destroyed us.

But did the tour not have redeeming features? What of Frank? Didn't he work out all right?"

"Oh, yes. Yes, He was fine." In her voice there was a trace of irony. "He was very successful with—with—" A blush reddened her cheeks. "But I've said enough.

I looked at her sharply her face was as red as though she had been skinned. Now my abdomen began to pain me again. Recently I had suffered from these pains almost every day, and they were getting worse. Oh, how they hurt. And I began to feel tears of self-pity trickling down my cheeks. "Is it that she has been unfaithful to me," I asked brokenly.

She was silent for so long a time that at last I looked at her and saw that the scarlet of her cheeks had vanished. Now they were a sickly white.

"You didn't suspect that I knew? I have known for a long time. A long time. And I cannot tell you how I have suffered because of it."

"No," she whispered. I had no idea that you knew. How could I?

"Because—let's not go into that, for God's sake. Now listen, I want you to tell me everything, everything that you know about Thede. And everything you suspect as well."

I waited for several minutes but still she hesitated. I was about to speak to her again when she said, timidly, "Well—I can only tell you that she went around with lots of men. And you know, one notices things. Or one overhears a strange word spoken with a familiarity which is difficult to understand."

"I know only of—of Frank," I lied.

"Who else? For the divorce court. No morbid curiosity."

She looked at me doubtfully for a moment. Then, she shrugged and said, "One can't be absolutely certain, but—well, you want to know about my suspicions. To start with, I am convinced that there was young Krikelaire." She paused. "Poor kid. Wasn't it simply dreadful about his father's death? And do you know, I am sure the father was interested in Olga. And, she knew it too. I know of no other man who has ever been interested in Olga and I have known her since 1927. And her *cello*! For her cello to have gotten drowned too. It is really too terrible.

For a time she was lost in memory. Then, "What was I. speaking of? Oh, yes. Thede's men." She sighed. "I don't know what she was able to accomplish on the road, but in Hollywood there was the cameraman. Herbert Guss. He was very upset when Thede left him for Wellwood Smith, one of the younger directors, who was quite angry when she left him for Josef Markesch, one of the older directors. The speed of all this was terrific. We were in Hollywood, you know, for little more than a month. Of course on the way to the studio one day she ran into an old friend"

"Enough," I groaned. Quite enough."

But Maia was caught in the rush of her thoughts and could not stop. "The spectacle of it got worse and worse," she cried. "There came a time when we were actually ashamed to be seen with her."

"Why do you think she acted like that? I mean, right out in the open. You'd think—"

"No doubt because she was trying to be rid of us. She had been offered a screen contract, you know."

"Never told me. Never said a word."

"Oh, yes. She would have accepted it too, but Otto warned her I have a contract too, he would say. We begged him to let her go, for God's sake. She was ruining everything. But you know how stubborn he can be. He insisted that we deliver her back to you, then she could do as she pleased."

Now Maia made a gesture of dismissal. "That's all, I guess. God, I'm tired."

I made her rest on the couch. Now I thought I would listen to rehearsal and closed the door and started down the stairs. But then I remembered the diary and I stole quietly back into the room and retrieved the little red book.

I descended into the music, into the irresistible music of Beethoven. There was a contour chair near the foot of the stairs and I stretched out on it and listened. The "Ghost" Trio was one of my favorite compositions.

But I found my attention drawn to the players. Olga, with her back toward me was the closest. As I listened to her groaning breathing, rhythmic with the music, and watched her grey head nodding with weariness, I saw a banked and failing fire. During a momentary pause in the music she jerked her cello angrily from the floor and chopped it into a different place. She had always refused to use a portable board for her cello's end pin. Said it limited her freedom. The floor, newly refinished during the winter, had already acquired several wounds that morning from Olga's sharp steel.

To hell with it, of what importance was the damned floor. The main thing was that she was not playing well today. Her pitch was dreadfully inaccurate and a gravelly undertone marred her usually immaculate sound. She looked at Otto as she jabbed again and I could see her face for a moment. Her weariness was something I had not known in Olga before. In her expression a tired anger held the only vitality.

I followed her gaze to Otto. He was lost in thought as his long fingers discovered and projected the music. A tiny, almost unnoticeable trace of the palsy remained. His hair was completely white now. The winter, in conquering the last red threads, had left behind the monotonous color of snow, stained only by the patch of rust which showed through his opened shirt front. He seemed to play absently, the fire of his tone drawn from another bow, or from some deeply buried substratum of his soul, hidden, volcanic, remote and it came to me that the greatness of Otto had lain not in his intellectual force but in the roiling of his spirit, in a vanished incandescence. What had happened to him?

With the ending of the trio, however, he became alert again. "Together," he cried, "together: Whatever you do, let the last chords be together. No matter what crimes one commits, a sparkling, precise ending will save the day." The second syllable chimed with the chord, to to*geth*er.

I shrugged. This kind of rehearsing was for amateurs. I thought of the decade which. I had spent with the quartet, from the first magnificent time to the shabby present. Now it seemed to me that all the miraculous artistry was no more, that it had dissipated like a precious essence from a cracked vial. A painfully wrong discord made me wince. I struggled out of the contour chair and stood so that I could see Thede. Ah, yes. She was chewing gum.

Well, enough of it, I had more important things to do. Maia came down the stairs with the translation and, lay down in the contour chair. Suddenly it struck me with great force that the translation would tell Maia of Andrea's affair with Otto. God in heaven, how could. I get it back from her. For-tunately it would take her some time to get to the affair. Maybe I would think of something. Nervously, and, with one eye on Mafia, I sat down on a sofa and began to read.

I turned the last page of the diary. Suddenly the words swam before my eyes. They seemed, impossible to believe and I raced through the page again. Then I lurched to my feet. "Stop playing," I cried "Stop playing. Listen to what I have found in Andrea's diary." Startled. Otto and Olga put down their instruments.

'"I have found out how Andrea died Listen to this."

September 7, 1950

And now I have tried everything. Everything. Only one thing has ever helped me worth a damn. Alcohol, lovely alcohol. Use as directed. Directed. But directed by whom? By chance. Perhaps? Ah, almost all gone. Gone. One little, *little* bottle left. And then what happens? Guess what happens? *Theodora* comes with an *extra* bottle. La, la. Left by *chance* in the rehearsal room. La, la. She is not *really* so bad, I suppose. As a matter of fact I *love* her, love her *madly*."

And now my voice failed and the last two ridiculous syllables came out in a feeble croak, "La, la."

The room was so quiet now that the innocent ticking of the grandfather clock became the sharp report of a whiplash. Louder it grew, and angrier until it struck at me with a monomaniacal fury. Everyone was frozen to their chairs and no one moved. Lifeless they were, and rigid, and for a crazy, fleeting moment I thought that my friends were dead and that I was in a waxwork.

Thede arose and walked carefully to the large window, delicately picking her way between the, music racks. She leaned against the crack in the glass with a forearm, her jaws never failing of their rhythmic movement as she stared at the landscape. But she chewed cautiously, as if she were afraid to make a sound.

Now the silence was abruptly shattered by the sudden swiveling of Otto's chair and the hissing release of Olga's breath. Still no one spoke.

At last Thede turned to face them.

"What's everybody looking at *me* for?" She said, desperately. "I didn't know she would *drink* the stuff. I stumbled and dropped the bottle. It broke so I filled another one with denatured and brought it to her."

No one replied to Thede's explanation. "She was drunk as a lord," she cried. "Drunk as an absolute lord." Still the silence. "What's the matter," she wailed. "Don't you believe me?"

I had moved to the piano bench and now, surrounded, by the steel bars of the music racks, I watched the frozen faces of my friends as the horror crept into them, the disbelief the slow realization.

Olga had been staring numbly at Thede. But now her face lost its grey rigidity. The hewn stone of it would crumble suddenly as she blinked with a nervous fierceness, then stiffen again until the next fierce blinking constrained a great and sudden closing of mouth and eyes. And once more she was a rigid mask, except for the sweat which oozed from the rock of her forehead.

Otto, trembling with an artificial calm, began to smoke cigarettes with the intensity of a drug addict, half a cigarette with each drag and a lighting of the next from the touch of the old. With shaking hands he would patiently and thoroughly ignite the troubled, paper until it gave forth grey little curls of smoke. Then came the new, swift inhalation.

And Maia, face shielded by her arms, wept softly, bitterly, as though her heart would break. One could only know that she was weeping because of the rhythmic, convulsive throbbing of her tiny body.

But Thede had regained her composure now and was looking calmly, indifferently at the turmoil of the others. I hated her with a purity of emotion which I had never known before. I knew somehow that she was not trying to dissemble, that she *was* indifferent that she didn't care in the least, not two cents' worth, about Andrea's death, about her own fault in the poisoning. God damn her dirty soul. And my fury washed over me in a great waves and I wanted to strangle the beautiful whore I had married, the beautiful murderess. She knew Andrea drank, damn her soul to hell.

I tried to speak softly, but my voice trembled with a rage I could not control as I whispered, "I understand that you made friends with several *charming* gentlemen on the tour. *Good* friends. And as sarcastically as I could. I shouted, "*Extremely* good friends."

How ugly her beautiful face could be. Like a fishwife she snarled at me "I've been sick of you for a long time. Mister Esca. Sick of you and your zombie quartet, since you want to make it public. But I have never been unfaithful to you."

"You are lying, you are lying," I screamed. My heart pained me as I tried vainly to control myself. "I don't *think*, I *know* of most if not all of your infidelities, beginning with Otto, on tour, in California—"

With a violent wrench I caught myself, horrified by my mistake. Almighty Lord, what had I done. The quartet ruined now, ruined, for good. Ruined. Billy, ruined Billy, ruined—

Otto groaned and turned his face to the wall. He said, almost inaudibly, "Now there is not even a trio."

Olga rose slowly to her full height. "A trio?" she said gently. "Do you think Maia would play with you? There is not even a duo anymore. At any rate not a duo which includes you."

She sat down at the piano and shoved me aside gently. Then she began, very softly, to play the wonderful slow movement of the "Ghost" Trio. "And it is not because of your—your wife, Billy," she said grimly, "but because of Otto. We are ded-icated, the three of us, but to different things Maia, and I to music, Otto to harlotry."

Thede said, "Your English is bad. What you mean is that he is dedicated to harlots. Preferably musical harlots."

Olga stood up violently, upsetting her cello on the stabbed floor. In a slow, stamping seesaw she turned to face Thede her face livid with rage. "I do not speak to you, tramp, murderess," she yelled.

It is impossible to describe Olga's yell. It was ear-splitting. The strings of the piano hummed.

But Thede smiled sweetly. "I wasn't the only one. He enjoyed a turn or two with Maia, you know. *And* Andrea. As a matter of fact, the old dear slept with *practically,*" here she paused insultingly, "with *practically everybody.*"

The workings of Olga's face were frightening. "You are a *liar!*" she bellowed, "a dirty *liar!*" She turned to Mala who lay face dawn, her shoulders racked with the effort to contain her violent sobbing.

"Don't be mad at *me*, honey," Thede said demurely. "I can't help it if men like *me*, and—"

"Whore," Olga screamed. "Be quiet, shameful, shameful whore." She seized a great sheaf of music and threw it to the floor, stamping and tearing it until she was forced to stop from lack of breath.

Thede was politely alarmed, "Do control yourself, Olga honey," she cooed. "You're too *nervous*." She smiled maliciously. "What you really need to do, sweetie pie, is to find yourself a man, a nice *big* man, and—"

Olga went berserk. She seized her cello in a great blind scoop and hurled it at her tormentor. There was a fearful, shattering crash as the cello struck with all of Olga's furious strength against a wall, the strings jarring loose, the wood splintering into jagged planks, the end pin clattering and rolling free on the floor. Then, with a swift lumbering, she seized Thede and began to strangle her.

For the fraction of a second Otto hesitated. Then he threw himself on Olga, wrenching at her hands, trying to separate the battling women. But with a terrible backward blow of her left arm the enraged giantess sent him stumbling so that he struck his head against the piano and fell senseless to the floor.

Now Olga threw herself on Thede again, her powerful fingers seeking a new stranglehold as she overwhelmed her enemy with her huge body. "Whore," she gasped, "whore, oh whore."

Maia, horrified, climbed out of the

entanglement of the contour chair and stood wringing her hands. "Stop, Olga," she cried, uselessly, "Stop."

Thede drowned in Olga's smothering bulk, had only one flailing, groping arm free. As I watched I had a dreadful premonition and scrambled to my feet. But I was too late. In her helpless beating and searching of the floor Thede had at last found the sharp steel of the cello end pin, and before I could reach her she had lifted it, paused in a momentary, frenzied aim, and driven it with a desperate strength deep into Olga's back, again and again.

I tried to tear the bloody pin from Thede's hand but Olga, rising weakly to her feet, gave, me a frightful shove so that I flew backwards, struck the piano with terrific force, then fell to the floor.

The next moment there was a dreadful, splintering crash. And my hazy, shimmering world was riven by a high-pitched, vanishing, accusing scream.

After a time I managed to raise myself to an elbow. I looked stupidly about the room and saw Olga, hunched quietly, eyes closed, sitting on the edge of the contour chair. Now I heard a shrill, repetitious, tearful voice. I got to my knees, and then I saw that it was Maia, crying frantically into the telephone, over and over, "Send an ambulance quickly, quickly, please—"

She cradled the phone at last and ran to Olga, who sat with a curiously thoughtful expression, feebly picking her nose. "*Please* lie down, Olga," she begged. "You *must* lie dawn."

I regarded her blearily. Idle silly thoughts floated through my mind. It seemed strange to me that I had not seen Maia all day except in tears. Funny. Why did she want to cry all the time? Then an even stranger thought occurred to me. Why on earth had Otto chosen the middle of the day to sleep on the floor?

I looked at him wonderingly. Then I shook my head and blinked for several minutes and gradually my mind became clearer. But now I remembered that there was something, something peculiar, something—

It teased me and nagged at me and I became angry and struggled and fought to capture the elusive memory. And suddenly I heard a splintering crash, a terrible scream I staggered to my feet. And as I saw the vast rent in the window, the scattered shards of glass, my brain came sharply into focus again. "Thede," I gasped. "Maia, for God's sake, where is Thede, what has happened to Thede?"

"Dead," she said callously, and nodded indifferently at the shattered window, with its terrible implication of what must lie below. But her attention did not waver from Olga and she dabbed with a wet handkerchief at the blood which oozed from the great bared back.

We hoped, uselessly, that Olga would live. For even after the glaze of death had, settled on the granite face the little finger of her left hand continued visibly to tremble.

At last the police had no more questions and we were permitted to retire to our rooms. Everyone wanted seclusion and was glad to go.

At five o'clock we were told that we could leave, and I telephoned for a cab. When it arrived I went through the music room, and there I saw the body of Olga. Tenderly I drew her sheet aside. And at the sight of the once huge face, shrunken in death, I was seized by a poignant grief. Poor, dear Olga. There she lay, her monstrous nose all the more in prominence, the prow of her final journey. Replacing the sheet I walked, slowly on. For a long moment I paused at the covered body of Thede. Then I passed on to the waiting cab.

As we bumped down the slow trail I was increasingly aware of my exhaustion. I felt that I never wanted to move again, that I was imprisoned in a curious death-like lethargy. It was almost the dreadful lethargy for which Olga had deserted us. Still, I thought, if Olga why *not* me? And Otto and Maia?

Their nearness irritated me. I would be glad to leave them and thought that if they went by train I would fly. Or if they flew, then—I could easily be driven to New York in two days. But why New York? Why not a plane back to California?

No, a jet. A jet back to the beginning.

* * *

He had finished typing and now he skimmed through the pages he had written. How frequently the word "inescapable" flashed into his mind.

But did he want to escape? Not yet. He wasn't finished. Not until he had written the story of Olga, and Andrea. The translation of their lives and the unfolding of meaning. A requiem for the quartet, and for the beautiful muse. The sonata, the sonnet. A new place in Canada, a burial place, in a new northern winter. And new friends among the silent pines, the sentient evergreens.

Alone at the oblong table, he buried his head in his arms. Good-by, my friends. Good-bye.

* * * * *

Printed in Great Britain
by Amazon

67472137R00244